RANDOM HOUSE
**LARGE
PRINT**

THE GHOST ORCHID

JONATHAN KELLERMAN

THE GHOST ORCHID

AN ALEX DELAWARE NOVEL

RANDOM HOUSE
LARGE PRINT

Cover design: Derek Walls
Cover images: © Radoslaw Lecyk/Shutterstock (cityscape), © Masterfile Royalty Free (house and pool), © KK.KICKIN/ Shutterstock (starry sky)

The Library of Congress has established a Cataloging-in-Publication record for this title.

ISBN: 978-0-593-86180-6

www.penguinrandomhouse.com/large-print-format-books

FIRST LARGE PRINT EDITION

Printed in the United States of America

1st Printing

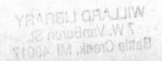

To Emmett

THE GHOST ORCHID

1

Nearly getting killed can change your life in interesting ways.

There's the physical healing, but that's tedious to think about. What fascinates me is how people behave when they know you've come close to death.

Some you haven't heard from in a while get in touch out of obligation. Most of the time they have no idea what to say or do and you end up assuring them you're fine and trying to make them feel better. Or maybe that was just me, reverting to the psychologist's role.

I'm close to only two people on the planet.

The woman I live with handled the whole thing beautifully, pulling off the perfect balance of caring for me and allowing me space when I needed it. Even more impressively, when Robin allowed herself to get angry at me for being in danger in the first place, she was able to talk about it reasonably.

My best friend, a homicide detective, was overcome with guilt. I'd been working with Milo when a lunatic nearly crushed me to death. No one's fault, reasonable precautions had been taken. Just one of those things that happen. But, still.

He'd worked hard at keeping the guilt in check but I could tell. Our conversations began ebbing into long silences, terminating when he told me I needed to rest.

Eventually, his visits tapered off, though he tried to keep up with regular phone calls. But he avoided talking about work, which peppered the calls with awkward silences.

Worst of all, he stopped calling me in on cases. The "different ones" where he tends to overestimate my talent. When I brought up the subject, he claimed the two new murders he'd taken on were open and shut.

Four months after being injured I sat with Robin on the second-story terrace that fronts our house, eating and drinking and enjoying the weather that keeps people in L.A., and said, "Still nothing from Big Guy."

She said, "Can you blame him?"

"I think he's overdoing it. Objectively, he did nothing wrong."

"Who's ever objective, Alex?"

I poured myself another finger of Chivas—the pricey gold stuff I'd never buy for myself. A guilt offering from Milo.

Neither of us talked for a while and I resumed rubbing the big, knobby head of our little blond French bulldog, Blanche. She's also been perfect. Sitting next to me as I knitted, silent and patient, careful not to touch the torn muscles in my chest. She's always been a wonderful companion, intuitive, perceptive, more keyed in to nonverbal cues than any human could hope to be. But this was more. She knew something was different and she cared.

Robin said, "All those custody cases came in but you're still bored."

"I could use some variety."

"Know what you mean."

That surprised me.

She said, "Why do you think I do what I do, baby? Every instrument's different, it's not like I'm making the same armchair over and over."

I said, "So you wouldn't mind if I diversified. Maybe got into macramé?"

She grinned and placed her small, strong hand over mine. Her hair's thick, auburn, and curly and when she's not in her studio, she wears it loose to the midpoint of her back. Tonight, the moon was medium strength and it gilded all those curls and limned her oval face, her pointy chin.

The slightly oversized milk-white incisors that had attracted me in the first place.

"Would I prefer if you never got involved in all the ugly stuff? Part of me would. But I'd be living with a very unhappy man."

"Unhappy fool."

She laughed. "Don't tempt me. Anyway, I'm sure he'll call when he really needs you."

"I'm not."

She poured herself another half glass of Zinfandel. Daintily polished off a stuffed grape leaf. Greek takeout, tonight. Blanche had scored bits of rice and lamb. Everyone happy.

Except me. I'd been faking serenity for a while, had never stopped feeling incomplete.

It took another two weeks for that to finally change.

2

The call came in at nine a.m. on a glorious Sunday. The familiar voice, tight with battle readiness but tinged with uncertainty.

"Too early for you?"

"No, been up for a while."

"How you feeling?"

"Great."

"Well . . . I've got one, been here since seven thirty, I figured maybe . . ."

"Sure."

"Also," he said, "not far from you. If you're feeling up for it. Back in the old days you probably coulda run over here."

I said, "Give me the address."

The trip was four point eight miles from my house in Beverly Glen. A feasible run B.C.—before crushing—but even then I'd have driven because I like to get to scenes fast.

I wheeled the Seville down the nameless former bridle path that winds down treacherously from our half acre, drove south on Beverly Glen past the skinny chockablock houses that line the road in our neighborhood, and transitioned to the grand estates just north of Sunset Boulevard.

At Sunset I hooked right and continued to the western gate of Bel Air, sped up Bellagio Road before turning onto a series of serpentine side streets. Reversing the process: eight-figure palaces followed by progressively more modest houses on limited woodsy lots.

Every crime scene's unique but there's also a sameness to them. The procedures, the activities of those who've chosen to work with worst-case scenarios. The emotional tone.

The first thing you see is what I've come to think of as Death's Parking Lot: detectives' unmarked sedans, patrol cruisers, crypt vans, hybrid compacts driven by coroner's investigators.

Behind all that, the inevitable yellow tape. Canary-bright and sadder for that.

This was my first crime scene in four-plus months and simply arriving tweaked my brain and made me feel alive. No point wondering what that said about me. I was imagining, wondering, lasering the layout.

This lot was so thickly wooded that no structure

was visible from the street. To the right of the vehicles, a burly young officer stood guard. The foliage hid neighboring properties, as well, creating an illusion of forest.

Cruelly peaceful.

Usually, Milo informs the cops that I'm coming and they lift up the yellow strand. Sometimes they even smile and welcome me by name.

This time I had to show my I.D. to Burly, who looked to be allergic to smiling.

He examined my driver's license as if it were written in hieroglyphics, re-read, checked me out squint-eyed, stepped away and made a call. Returning, he favored me with a lemon-sucking frown, said, "Okay," reluctantly, and left me to lift my own damn tape.

Trying not to read too much into any of it, I ducked under and picked up my pace, ignoring the twinges in my ribs that followed each footfall.

Aiming myself toward the old days.

The forest turned out to be little more than a poorly trimmed amalgam of ficus and eugenia backed by huge, shaggy silver dollar eucalyptus. Decades ago, a plague had killed off most of the eugenia hedges in Southern California but a few survivors remain. The ficus tack-on said someone had settled for a quick fix in lieu of re-landscaping.

Getting past the greenery landed me in front of

a small, flat lawn fronting a one-story, cedar-sided ranch house.

In a suburban setting, another dated sixties throwback. In Bel Air, five million bucks if you hired the right real estate agent.

A second tape barrier ran across the front door. A black Maserati convertible sat in a gravel driveway to the left of the house. Newer model, the name of a Beverly Hills dealer framing the license plate. Littered with dust and leaves. Tennis racquet and balls on the passenger seat.

When the driveway reached the house, it converted to concrete and continued, ungated, toward the rear of the property.

The only feasible entry this morning. I walked along the house. Thought about easy access to a killer.

No sign of Milo or anyone else until I reached the end of the drive and turned right and there he was along with a pair of techs, a C.I., and half a dozen uniforms with nothing to do but look official.

Milo looked the same; why wouldn't he? Tall, mastiff-jowled, top-heavy above oddly thin legs, he wore wrinkled khakis, pink-soled desert boots, a spinach-green sport coat, a white wash 'n' wear shirt with a defeated collar, and a skinny black tie patterned with something hard to make out.

Sunlight waged a full-on assault on his pale, pocked face, having its way with every pit and lump.

His black hair, slicked down hours ago, had rebelled and bristled. A limp flap in front diagonaled a brow the texture of cottage cheese.

He was on his phone, saw me and nodded. Grimly, I thought. But maybe not. Who cared, anyway? He'd called. Time to focus and not get sidetracked.

I got close enough to see the tie pattern. Goose heads. Rows of beaks pointing to the right. He clicked off and said, "Thanks for coming."

Like there'd been a doubt.

I said, "What's going on?"

Instead of explaining, he waved expansively. **Check it out.**

Not much more to the backyard than a kidney-shaped swimming pool and concrete deck. Small, cup-shaped spa at the front of the pool.

A few feet from where we were standing, a naked man lay facing the sky. A single sizable crusted hole dotted the upper left quadrant of his chest. Blood spidered from the wound, running down from left to right and collecting on the ground. The flow dictated by the body's slight rightward cant.

No positioning. Shot and left to drop.

The blood on the deck had pooled to an amoeboid blot congealed and turned rusty with lingering scarlet highlights. The man's skin was gray, with faint pink traces of lividity visible beneath his left buttocks and thigh. No rigor or decomposition I could see.

"Is the pool heated?"

"The pool and the Jacuzzi."

Last night's temperature had floated in the mid-sixties. Warm enough for a swim but cool enough to slow down breakdown. Weather and exertion could've hastened muscle stiffening and caused it to fade more quickly. If rigor had come and gone, death had occurred sometime late at night or during the earliest morning hours.

Either way, in the darkness.

Partial darkness; a pair of outdoor fixtures just below the house's rain gutter were still on and so was a light in the pool.

The body lay five feet or so from a rear bank of sliding glass doors. One panel was open.

Stepping out of his home into the warm night air and . . .

Something small had been yellow-tagged to the left of the corpse. I bent and took a look. Unrolled condom.

Stepping out into the charitable night air, ready for fun.

He was young, late twenties or early thirties, with a black buzz cut and a three-day beard the same color. Midsized, lean, muscular with a long chiseled face centered by a strong, slightly hooked nose. Hispanic, Mediterranean, or Mideastern.

Rose-vine tattoo around his left ankle.

He lay flat on his back, mouth open, eyes partially shut, what was visible of the sclera, dark brown.

A black terry robe had been tossed carelessly over a chaise lounge chair that faced the pool. Next to the lounge a table held two crystal highball glasses, a bottle of Campari, an ice bucket half filled with water, and two cans of Pellegrino. Abutting the cans, a dish of small, ocher olives. The absence of pits said untasted.

Beyond all that, a naked woman occupied an identical lounge.

Prone and shot in exactly the same spot, head facing left, right arm dangling.

A bit older than her companion—fortyish—she was equally trim with crisp angular features and the kind of symmetrical beauty that cameras love. Blood of the same color and consistency striped her left breast and ran onto the chair, which was some sort of woven vinyl. Spaces between the weave allowed the rusty clot to settle on the deck below.

Her thick mahogany hair was scrunched up in a high pony. Her fingernails were polished pink, her toenails black. A black robe identical to her companion's was draped neatly over the top of a third lounge.

No body ink I could see; any obvious adornment came from the carbon glinting on her left hand: a sizable rectangular diamond ring above a pavé wedding band.

Holes in her earlobes but no earrings.

I took in the rest of the layout. A few leaves floated on the pool surface. Only a few, because unlike the front of the property, the sliver of space was concrete, much of it cracked. It butted up against ten-foot redwood fencing that continued on both sides. Several feet behind the back fence, massive, bushy podocarpus asserted themselves. Layers of them, from the near-black density. They're clean trees but slow-growing. These had to stretch back decades.

I said, "Who lives over there?"

Milo was surprised by the question. "No idea, Alicia's canvassing. Anything right here intrigue you?"

I took a closer look at both bodies and a few of the uniforms took closer looks at me. "Big holes. A .38 or larger?"

He strode to the northern fence and pointed out a splintered divot in a plank. "Pulled out a bullet, no casings, mashed up but looks like a .38."

"A revolver . . . there's a precise feel to it. Confidence that one shot would take care of business and pinpoint accuracy. Where's the other bullet?"

"Still inside her," he said. "The back of the chair blocked exit, it's wedged up against the plastic." Shaking his head. "Miracle fiber, who knew."

"Who found the bodies?"

"Pool guy at six forty-five. He comes twice a month, this is the first stop on his route, he's careful to be quiet. Says with no plants it's an easy job, he's in and out, has never actually seen or spoken to anyone, his company handles all the arrangements."

He tapped his foot. "How do you see it happening?"

"My guess would be he got shot first."

"Mine, too. Subduing him first would be safer."

"His position suggests he'd gone inside, maybe for the condom, reemerged and was confronted. The killer could've been concealed at the side of the house and still had an oblique view of the yard. What time do you figure it happened?"

"C.I. guesstimates eight p.m. to two a.m., doubts the pathologist will be able to narrow it much."

"No rigor."

"There was some when I got here but it faded soon after, so I'm figuring on the earlier end."

I said, "Either way, it was dark and they were preoccupied and less likely to notice an intruder. He waited until the time was right—after the male victim stepped out—came forward, and pulled off a quick shot to center mass. She was relaxing in the chaise, naked and vulnerable. She froze, the shooter walked up to her and finished what he'd come to do. I asked about the neighbors because if it's also a small property, someone might've heard the gun go off."

"No 911 calls, but we'll check it out."

"Her ring is sizable but it wasn't taken. Anything lifted from the house?"

"Nothing obvious. Want to see for yourself?"

Without waiting for an answer, he gloved up, handed me a pair, turned and led me through the open glass door.

3

Inside, the house was small and boxy with an L-shaped living area feeding to a white-on-white kitchen on one side, a brief hallway on the other. Pink-beige tile covered every square inch of floor. The furniture was somber and angular: gray tweed stools pushed against a breakfast bar, three-piece sectional of the same fabric, two black leather deco-revival chairs, three occasional tables fashioned from a charcoal-tinted resin.

White walls were mostly blank, except for a few of the inoffensive abstract prints you see in chain hotels. A sixty-five-inch flat-screen faced the long arm of the sectional. On the floor beneath the TV sat a pair of squat little Sonos speakers. No attempt to hide wires.

I said, "Not much personal investment. A rental?"

Milo said, "You're on a roll. Found the lease in a nightstand along with the guy's wallet and an Italian passport." He consulted his pad. "Giovanni Aggiunta, twenty-nine a few months ago."

He spelled the surname. "In answer to your next question, don't know anything about him yet."

I looked around. "Don't see any sign of disturbance."

He pointed to the hallway, left me to follow. One door to the right, on the left a nondescript beige bathroom followed by a nondescript beige bedroom.

Giovanni Aggiunta's sleeping chamber featured the same tile floor. A pair of windows facing the backyard were blocked by accordion shades. I lifted a few pleats on each. Both casements were shut tight and held fast by latches.

Not even cheap art in here, no chest or dresser, the only furniture a pair of chromium-legged black marble circles serving as nightstands. Rust-specked chrome. I'd seen budget hotels given more consideration.

A pair of wide double doors took up most of the facing wall.

Milo pointed to the bed. "Guess this could technically be counted as disturbance but not the type I'm interested in."

The king-sized mattress was made up with plum-colored sheets and pillows that had seen recent use. The pillows were bunched up against a black lacquer headboard. A corner of fitted sheet had come untucked, exposing the mattress pad. At the foot of the bed, a quilted, purple-brown silk spread humped where it hadn't trailed to the floor.

On the floor, neatly arranged a few feet from the bed, were a pink velour jogging suit, padded mini-socks, black-and-pink Asics running shoes.

The nearer stand hosted a matte-gray vibrator, a box of ESP condoms, a jar of Nivea crème, and a vial of something called Sweet Touch Love Oil. On the farther stand, a pink leather fanny pack.

Next to the pack were a diamond tennis brace-let and matching anklet, a platinum cocktail ring set with two serious diamonds and an even larger sapphire, and off to one side, a simple chain neck-lace set with a small purplish amethyst. The necklace seemed markedly lower-caliber. Maybe sentimental value.

Milo said, "No reason to go for small stuff when this was in plain sight but doesn't look as if there was ever a laptop or a desktop, just that tablet in the living room. All that's on it are the apps it came with and one that turns it into a remote. No evidence the bad guy ever came inside. So much for classic motive number one."

He lifted the fanny pack, tweezed out the con-tents, arrayed them on the bed.

Three twenty-dollar bills folded in half, shiny gold Gucci lipstick tube, brushed-gold container holding one point six ounces of Gucci Guilty perfume, the California driver's license of Meagin Lea March, blond/blue, five-six, one thirty, DOB forty-one years ago.

I said, "No phone?"

"It was on the stand next to the jewelry, techies pulled up prints on the case so they bagged and tagged before I had a chance to eyeball. I asked for a call-dump and a zip drive."

I read the address on the license. Guarida Lane, 90077. "Right here in Bel Air."

"Little under a mile and a half south over in the high-priced spread."

I said, "Who drives the Maserati?"

"Titled to a leasing company in the Palisades. Signor Aggiunta gets to use it for twenty-four months."

"So either he drove her here or she walked or jogged over."

"Fresh-looking grit in the soles of her running shoes says she's been using them somewhere recently."

He looked at the clothing on the floor, then the rumpled bed. "Physical fitness."

I said, "Both of them naked and him bringing out the condom says they were ready for chapter two. Wonder why she took all her jewelry off but left her wedding rings on."

"I wondered about it, too. Figured maybe they were too tight. But I checked and they weren't. So maybe that was part of the thrill."

"Not thrilling for the husband."

"Exactly. Classic motive number two. Once I'm outta here, learning about hubby is priority one." He looked at his Timex.

"Jealous spouse," I said. "Could turn out to be straightforward."

He crossed his fingers.

"What is it you think I can help you with?"

"Nothing specific, just spread your aura."

That sounded like tokenism and it made me wonder.

He said, "Anything else you wanna see?"

I opened the double doors to a generous closet. Hanging space to the left, drawers to the right.

Milo said, "Been through it, nothing in the pockets except more condoms. Two packets for each jacket and a couple more boxes in the medicine cabinet. Italian design, Swiss manufacture. Gluten-free and vegan."

I laughed.

He said, "I'm serious. And maybe the poor guy was onto something because there was nothing interesting medication-wise. Guy didn't even seem to have headaches."

I examined the clothing. Not much quantity but plenty of quality.

Three unstructured Brunello Cucinelli cashmere sport coats were paired with brightly colored slim-fit slacks, a black calfskin jacket was coupled with black Stefano Ricci jeans. No ties, no dress shirts but for a Prada wing-collar formal under a navy-blue tux. Both crisp enough to be unused. A handwritten receipt on high-quality paper hanging from a button inside the tux jacket supported that. Handmade for **Sig. G. Aggiunta** by a tailor in Milan. Thirty-four hundred euros.

The drawers contained black T-shirts, mostly silk, a few linen and cotton; black silk bikini underwear, turtlenecks, cashmere sweaters, fitted polos in the same bright hues as the pants.

In contrast with the limited display of textiles, shoes filled every inch of floor space and two upper shelves. Tennis shoes for exercise and for show, suede drivers, supple loafers, woven oxfords, glossy wingtips, lace-up boots. Four pairs of Chelsea boots. Peanut butter leather, gray leather, crocodile, ostrich hide.

Milo said, "Maybe married women weren't his only fetish."

I pointed to a mustard-colored jacket coupled with scarlet pants. "No suits, what the Italians call **spezzato**."

"What?"

"Unmatched components."

"And you know this because . . ."

"Evaluated a family originally from Rome a while back. The husband was into it, one point of contention was he wanted to dress his ten-year-old son the same way. The wife thought it was vulgar. Like him."

He looked down at his own contrasting getup.

I said, "Ahead of your time."

"Live long enough, everything comes 'round."

"I mentioned it because apart from no business wear, his tux looks unused and he doesn't own a tie. Whatever he does to make money doesn't require formality."

"Maybe he's Cobbler to the Stars . . . so far, haven't found evidence of any kind of job."

"The clothing's expensive, so he's got an income from somewhere."

"Yeah, alligator boots have to cost three figures . . . poor lizard. Anything else you wanna check out?"

"What's behind the closed door?"

"Nothing. Empty space."

"Then I'm fine."

"Then outta here has arrived."

I followed his unmarked Impala to the West L.A. station on Butler, where he key-carded both of us into the staff lot. We crossed the street, entered the building, took the stairs up to the second floor where he'd been banished years ago by a corrupt police chief about to retire.

The exile had followed his work on an old case murder that unearthed pension-jeopardizing dirt on the chief. Off-the-record negotiation had led to his promotion to lieutenant sweetened by the ability to keep working murders and avoid the paper-shuffling obligations of rank.

The downside would be isolation.

Sequestered above the big detective room in a windowless office the size of a broom closet, he'd have no authority over anyone and lack the ability to assemble a team without permission from his captain. Every single time.

The chief, known to be petty, had figured he'd stuck it to Milo but he'd failed to do his homework and had no idea he'd handed my friend a gift. Closet notwithstanding, the ability to come and go as he pleased was a boon. Who needs a view and square footage when you're free to do your own thing?

Subsequent chiefs bristled when they learned of the arrangement because police departments are paramilitary and crave regulation. But Milo's solve rate, the highest in the department, to the chagrin of the hotshots at Parker Center, had prevented any change.

Barely able to accommodate Milo's bulk, the space shrank to a claustrophobic box when anyone else entered. Anyone else usually meant me and I'd accommodated myself to a small, hard chair in the corner facing Milo's back as he hunched over his undersized, cluttered desk.

He plopped down, rolled back just short of impact with my toes, pushed himself back and swept a stack of papers into a wastebasket. Wheeling around sharply, he faced me. A cellphone in a fuzzy black case had materialized in his hand.

"No prints so I got to take it. Let's have a look at what's in plain sight." He began scrolling. "Everything older than two weeks has been deleted . . . most recent calls are a ton of numbers, gotta be international . . . code 39."

He swiveled to his keyboard, typed, swung back. "No surprise, Italy. I'll check that out later, let's see who he communicated with on this continent."

Giovanni Aggiunta's domestic communications were limited to outgoing calls to a Whole Foods and a sushi bar in Santa Monica, an Indian restaurant in Brentwood, a Spanish restaurant in Midtown, a Moroccan restaurant, a florist, and a dry cleaner in Westwood, the Beverly Hills Tennis Spa, and the cocktail lounges at three luxury hotels: the Peninsula and the Waldorf in B.H., and the Bel-Air.

"You and Robin go there. Ever see him?"

I smiled.

He said, "Even if he was there, I'm sure you two had eyes only for each other."

He returned to the phone. "Everything's outgoing and non-personal. So he deleted his incomings. That feels like something to hide."

I said, "Affair with a married woman, be careful. Didn't see any booze in the house. Did I miss it?"

The question threw him. "Why would that be relevant?"

"Trying to get a feel for him. There was tennis stuff in his car. It's shaping up like days devoted to recreation and nights to drinking in five-star lounges."

"Fine dining and a tennis spa," he said. "Nope, there wasn't much juice in the house and no flashy bachelor wet bar. Another Campari, coupla bottles of wine, some vodka, all in a kitchen cabinet."

I said, "Maybe no need to pretend the house was used for anything but sex."

"Party hardy, meet up for some illicit amore, take a dip, sleep late? Yeah, the place does have that self-indulgent feel to it."

I said, "Didn't see flowers in the house so his calls to the florist mean someone else got blooms."

"The old charm offensive? You're thinking I've got myself a playboy victim?"

"I was thinking gigolo financed by his clients. The house is no palace but it is secluded and a Bel Air address might've made wealthy women feel at ease. And in Ms. March's case, close enough for convenience."

"It's no palace, Alex, but the rental was eight grand a month."

"Doesn't mean he paid it," I said. "Or I'm wrong and he was just a young guy with an independent income."

"Don Giovanni," he said. "Enjoying the good life and never imagining." He shook his head. "Okay, let's see what the cyber-gods have to say about poor Meagin. Creative spelling should make it easier."

The data-gods held back, **meagin march** pulling up only two hits: a Planned Parenthood silent auction and a 5K run for a group that fostered and homed stray dogs called The Paws That Refresh.

On the donor list of both, Meagin and Douglass March. Five grand a pop.

"Another inventive speller," said Milo. "Maybe that's what the two of them bonded over."

A search for **douglass march** produced six small-print legal postings related to real estate syndications organized by Venture Quest Properties.

B. Douglass March, MBA, CEO and Primary Operating Partner. Corporate headquarters in Elko, Nevada.

The company had invested in large-scale residential complexes. Memphis, Orlando, Reno, Spokane.

Milo said, "Guy doesn't believe in keeping it local."

I said, "They're all in places with no state income tax. If March is hands-on, we could be talking a frequent flier and another layer of convenience for her."

"Feline's on the jet, the rodents pet? Makes sense. Maybe her phone will be more productive. I get freakishly lucky, there'll be deceptive calls to hubby on the same day she's setting up trysts with Giovanni and a tower ping that puts Dougie-with-two-esses near the scene last night. Though if he was home, we could be talking the same tower."

"Why were there no prints on Aggiunta's phone?"

"The more fibrous the surface, the worse for lifting." He produced the black case. "Cashmere. And whatever was on the face had smudged. Maybe due to hot hands."

He pushed hair from his forehead, sat back nearly bumping into his monitor. "Those Italian numbers could include his parents. Notification's bad enough but long distance is the worst. And what if they don't speak English—hey, do you know Italian?"

"Sorry, no."

"Just that **spezzato** thing, huh? I'll have to remember that and tell Rick. He'll be stunned into silence. Anything else come to mind?"

I said, "Who cleans the house?"

"Pool guy said he'd seen a service a few times but didn't know how often they come. No paperwork in the house. Nothing in the house but the lease so maybe you're right and someone else pays the bills. He does have three credit cards, hopefully they'll teach me something."

He stood, stretched upward, hands nearly brushing the oppressive ceiling. "Ready for some lunch? I'd say Italian but that feels wrong. Like we're minimizing the poor guy."

5

By the time we'd walked to Santa Monica Boulevard and covered a block, he said, "Changed my mind, I'm thinking Italian will be an homage."

That epiphany had occurred a few feet from a small Italian-deli-**cum**-café. Aromas spilled out to the sidewalk. Strong cheese, fresh tomatoes, followed by the earthy perfume of truffles.

In most of the eateries Milo frequents he's treated like a homecoming hero. Payoff for a police presence proprietors view as a deterrent to problems.

More important: huge tips.

The proprietors of Mangiamo were a husband and wife in their sixties. He ran the counter and she made pasta from scratch. A long-haired guy in his twenties who looked like an actor in a soap opera served and bused. All three beamed and shouted

"**Buongiorno!**" as we stepped in. The older man raced from behind the counter, seated us, and endowed Milo with instant promotion.

"**Capitano!** Sit, relax, today we have the **tartufo nero.**"

"Good news is always welcome, Marco. What are you putting it on?"

"I recommend tagliatelle, if you want smaller, you could do tagliolini."

"I have found," said Milo, "that less is not more. Tagliatelle."

"Perfect. And you, signor?"

"The same."

Marco hurried back to deliver the good news to his wife. Soap Opera came over with bread, butter, and olive oil. "What would you like to drink, please?" Perfect English, marked accent.

Milo said, "Pitcher of iced tea, two glasses."

"Immediately."

When the tea arrived, Milo had Giovanni Aggiunta's passport flipped to the I.D. photo.

"Has this gentleman ever been here?"

The waiter peered carefully. "No, sir." His eyes shifted to the name beneath the photo. "Aggiunta. Like the shoes."

"Shoes?"

"Expensive shoes." He looked down at his own dusty black lace-ups and smiled.

"Are they sold locally?"

"I don't know, sir. Maybe Rodeo Drive?"

"Super high-end, huh?"

The waiter whistled.

Milo put away the passport. The waiter's curiosity had been stoked but he knew better than to push it. "Anything else, **Capitano?**"

"We're fine, thanks. What's your name?"

"Bartolomo."

When we were alone, I said, "Cobbler to the Stars."

"All those shoes in the closet," he said. "All I had to do was examine the labels."

He poured tea for both of us, lifted his glass, put it down. "Here I was writing him off as a boy-toy and the guy turns out to be a serious businessman. Probably has an office in Century or B.H. Probably has a business phone."

I said, "The house is still no great shakes."

"You keep coming back to that."

"Fashion's all about promotion. Someone representing a high-end manufacturer in L.A. would be entertaining conspicuously. That place doesn't fit."

"Meaning?"

"I'm just guessing," I said, "but it's possible he's got a token job."

"The dumb son."

"Or just a son not interested in the family business. Alternatively, what if he got into some sort of trouble back home so they sent him here with a housing allowance, a leased car, and a fund that paid all his bills?"

"Trouble," he said. "With someone like Meagin."

"The thought crossed my mind."

"He crossed a husband in Italy with a short temper and a long memory? God, I hope not, Alex. Last thing I need is my suspect list expanding to international."

The waiter delivered two plates of golden-tinged pasta topped by shavings of black truffle.

Milo said, "Thanks, Bartolomo."

"Pleasure, sir. Enjoy." Still curious. Still discreet.

Milo coiled tagliatelle onto his fork and held it, suspended.

I said, "Something the matter?"

"Waiting for you to start."

"When did that become a thing?"

"Hey," he said, "it's not often you actually order something sinful. I want to see if it transforms you."

I tasted, smiled. "Do I look different?"

He said, "Yeah, like a bon vivant. Or whatever that is in Italian."

I ate.

He said, "You live with an Italian girl and don't know how to say it?"

"Robin's fourth-generation Californian and her mother was English."

He worked his phone. "Same thing, bon vivant."

I said, "Speaking of my girl, when did she call you and suggest you call me?"

His eyes, always a shockingly bright green, slid to the right. Seasoned detective giving off a liar's tell.

He nibbled with atypical precision. Chewed even slower.

I said, "It wasn't a trick question."

"You're making this assumption because . . ."

"The case doesn't feel different. And no more about aura, please."

"**Someone's** testy . . . when did she call? I wasn't supposed to let on but now you'll go home and badger her, so fine. A week ago. She said you were champing at the bit. Assured me you were okay then wondered if I'd lost my nerve."

He smiled. "She comes right to the point, Robin does."

I said, "I appreciate your wanting to protect me but she's right. I'm ready to go."

He drank tea.

I said, "The problem is . . ."

He put down his glass. "I keep turning it over and over, wondering how things screwed up so badly that you were nearly . . ." He waved away the rest of the sentence. Specks of moisture had collected in the corners of his eyes.

"Nothing screwed up. It was unpreventable."

"So you say."

"Have you come up with anything that could've stopped it?"

"No and that's the problem. My line of work, stuff happens. But it's not part of your job description."

"I'll be fine."

Silence.

I said, "How about this: I'll keep my distance from anything remotely resembling danger. Though I'm not sure how that'll affect riding with you and your damn lead-foot."

Queasy smile. He'd stopped eating.

"And if you get to go to Italy, I'll stay home."

He rubbed his face, looked up at the ceiling then down at the table. Pushed his plate away.

"No, no, no," I said. "Don't tell me you lost your appetite."

He patted his gut. "That would be so terrible?"

"Indeed it would," I said. "The world's tough enough without having my faith challenged."

"Wiseass."

"You used to say wise man."

He stared at me. I stared back. We broke into simultaneous grins.

From behind the counter, Marco said, "Ah, you like the **tartufo.** Fabulous!"

We both cleaned our plates. Bartolomo came over to bus.

Milo said, "Where you originally from?"

"Sardinia. But I lived in Rome. Studied architecture."

"No architecture jobs?"

"If only. I hope to certify here but it takes time."

Milo handed him a wad of cash. "Whatever's left is yours."

"**Capitano,** I cannot—"

"No big deal, stay healthy."

Bartolomo left looking stunned. Murmured conversation rose from behind the counter. Moments later, he was back with two small plates. A pair of cannoli on each, coated with pistachio bits and dark chocolate.

Milo said, "Thanks but not necessary."

"Life, **Capitano,** is not about necessary."

The moment his back was turned, Milo polished off one pastry and was reaching for another.

All was right in the world.

As we walked back to the station, Milo checked in with Detective Alicia Bogomil.

"Anything on the canvass, kid?"

She said, "I wish. The properties are spread out and maybe twenty percent of the houses seem to actually be occupied. Of the people I did make contact with, no one heard a thing. What's with the ghost-town atmosphere, Loo?"

"These are second- and third-home people. Did you get to the neighbors directly behind the scene?"

"Yup. Ginormous place, older couple with three German shepherds. They had no clue, were totally freaked out. It's like two acres from their house to the fence line and the back is like a forest so I can see them not hearing the shots."

"The dogs didn't bark?"

"These dogs, Loo, are about the same vintage as their owners. One had filmy eyes and just sat there, another licked my hand and rolled over for a tummy scratch, and the third dragged around looking totally out of it. Also, they sleep in the bedroom and there's a noise machine going."

"Everyone comfy, cozy, and unaware."

"You got it," said Alicia. "I felt bad having to tell them, they really got spooked. But better to be prepared, no? Not that they're likely to be targeted, this feels focused, don't you think? Not some maniac on the prowl."

"Agreed," he said. "Learned something about the male victim." He told her about the shoes.

She said, "Aggiunta? Never heard of them."

"Maybe they only make men's stuff."

"Probably," she said. "Women's, I'm an expert."

"That so."

"Believe it or not, Loo, off the job I can get girlie. Scored myself a pair of Jimmy Choos at the Nordstrom sale last year. Big heels, you know how tall Al is. Want me to look into the company?"

"Appreciate it. Where are Moe and Sean?"

"Moe was canvassing with me and Sean was on his way but both of them got called in, don't know for what."

"Not you."

"Well," she said, "sometimes I get **so** much static on my radio."

When we got to the staff lot, Milo said, "You up for checking out Meagin's place? If I get lucky, Dougie-with-two-esses will be sitting there with a guilty look on his face, on the verge of confessing. It's right on the way back to your place so we'll take separate cars."

"Makes sense."

"Also," he said, "God forbid my lead-foot should cause anxiety."

The residence of Meagin and Douglass March was a two-hundred-foot-wide, Palladian Revival manor. Three stories of cream-colored limestone were lidded by a stout slate roof. A columned entry sheltered a massive glass-and-brass door. On either side of the structure were wide passageways angling around the house.

Stained stone and darkening at the seams created a patina you couldn't fake. This was one of the original Bel Air dream palaces erected during the twenties. The decade had started off grandly only to be murdered by the Great Depression.

The front of the property was walled with ten feet of piled rock that, combined with an even higher iron gate, discouraged drop-ins. Through the slats of the gate, a park-like stretch of lawn was centered by a sinuous driveway lined with topiary balls.

Milo was parked, reading his notepad. I slipped

behind him and the two of us walked to the gate where he stabbed the call-box button.

Five phone rings before a woman's voice said, "Yes?"

"Police, ma'am. Please let us in."

Most people hearing that ask questions. This time the line went dead. Seconds later, the front door swung open and a woman in a pale-blue maid's uniform stepped between the columns and peered out.

Milo gave a small wave and held up his badge.

The woman took a few steps closer, studied us some more, returned to the house and slipped from view.

The gate glided open and we hiked to the front door. When we'd reached midway it reopened and the maid stood there watching us.

Milo said, "Lieutenant Sturgis, ma'am. This is Alex Delaware."

She nodded but her eyes were tight. Thirties, Hispanic, fresh-faced, pretty. Someone materialized behind her. An older woman, shorter, dressed in an identical uniform. Equally apprehensive.

"May we come in, please?"

Both women shifted to the right, as if trained to be a welcoming party.

The entry hall was a thirty-foot disk of white marble inlaid with small black squares. An elaborately carved and gilded center table held a three-foot crystal vase filled with silk flowers.

Behind the disk, a double marble staircase climbed to a window-backed landing. A Persian runner centering the steps was held fast by brass rods.

The bordering walls were hung with a tapestry on each side and tall paintings. Portraits of elaborately dressed, pallid, flat-faced people. Most likely imaginary ancestors. The kind of artwork that looks impressive at first glance but fetches low prices at auctions because who wants to be surrounded by dyspeptic Victorians?

On both sides of the entry were cavernous spaces that defied labeling. Great room? Living room? Salon? Indoor football field?

Identical six-foot black granite fireplaces at both ends, the mantels topped by silver torchères and another pair of judgmental faux forebears.

Milo pointed to the nearest portrait. "Family?"

The women giggled. The older woman said, "He buys."

"Mr. March."

"Si— yes."

Milo said, "Is Mr. March here?"

The younger woman shook her head.

"Where is he?" Smiling and keeping his voice soft.

"Traveling."

"Any idea where?"

She looked back at the older woman. Dual shrugs.

"Any idea when he'll be back?"

The younger woman began to shrug again but stopped when the older woman touched her shoulder and said, "He say Tuesday. But sometimes he doesn't."

"Sometimes he doesn't arrive when he says he's going to?"

Nods.

Milo said, "Do you have a number where he can be reached?"

The younger woman left, walked to the left of the staircase and around.

The older woman said, "In the kitchen."

"Got it. Thanks."

She gnawed her lower lip. "This is about Missus?"

"You're concerned about Missus."

"She go out running, no come home."

"That hasn't happened before?"

She looked at the floor. "Sometime she home late but always she come home."

"She likes to run at night."

Silence.

The younger woman returned with a white business card. Milo read it, raised his eyebrows, and handed it to me. The moment I touched it I knew what had surprised him. The paper was so flimsy it threatened to dissolve under my fingertips. Flat printing, no embossing. Like something a high school student might run off on a home computer.

Guy lives in a house like this and economizes on paper?

He'd also held back on the details of self-promotion.

B. DOUGLASS MARCH
VENTURE QUEST PROPERTIES, LLC
P.O.B. 467-89 B, LOS ANGELES, 90067 888
545 6201 EXT. 632-D

Milo stepped a few feet away and punched in the number. What he heard made him frown. Leaving an inaudible message, he glanced toward the right-hand cavern and headed there. I followed. The maids remained in place.

The room was at least fifty feet long and half as wide, set up with multiple conversation zones formed by careful arrangements of brocade, velvet, and suede seating that looked as if buttocks had never dared intrude. Twenty or so tables of various materials hosted boxes, paperweights, glass animals, silver ashtrays, enamel figurines.

One exception, the table that interested Milo. Nothing but a lone photograph in a silver rococo standing frame.

Full-body view of the woman we'd seen a few hours ago, captured bright-eyed and vital. In death, Meagin March's good looks had been a sad abstraction. In life, Meagin March had been gorgeous, graced by the kind of confident beauty that results when great genetics melds with a high level of self-care.

Her skin was clear and tan, her smile broad, white, warm, spiced by a hint of impishness. A long, smooth neck supported a perfectly proportioned face, the cheekbones high and pronounced, the eyes pale blue. The hair she'd pinned up carelessly in preparation for lovemaking, followed by a swim, was upswept in a soft but obedient chignon.

Shoulders bared by a black sleeveless cocktail dress were square, strong, and tanned. Some of the diamonds we'd seen a few hours ago glinted from strategic locations and the amethyst necklace settled perfectly in the V of the dress, as if the garment had been tailored to accommodate it. The dress was knee-length, fitted as snugly as a wetsuit. Red shoes with serious heels elevated her a couple of inches above the man whose arm she clutched.

Milo turned to the maids. "This is Mr. March?"

They hesitated for a second, then approached.

"Yes," said the older woman.

"Where was this taken?"

Head shakes.

"Looks like a party."

Silence.

Milo said, "Do Mr. and Mrs. March go to a lot of parties?"

The maids looked at each other.

The older one said, "Not a lot."

Out came his pad. Working to maintain his smile. "What are your names, please?"

"Irma," said the older woman.

"Last name, please?"

"Ruiz."

He scrawled. "And you, ma'am?"

"Adelita. Santiago."

"Why you need names?" said Irma Ruiz.

"Just for the record."

"Something happened to Missus." A statement, not a question.

"I'm afraid so. That's why I need to talk to Mr. March."

"Yes," said Irma Ruiz. "I think Memphis. But not sure."

"Great, thanks, very helpful. Is he at a hotel?"

"I think."

"Any idea which hotel?"

"No."

Adelita Santiago said, "There are ducks."

Irma Ruiz looked surprised.

Milo said, "Docks, like boats?"

Adelita Santiago wiggled her fingers and pantomimed flight.

"Ducks? Like the birds?"

Nod.

"He's staying at a farm."

"No, a hotel."

"A hotel with ducks."

Nod.

"Okay . . ." He returned to the photo of the Marches and I got out my phone.

When I clicked off, I studied Douglass March's image.

Slightly built and at least five years younger than his wife. Handsome in a starving-poet way, with limp, sandy hair worn longish, narrow dark eyes, and a waxy complexion suggesting susceptibility to infection. He wore a black suit, a black shirt striped with white, and a royal-blue tie. Reacted to the camera with the stingiest upturn of lips.

Smile!

Don't bug me.

The contrast with his wife's full-on photogenic glee was striking. Fissures in the relationship well under way?

Milo edged closer to me and spoke just above a whisper. "I was expecting a Daddy Warbucks twice her age and this guy's what—thirty? Looks more like a boy-wonder math prof than a real estate tycoon."

He took in the vastness of the house. "Making it young and thinking he's got it all."

I said, "Or not. He doesn't look overjoyed."

He studied the photo. "Good point. So maybe he already knew something was up when she went out running and there's the motive . . . they do look kinda mismatched. Wonder when this was taken."

He picked up the photo and walked over to the maids, still standing in the entry, immobile. "When's the first time you saw this?"

Adelita Santiago said, "Missus told me to find a good place for it . . . maybe . . . I don't know for sure."

"Doesn't have to be for sure," Milo said gently. "Even a guess."

Silence.

"Is it new or from before?"

"Before. Maybe . . . two months ago?"

Irma Ruiz said, "I think maybe three. They went to a party in Mister's car."

"Where is Mister's car?"

"In the garage. Missus's, too."

"Got it. Anything else you want to tell us?"

Silence.

"Okay, thanks, you've been helpful."

That assessment made both women tighten up.

I said, "What's wrong?"

Adelita Santiago said, "We not supposed to talk to people. To let people in."

"Makes sense," said Milo. "But we're not people, we're the police."

Her mouth quivered. "Something happened to Missus."

Milo thought for a moment. Glanced at me. I nodded.

"I've got very bad news for you, ladies. Missus is **muerta.**"

Irma Ruiz clutched her chest. "No."

Adelita Santiago clutched the sides of her face. "No, no, no."

"I'm sorry," said Milo.

That opened the spigots. Both women broke down and sobbed.

7

Leaving me with the maids in the entry, Milo traced the same route Adelita had taken to the kitchen. The two of them spent the time crying and hugging each other, were still doing so when he returned with a box of tissues and two bottles of Fiji Water.

The women wiped their eyes but held on to the water, unopened.

He said, "Anything you want to tell us?"

Neck-straining head shakes.

Neither had asked any questions about Missus's death. Some jobs are based on not asking.

Milo laid his own business card on the center table. "If there's anything else you want to say, please call."

The maids stood there, glassy-eyed.

"We'll get going now. Could you please open the gate for us?"

"Black button," said Adelita. She remained in place, as did Irma.

Neither of them budged as we saw ourselves out.

The black button took a moment to locate. On the side of a stone post, tucked near the junction with the wall, several feet above the motor that activated the gate.

When we were through, he said, "Ducks? Must be a language problem."

I said, "The Peabody hotel in Memphis has a twice-a-day ritual. The birds march off an elevator, walk across the lobby, and swim in a fountain. Then they go back. Morning and evening. Apparently it's a big attraction."

"Unbelievable. How do you know this?"

"You pick stuff up."

"Ducks. I verify him in Memphis, he didn't pull the trigger. But a guy of his means would have no problem hiring someone. And like you said, there's a precise feel to it. Big money buys the best."

Leaning against the unmarked, he phoned the hotel, asked for Douglass March, waited. "Okay, please tell him Lieutenant Sturgis from the Los Angeles Police Department called. Here's my number . . . that's it, no additional message. Thanks. By the way, how're the ducks doing . . . ?"

Nope, haven't, just heard about it . . . yeah, I definitely will if I ever get over there . . . I believe you, sounds like fun. Bye."

He hung up. "Mr. March is registered but out of his room. The ducks are in fine form. And notice, I made no cracks about **l'orange**."

He walked me to the Seville. "Hopefully March will get back to me soon. I'll let you know and we can do a face-to-face."

We. Good sign.

I said, "Aren't most contract executions usually headshots? If not the first bullet, then the coup to the back of the skull?"

"The few pro jobs I've seen have been that. But there are always exceptions."

"Granted," I said. "But the question is why deviate and two possibilities come to mind, starting with symbolism. You broke my heart, I'll destroy yours."

"Dougie gave the hit man instructions? Yeah, I like it. What's the second?"

This you won't like. "Who gets training to aim for center mass?"

His face tightened. "Fine, we do. Most departments do. Aim to stop not just to kill, minimize corollary damage. A cop-turned-hit-man? Sounds like a movie."

I said, "Maybe, but we're likely dealing with a .38 revolver and what's the most common type?"

"S and W Police **and** Military," he said. "Note the emphasis on **and**. Every branch of the military used 'em. Plenty of private citizens, too. There've got to be millions of them out there. Look **that** up in the Bible."

He waited, shoulders bunched, as I ran a search. "Close to seven million manufactured."

"There you go. Walk into any damn gun shop or show and buy dozens. Not to mention private sales. Okay, thanks for your time. Let's both take a break."

Once home, I took the rear steps down to the garden, paused to feed the koi, and continued to Robin's studio.

Usually she's got several projects going, working on a mix of electric and acoustic instruments. For the past three weeks she'd been busy with one: restoring a hundred-and-fifty-year-old Antonio Torres classical guitar with a tissue-thin top and a history of ownership by several major composers and players. The challenge: alter as little as possible but do enough to resuscitate tone destroyed by wood-butchery in Barcelona.

Not her usual gig but the Swiss-born artisan in New York who used to take on that kind of thing had retired and forwarded clients to Robin.

If she found the assignment intimidating she didn't let on. But hours spent in the studio had been stretching later than usual, the roar-and-buzz of power tools replaced by the click-clack of tweezers and scalpels.

I opened the door slowly and paused in the doorway to make sure I didn't startle her.

Blanche had also gotten with the program. Instead of her usual jump off the couch followed by a heavy-breathing waddle toward me, she remained in place. Glancing at the workbench where Robin sat wearing magnifying goggles and holding a tiny tessera of inlay an inch above the Torres's sound hole. Repairing the rosette, a masterpiece of inlay that had warped. Hundreds of snippets of dyed wood and ivory no larger than toothpick tips requiring painstaking reinstallation.

She smiled. "It's okay, girlfriend, do your romantic thing. Same for you, darling."

But both of us waited until she'd set the sliver.

Removing the thick specs, she breathed out, rolled her shoulders, knuckled her eyes, finally smiled.

"How'd it go, babe?"

The reunion you set up?

I kneeled and received slobbering affection from Blanche. "Interesting case."

"That's great." Walking away from the bench, Robin untied her hair, shook it loose, removed her apron, dusted off black overalls.

I said, "Kicking off early?"

"Maybe," she said. "Or maybe I'll resume later. It's a gorgeous little thing, isn't it? Can't wait to hear it once it's playable."

I stood, took her in my arms, held her and kissed her, breathing in perfume and sawdust and oddly aromatic sweat.

"You have lunch with Big Guy?"

"Italian."

"Pizza the size of a manhole cover, you eat a slice or two, he demolishes the rest?"

"Pasta with black truffles."

"Ooh," she said. "Now I'm jealous." She rubbed the back of my neck. "Looser than it's been in a while, good for you. Not that it'll stop me from guilt-tripping you as I pry open a can of tuna with aching fingers and pair it with dry crackers."

She feigned coughing.

I cracked up.

"Glad someone thinks it's funny." Grinning.

I said, "How about dinner as atonement? Maybe the Bel-Air? Restaurant or bar, been a while."

"That might partially compensate. If you toss in special devotion."

"Dessert?"

"More like some serious calorie-burning afterward."

"I'm free now."

"And I'm starving and will soon have fish breath. Sure, let's do the bar, keep it light, catch some music."

"Perfect." In more ways than one.

We left the studio, entered the house, and went into the kitchen. I said, "Mea culpa, culpa mea," as she reached for the tuna can.

"You're on the right track but have a way to go."

I drank coffee as she ate, remained at the kitchen table when she went to freshen up. When the shower began running, I texted Milo and asked him to send me Giovanni Aggiunta's and Meagin March's headshots.

Why?

I told him.

Doctor Romantic.

The emoji that followed stuck its tongue out in disgust.

If you don't want me to . . .

Fine, on their way. Any shame's on you.

8

The bar at the Bel-Air was half empty when we arrived, nearly full by the time we'd had our first drinks.

On the menu, tagliatelle with black truffles.

I said, "Karma."

Robin said, "Did you plan it?"

"Wish I was that prescient."

She stared at me. "I guess I believe you. What are you going to have?"

"Black bass sounds good."

"I may steal some of that, too."

She leaned over and kissed me. "This is great, I'm so glad you're back in the swing."

Midway through the food, the entertainment arrived. Solo pianist, older guy, bad suit, great touch, long memory. My opportunity came when he took a break and Robin said, "'Scuse me, back in a sec."

The restrooms at the Bel-Air are outdoors, a short walk from the bar and a right angle beyond the restaurant.

More than a sec required. I went up to the hostess and showed her the photos.

She said, "Gio? He comes here. Her . . . don't think so . . . nope, never. Why?"

"He and my girlfriend have kind of a history and bumping into each other could be, you know." I smiled and shrugged.

"Awkward City, got it," she said. "I haven't seen him for a while and he's always with a date. Would that hurt or help?"

"Definitely help, she's the one who ended it."

"Good for her. When I say dates I mean different women."

"That fits. Thanks."

She looked me over. "Treat her good."

"Promise."

A group of four middle-aged men in expensive suits and gut-flaunting T-shirts stepped up behind her, laughing.

"Welcome, guys, we've got a nice table over by the bar."

One of the men said, "Closer the better, gorgeous."

Laughter all around. The hostess forced a smile.

I was back at our table when Robin returned.

Later that evening, after we'd burned calories and showered together, she slipped on a robe and tied her hair up. "I thought I'd sneak over and take a look at the Torres. Shouldn't take long."

"Go for it."

When she was gone, I phoned Milo at home.

"What's up?" he said. Clogged voice. Weary.

I said, "Aggiunta goes by Gio. He was a regular at the Bel-Air bar and took lots of women there. Not including Meagin."

"How'd you find this out?"

"A not-so-confidential source." I told him about the hostess.

He said, "Covert operation while your true love's in the ladies'? Of course you told her what you were up to. Not."

I said, "Need-to-know basis."

"You also didn't tell her you figured out she called me."

"Same criterion."

"So the guy's a big-time player, no surprise."

I said, "What I find interesting is he never took Meagin there and she was one of many. So maybe there was no long-term affair. They met jogging or at some other chance event."

"Maybe . . . you realize what that does. Expands the jealous-husband thing way beyond Mr. March."

"On the other hand, it was Ms. March who got shot."

"Coulda been wrong place, wrong time."

"Two straight to the heart?"

"The bad guy likes patterns."

"I guess."

"So what, you like her as the main target or not?"

"Don't know."

His exhalation came through the phone as a wheezy gush. "Two victims and no clue which one to focus on. Guess now it's officially different, amigo, so you no longer need to worry about me doling out alms. Anything else?"

"Not for now."

"Long as we're chatting, I'll catch you up," he said. "Zilch from the canvass, tried every Italian number in Giovanni's phone and got a whole bunch of Italian voicemail. Hopefully someone'll understand a message in English. What does intrigue me is no callback yet from Douglass March."

"How much detail did you give him?"

"Just that I need to talk to him. You get that outta the clear blue, you don't respond? Or at least check it out?"

A beat. "Hopefully he hasn't ducked out."

I was putting the phone down when Robin came into the bedroom.

"Three guesses," she said. "Milo, Milo, or Milo. Anything interesting?"

"Unfortunately not."

"You called him."

"Just checking in."

"At ten p.m.," she said. "In pajamas."

"How's the guitar?"

"Point made," she said. "How is it? It's talking to me in a much friendlier voice. I tucked it in, kissed it, said nighty-night."

She slid in beside me, laid her head on my chest. "Pleasant dreams to you, too, my fellow compulsive."

CHAPTER

9

I woke up early on Monday, took a brief run while trying to ignore the lingering buzz in my ribs. Had coffee and a couple of scrambled eggs and spent the next four hours writing reports and talking to judges.

Two active custody cases had finally been put to rest, same for the evaluation and treatment of a bright, gentle five-year-old boy who'd been injured in a freeway pileup that had broken his mother's legs. The damage to him had been less severe: soft tissue bruising. Which I could easily relate to. His body had healed quickly, not unusual for kids. Emotional injury had endured.

Once I sign off on custody recommendations, I rarely see the kids they affect. No matter how careful and fair I try to be, someone's bound to be resentful and it's best to fade out and permit a new beginning. Injury cases, on the other hand, often do become treatment cases because of my training in pediatric trauma. The freeway disaster had led to three and a half months of rapport-building and intervention aimed at restoring security and mastery.

Addressing and sealing three legal-sized envelopes brought satisfaction. I was waiting by the gate when the courier service came to pick them up. A driver who'd been here before. Per usual, I had a can of Perrier ready for him.

"How's it going, Frank?"

"It's going." He took the can. "Not necessary, Doc, but thanks, you rock. So . . . these to the court, this one to a lawyer on Seventh. Keep working, Doc. Helps me to do the same."

As he drove off, my phone buzzed.

Milo said, "Finally heard from ol' Dougie. He's on his way back, should be here by five, said meet him at his place."

I said, "How'd he react when you filled him in?"

"He didn't because I didn't. There was no conversation, just him informing me of his plans. When I redialed I got Ms. Robot. Speaking of which, his voice was kinda flat."

I said, "Maybe she's actually his assistant."

He laughed. "We go to his office and it's all automatons in hipster clothing? Which actually sounds like Silicon Valley. Anyway, back to his demeanor. Totally matter-of-fact, no curiosity when the police call. Bizarre. Can you make it at five?"

"Sure."

"Convenient, huh? You living so close. Gonna try to jog it this time?"

"Got that out of the way this morning."

"Did you," he said. "My aerobic challenge was waking up."

At three p.m., he called again. "Turns out Mr. March caught a direct flight from Memphis and plans to be home in forty minutes. Allegiant Air, I looked it up, discount outfit, hundred and fifty bucks. That house, you'd think he owned his own jet or at least chartered. Guy's full of surprises. Either the worst kind of suspect or the best. Can you make it in forty?"

"No prob."

He hummed the first few bars of "Hail, Hail, the Gang's All Here." "Glad we're doing our thing again."

Click.

I arrived on time at the March estate. Milo had beat me to it and was parked in the same spot.

This time the gate opened after a single ring. No inquiries from within.

When we reached the front door, it was shut, requiring another button-push.

Several moments passed before Irma Ruiz opened it. Looking no less uncomfortable than she had yesterday.

Behind her, Adelita Santiago, likewise.

No one else in sight.

Irma said, "Please come," and led us around the left side of the double staircase into a second circular reception area. Black marble checked with white, smaller than the grand hall but still generous at twenty or so feet in diameter.

In lieu of more portraits, Gothic niches show-cased vases and urns. Beyond the space was a domed, window-backed room paneled in nearly black walnut inlaid with brass. Bookshelves on the side walls, most of them empty. The same kind of overstuffed furniture as in front, arranged in three groupings. One fireplace with a black granite surround.

Beyond the glass a columned patio larger than some apartments looked down on several acres of green grass. A sprinkle of trees: mature olives, a favorite of landscapers because their root balls are small and they transplant easily. A pair of fifty-foot pines was sited too precisely to be Mother Nature at work. A cobalt-tiled Olympic-sized pool featured a swim-up bar at the deep end. Meagin March hadn't run to Gio Aggiunta's place for the water.

Much of the property's back border was taken up by a two-story mini-me of the main house. Accessed by a motor court at the end of the left-hand drive. Rooms on the second floor, six-car garage on ground level.

Irma stopped and said, "They here."

A man sitting near the fireplace sat up and made himself visible. Staring at us for a second, he stood and came forward.

In the flesh, Douglass March looked even younger. Mid- to late twenties, five-six, a hundred thirty. His mouth was narrow, the lips plump and dark and set in a lemon-sucking pout. Smallish hazel eyes were blurred by the lenses of black-framed specs.

March's hair, lank and colored a strange beige, had grown out since he'd posed for the photo, now trailed an inch below his shoulders. The front flap swooped across one cheek, nearly concealing one eye. He wore a wrinkled white shirt with sleeves rolled to the elbows, skinny blue jeans that bagged on skinny legs, and white Reeboks grimed gray in spots.

Easily taken for a struggling grad student.

Milo said, "Lieutenant Sturgis." He held out his hand.

March nodded but kept his hands at his side. "Doug." Surprisingly deep voice.

Milo withdrew and looked at me. "This is Alex Delaware."

Doug March didn't follow his gaze. "We can sit down." As if he'd been debating it.

He led us back to the fireplace. Warm day but a fire raged. Curious. Then I noticed the oddities:

silent, not a hint of crackle; no logs or gas jets or any other type of fuel. Pale licks of blue-tipped flames peaked uniformly.

Some kind of holographic gizmo.

March returned to a corpulent brocade armchair. He had the kind of bony body that seems to diminish when it settles, as if inadequately supported by musculature. Crossing his legs had the effect of compressing him further.

When we'd sat, he said, "Who killed my wife?"

Milo said, "You know about it."

"A police detective supposedly calls me from L.A.? I check him out."

"Supposedly."

"I get all sorts of bogus calls. Obviously, yours wasn't. I learned you handle homicides. Add to that Meagin not answering my calls and it wasn't hard to figure out."

"Ah," said Milo. "Sorry about your loss."

"Thanks," said March. "Though I'm sure you say that to everyone. So what happened?"

"Your wife was shot to death either late Saturday night or early Sunday morning."

"Where?"

"At a man's house. He was killed, as well."

Doug March blinked. Swept hair away from the hidden eye and looked at the faux fire. "A man. May I ask who?"

"His name was Giovanni Aggiunta."

March shook his head. "Means nothing to me."

Studying the flames had swept his eyes past me. Now they swept back and focused on Milo. Someone used to dealing with bosses, no time for underlings.

Which was fine. More opportunity for me to study him.

His eyes were dry, his narrow, pale face, inert. The only trace of anxiety, rapid clenching and unclenching of pale, delicate hands.

"A man," he said. "Were the circumstances what I assume they were?"

"What do you assume, sir?"

"A liaison," said Doug March. "Where does this guy live?"

"Not far from here," said Milo. "Maybe a mile and a half north."

"Bel Air."

"Yes, sir."

"A mile and a half. Well within Meagin's running ability. She'd started running at night. I didn't suspect anything but looks like I should have. Why change her routine all of a sudden? Why run at night when she had all day to do it?"

"When did the routine change, sir?" said Milo.

Doug March said, "You don't need to call me sir. No one in my company does that, it's stuffy."

"What would you prefer?"

"You don't need to call me anything. I'm sure some people need that kind of thing—shallow acclaim. I don't."

March's pouty lips twisted in what might've been

intended as a smile. "Alternatively," he said, "we could go with Your Majesty."

He waved a hand awkwardly. "Sorry, that was snotty, don't mean to be a jerk. This is horrible for me, I'm just working at keeping afloat."

Or taking charge of the situation? Meanwhile, Milo's question had gone unanswered.

He repeated it.

March said, "When did she change? I really can't be sure because I'm gone so often."

The fingers of March's right hand began tapping those of the left. "The earliest I'm aware of would be . . . I guess around two months ago. Pretty close to that. I'd been in Texas looking at properties, came back at night and found her gone. The ladies said she went running. When she showed up, she was in her running outfit and pretty sweaty."

He sat up hard, blinked hard and frowned before sinking back into the embrace of the chair.

Sudden insight into the real source of his wife's perspiration?

Milo said, "Two months ago."

"Approximately. If you wait, I can fetch my phone and look up my schedule—no, I don't really need to do that, I can figure it out, let me think . . . after Austin came Tulsa . . . then Nashville . . . then Memphis, I settled on Memphis and that was . . . nine weeks ago. That's as close as I can get without checking."

I said, "After that Meagin continued to run at night."

March kept his eyes on Milo. "I never questioned her about it, just told her to watch for cars. There didn't seem to be a reason to question her. In retrospect this probably sounds crazily naive but I trusted Meagin. We've been married for a year and a half and there'd never been a rough spot."

Sad smile. "She always seemed happy to see me. That time, too. Sweaty but happy."

His lips trembled and turned inward. The hyperactive hands had stilled. As if his body could handle just so much reaction.

"This is so . . . I can't find an adjective. We had breakfast three days ago and now—the **gone**-ness of it all. It's . . . and now I find out she was betraying me? How old was this Italian?"

Milo's brows arched. "Twenty-nine."

"That's crazy," said Doug March.

Milo said, "How so?"

"Exactly my age. In the past, she'd always gone for older men. When we met she joked about cradle-robbing. Joked about having me dye my hair gray. Told me I was tolerable because I had an old soul."

He blinked. "Did this Italian have an old soul?"

"No idea, Doug."

"Older men," said March. "Or so she claimed."

"You doubt it?"

"I doubt everything, now."

He sprang up and hurried out of the room. Hooked right at the base of the staircase. Seeking a restroom? Taking the route that had led Adelita to the kitchen? Or continuing into the bowels of a massive service wing?

A house big enough to disappear in. But March returned at a near-trot moments later, carrying his phone in one hand, an open bottle of beer in the other.

Bud Light. Discount airline. Man of the people? Or striving to pretend?

Back in the chair, he downed half the bottle. "I need at least this level of alcohol to smooth out the edges. When you leave, I'm going to continue until I'm drowsy enough to sleep, but right now I want to be coherent."

He lofted the phone. "Checked my travel schedule and I was pretty close. Sixty-one days ago is when I returned and found out she'd taken a night run. But I can't tell you she never did it before. As I said, I'm gone so often."

"Looking at properties."

"You know about that."

Milo smiled. "Checking goes two ways."

Doug March thought about that. "Okay, I'll buy that. Yes, that's what I do. Size up opportunities and exploit the best ones. Large, well-run residential projects in areas primed for growth. I put my own money in for part of the purchase, finance the rest by taking on limited partners. I also handle management and charge for that. Ideally, I hold on to the properties no longer than three years and, having improved them, sell at a profit."

Long speech in his native language. It calmed him.

Milo said, "How often are you gone?"

"Once again," said March, "I'd have to check but my best guess would be two hundred and forty-four days out of the year. That's two-thirds of three sixty-five."

"Did Meagin ever travel with you?"

"I made several trips to Florida. Meagin wanted to go so she came along on . . . two of them. She brought her bikini and enjoyed the sun. One time she came to Austin when I examined possibilities on Lake Travis. That's it."

"The two of you were apart quite a bit."

Doug March's eyes slitted. "Are you saying I should have expected her to cheat?"

"No, sir—"

"Meagin never indicated she felt neglected. Just the opposite, between her exercise and her art and her friends, she kept busy. So why would I have expected anything?"

"No reason," said Milo.

"You're saying absence **doesn't** make the heart grow fonder?" said Doug March.

"Sorry if this seems intrusive but we're just trying to collect info—"

"Obviously you're right. About **our** absences.

But how was I to know? Every time I came home she was happy to see me. Made that **clear.**"

Pink blotches rose on March's waxy skin. "Our physical life was excellent. I don't understand any of this."

We said nothing.

"She was happy to see me every single time," he said. "Sixty-one days ago, as well. The only difference was she wasn't there to greet me."

He shook his head. Hair swung and settled over both eyes. He brushed it away furiously. "I'm an **idiot.**"

Milo looked at me.

I ran a finger across my lips.

We sat there as Doug March squinted and grimaced and finished his beer. Lifting the bottle high over his head, he flung it at the fireplace. Stiff, clumsy throw. It bounced, rolled, and came to a stop near a five-foot andiron.

"Can't even do that," he said. "Can't even do fucking **that.**"

10

We waited for Doug March to compose himself. That didn't happen; instead he sank into inertia and stared at his lap.

Milo said, "You're going through incredible stress, Doug."

A muffled, "So what?"

"So it's best that you go easy on yourself."

March's head snapped up, face pinched with anger.

"Go easy? What, I'm a snowflake? Feeling unsafe? Give me a break."

He began to stand, tottered, made it to his feet and left. When he returned, he was marching stiffly. Swinging beer number two at his side. Already down by half.

Plopping down heavily, he said, "Now what?"

"If you're okay with it," said Milo, "we'd like to ask you a few more questions about Meagin and yourself."

"What kind of questions?"

"Let's start with how you met."

March said, "Can't see how that's relevant but no sense prolonging this. We met by accident at the Waldorf bar. I'd finished a business meeting, wanted to go over some paperwork."

He held up the bottle.

"I took a quiet table. Meagin was with some friends nearby. A table of women. The rest of them ignored me. She didn't. I saw her looking at me. Looked at her and smiled. She smiled back. So I bought drinks for the table. Pretty smooth, huh? First time I'd done it. First time a woman had noticed me in a bar. Before that it was girls in college and grad school, then meeting women in the real estate world—way too much assertiveness."

"Meagin wasn't assertive."

"Meagin was self-confident so she didn't need to be assertive," said March. "Meagin was soft-spoken and gorgeous. Why did she notice me?" He shrugged. "She said she'd always gone for older men and that hadn't turned out so well. She thought I was younger than I actually was." The blotches deepened. "What she told me later was, 'I was going through a dry patch, Dougie, figured why not try the cougar thing?'"

His eyes hardened. "And no, it wasn't about

money. She also figured I was some kind of gofer or assistant right out of school. Actually, I was right out of school. Two years after my M.B.A."

"But not an assistant."

March said, "No, not that."

He drank beer, waved a limp hand around the room. "It wasn't this house, either, because I didn't live here, I had a one-bedroom apartment in the Palisades. I owned the building but no great shakes. This place I bought right after we got married. Got it from the heirs of a former client. Mint condition, fully furnished, the sale benefited their asset division, for me it was the deal of the century. When Meagin saw it, she said, 'You've got to be kidding,' and laughed. She was always laughing about it. Making size-matters jokes. So it wasn't about the money, not at all. Not one bit."

His voice had begun to rise at the end of each sentence. Straining to convince himself.

Another bottle drained. March looked toward the exit, fidgeted, remained in place.

"So if things were so great, why did she cheat? Good question. Maybe you'll **detect** the reason."

He placed the bottle on the floor. "The Italian, was he some kind of Mafia lowlife? Didn't know you had them in L.A. Thought your old boss back in the fifties, what was his name . . . Parker. Thought Parker got rid of them and they never came back big-time."

Milo said, "Before my time, Doug."

"Not before mine," said March. "I get to know every city I invest in from stem to stern. Not just the market history, the social and political history, the zeitgeist—overall atmosphere. When I came to S.C. to do the M.B.A., I thought L.A. was insane. Not a real city, more like a sprawling piece of . . . intentions."

I said, "You used to invest here."

He looked at me quizzically.

"The apartment in the Palisades."

"Oh, that," he said. "Nothing big, I leveraged a few apartments, made my profit, dumped them. Too much hassle, oppressive rent control. I'd actually been considering moving out of state. Then I met Meagin and she liked it here, so . . . why does any of this matter?"

I said, "Where was Meagin from?"

"The Midwest," he said. "And since you're obviously going to ask, I'm from Tuxedo Park. That's New York."

"The women Meagin was with the night you met her. Are they still her friends?"

"No idea."

"Who else did she socialize with?"

The wax turned florid. As if combusting from within.

March said, "What's the deal here? He's all sympathetic and you ask pointless questions? Why the hell do her friends matter? They didn't kill her, some Mafia scumbag probably did!"

Milo said, "The more we know about Meagin, Doug, the likelier we are to find out who murdered her."

"That," said Douglass March, "sounds random. If I ran my business that way, I'd be broke."

We remained silent.

March took another look at his exit route. The color in his face had begun to fade but he looked queasy, gripping the arms of the chair.

"You okay, Doug?"

"Not really. I feel like throwing up."

Milo said, "Whatever you need to do."

"I didn't mean that literally. I meant the whole thing is utterly sickening. My wife's gone and I have to wonder about why she cheated on me and did that lead to . . . what happened."

Milo nodded.

I said, "You mentioned her art."

"She painted, okay? But unless you're going to tell me someone poisoned her paints, I don't see . . . forget it, what's the use, you've got a playbook to follow."

Milo said, "Did she keep a studio, here?"

"Upstairs," said March.

"Would it be okay if we had a look at it? At any of her personal space that you think might be relevant."

"I think none of it's relevant. What if I say no?"

"Your right but we'd wonder why, Doug."

March's fingers drummed the chair arms. "Fine.

I keep saying that. Nothing's fine. Everything's for shit."

He bent low, covered his face with his hands, and wept.

It took a while for him to stop snuffling. When his shoulders ceased heaving, he looked up, tear-streaked, smiling crookedly.

"Guess you're still here. Guess you're set on doing your job. So few people are, I appreciate your making the effort so I'll stop being an asshole. The studio is her only personal space, unless you count clothes in her walk-in closet. Whatever you want to paw through, I've got nothing to hide."

He stood. "This place isn't really a home, anyway. Just a stopover."

We climbed the left-hand staircase to the window-backed landing. Another broad, circular disk surrounded by curving walls. Polished walnut inlaid with a marquetry star. Antique demilune tables tucked snugly at strategic points. High, broad, carved walnut doors punctuated the space. Eight upstairs rooms.

Doug March pointed at the inlay. "Lone Star. The family was from Houston, big in oil, they redid the house when they moved in thirty years ago."

The windows offered a full view of the property. Seen from above, it looked vast. All the doors were open, offering peeks inside. On the right, large, carpeted bedrooms, each with canopy beds. At the end, a home gym. The mechanical severity of exercise machines stood out against carved, gilt-edged furniture so ornate I imagined Louis XIV begging for simplicity.

On the left, two sets of double doors. The master bedroom. Doug March stood back and said, "Here."

The space he'd revealed was small, painted flat white, and softly lit by northern exposure. Minimally set up with an easel, a chair, an oak flat file, and a couple of taborets on wheels.

No bite of linseed oil. Acrylics.

A scatter of unframed canvases hung on the walls. Colorful, workman-like renderings of still lifes, seascapes, forests, cozy villages filled with tumbledown cottages.

Well done but lacking surprise.

Something different on the easel.

Doug March said, "Guess she was talented. That was a surprise."

Milo said, "Why's that?"

"Because in this city, everyone thinks they're creative and they're not." He laughed harshly. "When Meagin told me she painted and wanted to set up a studio, I thought, 'Here we go. Sure, indulge her.' No skin off, it's not like we lacked space. I offered her any space she wanted."

He pointed across the landing. "The bedrooms are huge but she wanted this, said it was intimate. It's dinky because it was originally an auxiliary closet. Mrs. Harrington used it to store her extra clothing. Standing racks crammed with ridiculous stuff that they left behind after she died. I was ready to dump it all. Meagin insisted on donating it to some animal thing."

Milo said, "I noticed a photo of the two of you—"

"Exactly," said March. "Raising money for wounded pets or whatever."

"Haven't seen any pets."

"I'm allergic. Okay, seen enough of the museum?"

I approached the easel and took a close look at the outlier.

Sixteen-by-twelve rectangle painted the deep dense gray of freshly watered concrete. Lighter gray blended with white for the subject. The lack of contrast made it struggle to materialize. An image struggling through a fog.

Unlike the other subjects Meagin March had chosen, this one was ambiguous. A small, stalky thing topped by a starburst and bottomed by what looked like pincers. Blurry and indistinct. Probably a work in progress—tentative rendering of an insect or a sea creature. The contrast with the other paintings was strange but when I looked over at Milo and March, neither showed any curiosity.

As they left, I hung back and phone-photo'd some of the paintings, including the exception.

March stopped and glared. "Why'd you do that?"

"What people produce can tell us about them."

"My God, more psychobabble bullshit? But sure, have it your way. Just don't put it on the internet."

Milo said, "Your wife's privacy will be guarded." Steel in his voice.

March flinched. "Sorry, I'm on edge. Got to get some sleep. You really need to paw through her clothes?"

"We'll do it quickly."

"Do I have to wait around?"

"No, go rest."

"Good, the girls can see you out." Crossing the landing, he entered one of the overstuffed bedrooms and shut the door.

Twin walk-in closets larger than most bedrooms, his dark wood, hers ivory enamel lit by a crystal chandelier. Lots of negative space in both. Doug March favored white shirts, jeans, owned a couple of nondescript suits and the tux in the photo.

Like her husband, Meagin March had filled only a quarter of her allotted space. Dresses, a couple of gowns, jeans, leggings, a dozen pairs of shoes.

Milo checked labels. "Everything high-end. Kinda like Aggiunta. Though that's probably not what they bonded over."

A rummage through built-in drawers unearthed plain wrap underwear and socks for him, designer lingerie for her. A pair of medicine cabinets in a massive white tile bathroom revealed that she was healthy and he was taking a single prescription med.

Milo held up the vial. "Norvasc. Prescribed by a doc in B.H."

"Hypertension."

"At his age?"

I said, "Could be something familial. And he is pretty reactive."

He put the vial back. "Wanna see anything else?"

"Nope."

"Then let's get seen out by the girls."

When we left the bedroom, Doug March was back in the landing, wearing a T-shirt and sweats and staring through the glass. Without looking at us, he placed his hands on his hips. "Is this the point where you tell me not to leave town?"

"Why would we do that, Doug?"

"Like I said, the rulebook. Don't you always look at the husband? Playing the odds, I get it. Obviously I didn't shoot anyone because I was across the country but what would've stopped me from hiring someone."

He swiveled. Milo stared at him.

March looked away. "This is probably a waste of breath, but I never paid anyone to do anything. I had no reason. Until you marched in here, I thought Meagin was the epitome of faithfulness."

If she hadn't been . . . ?

Milo said, "Sorry for having to deliver bad news, Doug."

"Whatever."

"Thanks for talking to us during this horrible time, Doug. Here's my card, if you've got any questions, call. I mean that."

March examined the card. "Sturgis. Like the motorcycle thing. I own a project in South Dakota. Have done really well with it— okay, I'm going to give sleep another try."

"Good luck, Doug."

Milo held out his hand. This time Doug March took it. But contact made him squirm and he looked relieved when it ended.

11

As we passed through the gates, I said, "Dry palms or moist?"

"Bone-dry but he was shaking. Any impressions other than he's an odd one?"

I said, "Tuxedo Park is gated, exclusive, expensive. Unless his folks were employed there, he comes from money. That would help establishing connections with big oil in Texas. And with bankrolling a real estate business right out of school."

He looked back at the mansion. "Not a baby-faced whiz kid, he did it the old-fashioned way? Maybe that matters, maybe it doesn't. What got me, Alex, was his claiming he needed a nap then he's waiting for us so he can deliver that parting shot. **Now** are you gonna tell me don't leave town."

He slapped his hands on his own hips. "What'd you get from his body language?"

"I dare you."

"Same here. Guy likes to be in control and he reacts to stress by getting mad."

I said, "Assuming it wasn't just a reaction to terrible news, he's definitely tightly wound."

"Like you said, not good for the blood pressure. So what if he just lied to us and knew all along that Meagin was screwing Gio? What do rich people do to solve problems? More dough, a higher-quality hit. Problem is, deep pockets also means more layers to hide behind."

He phoned Alicia.

She said, "Good news, Moe and Sean are back. It wasn't a case that pulled them off, it was a seminar on sexual etiquette. Not exactly learning to bow and curtsy."

"Must've missed the memo."

"Lucky you. Two hours of PowerPoint from a consultant the department hired. If there's another one scheduled, I'll probably have to go."

"Probably?"

"Well," she said, "sometimes the cell towers just don't catch the waves."

He laughed. "I need deep digging on the victim's husband."

"I can do it, L.T., but I'm still checking out Aggiunta Shoes. Want to hear what I've got, so far?"

"Shoot."

"Most of what's posted is in Italian and you know internet translations. But from what I can gather, it's a family enterprise, been around generations. You can go to Florence and they'll make a pattern and fit you bespoke. That's called **scarpe**—let me get this right—**scarpe personalizzate**. Regular stuff, they export but not in any great quantity. I found high-end retailers in Singapore, Dubai, Monaco, and Paris. In the U.S., only three places: a fancy-shmancy boutique in New York—Soho—similar on Michigan Avenue in Chicago, and here at a place near Sunset Plaza. **Veddy** expensive. I was about to go over there but if you'd rather, I'll start deep-diving on Mr. March. Alternatively, I can call one of the boys in on that."

"The boys," he said. "I'm hearing sexually loaded language. Maybe you do need that seminar."

"Ha! So what's your choice, L.T.? Oops, I almost said, 'What's your pleasure.'"

"There's a lot to learn about March so call both of the lads in before another memo pollutes the environment and go look at shoes."

"Will do," she said. "Got to be the most pleasant day I've had in Homicide."

When he hung up, I said, "One boutique doesn't require a full-time rep."

"Like we said, a make-work job?"

"Or he actually got sent here to drum up business."

When we reached the unmarked, he said, "Who're you betting on as the prime target, him or her?"

"No strong feeling either way so I'm staying away from the table."

"I think it's her and I think Dougie arranged it. If that leads to a mundane case, sorry for wasting your time."

His cell tooted abuse of Rossini. He picked up, listened for a few moments, muttered thanks, and clicked off shaking his head.

"The lab just I.D.'d the bullet pulled out of Meagin. No big challenge because it ain't rare ammo. MKE 9.65 Normal, full metal jacket."

It's not like him to fall back on jargon.

I waited.

He said, "Yeah, yeah, standard for the S and W Police and Military. Like I said, millions of 'em out there. They'll run it against prior shootings, fingers crossed."

He opened his driver's door, stood there grinding his jaws. "Pray it's not gonna be another McKinney and Lynk."

A couple of years ago, a pair of Sheriff's deputies fired for ethics violations had sought new careers as hit men in Compton. Taking on jobs for the town's biggest drug gang, only to be gunned down by an opposing group of thugs.

I said, "Time to go through Meagin's phone?"

He looked at me. "Changing the subject to relieve my anxiety? Very therapeutic."

"Always happy to help but it was a real question. Doug claims not to know any of her friends but Verizon might."

Back at his office, he removed the pink phone from a desk drawer, began scrolling, and stopped. "Looky here." Showing me the screen, he resumed. Stopped several times at specific calls.

To and from "G."

He said, "Let's count . . . twice a week, every week for the time span I've got, which is . . . four weeks. I'll subpoena her account and find out how long the affair's been going on."

I took the phone and reviewed the correspondence. "Sometimes he initiates, sometimes she does. The most recent pairing was him to her Saturday at five forty-two p.m. followed by her reply at six twenty-eight."

"Setting up the date. Too bad she didn't text. I'm hearing 'Ready, baby?' and 'Jogging over, can't wait.'"

I said, "She was careful enough not to text but didn't delete the calls. Maybe she was confident Doug wouldn't find out because they led separate lives and he'd never been interested in hers."

He thought about that. "Then he got interested because something got him suspicious. Like paying the phone bill and noticing a pattern."

I said, "Handling household bills sounds like

below his pay grade. More likely he uses auto-pay or farms it out to an assistant."

"Even better," he said. "The assistant notices and tells the boss. Or maybe he was already suspicious, to hell with pay grade, and decided to check. For all I know, she had a stable of Romeos and got careless. Let's see who else she talked to."

Examining a month of Meagin March's correspondence produced a slew of calls and texts ordering takeout from Grubhub and directly from restaurants throughout the Westside. Thai, Indian, vegan, health-conscious.

Nearly all her remaining contacts were also commercial: a nail salon in Brentwood, a day spa in Santa Monica, a dermatologist on Camden Drive in Beverly Hills, lots of shopping in all three neighborhoods with B.H. the clear favorite.

Gucci, Chanel, Armani, Vuitton, and Hermès on Rodeo Drive, lesser mono-brands and boutiques, including a bikini store, one street east on Beverly Drive.

I said, "For all that, not much in her closet."

"Shopping as a hobby."

"What isn't here is Tiffany or other jewelry sources. That could mean what we saw in Gio's bedroom were gifts from Doug."

"All the more motive," he said. "Guy lavishes her with bling, finds out how she repaid him, and blows."

His thumb picked up speed. "All right, finally some personal calls."

Three contacts, the most frequent contact "The Hub." Calling the number pulled up Doug March advising anyone interested to leave a message. In a tone that said **I don't care.**

Milo said, "Not the number I have for him."

I said, "Could be his personal cell."

"Doesn't sound personal, wonder if he even knows what that means." He counted. "Eleven calls from her to him in four weeks. A bit more than to Gio but it still doesn't shout domestic bliss."

"Any pattern related to her calls to Gio?"

"As in?"

"Same-day pairings."

He scrolled, read, eyes widening. "See what you were getting at. Every contact with Gio was followed by her checking in with Doug. Keeping track of him so she could fool with Romeo. Crafty . . . okay, the other two contacts are 'Toni' and 'Lana,' so maybe I'll get lucky and they're pals she was with when she went fishing for Doug and hauled him onto the dock."

I said, "No other recent Romeos, that could make your life easier."

"Unless there's an angry ex-Romeo from longer than a month ago."

"If there isn't, it could mean that what Meagin and Gio had was more than recreational."

"Amore? Why not?" he said. "Guy's got good

looks, nice clothes, no responsibilities, and a condom collection. What else do you need for a meaningful relationship? Okay, let's check out Toni and Lana and hope they're gum-flapping gossips."

Six outgoing calls had gone to "Toni," five to "Lana." As with Gio Aggiunta, sometimes Meagin had reached out, other times the women had called first.

That made me wonder about something. I said, "One second," went back and examined the spousal correspondence.

Doug March had accepted his wife's calls but had never once taken the initiative to phone her.

Milo said, "Inattentive."

"Which could explain her being confident he wouldn't snoop. And if he can be believed, he never did. He just claimed that when he asked where she was from, 'the Midwest' was enough detail."

"Rich guy, so much at stake, and he doesn't do any research. Weird."

I said, "Maybe he just didn't care. Or he saw himself as a shy loser when she picked him up and was awestruck. Then, as the relationship continued, she made no demands and was sexually available. He made sure to let us know she was, when he happened to be home. Given all that, why shake things up?"

"Especially when you really don't care," he said. "And she made no demands because she had plenty of entertainment on the side. King's out conquering territory, Queen's holed up in the castle and finds herself a knight."

That sounded like a riff on chess.

I said, "A castle filled with relics of strangers' lives. What's the first thing people of means do when they get a new house? Personalize it. Meagin and Doug moved in and made no changes at all. No mystery why Doug would be okay with that, he told us. It's not a home, it's a stopover. To him, real estate is currency. Want to take odds he'll be selling the place soon and trading up with some sort of tax-free exchange? But to Meagin it might've driven home how unstable her situation was. How little power she had in the relationship. So she explored."

"Not Ms. Domestic," he said. "Let's try to find out who she **was**."

12

"Hi, this is Lana . . ."
"Hi, this is Toni . . ."

Milo left identical messages, identifying himself as an LAPD detective but not specifying the nature of his call. Hanging up, he tapped his foot and drummed his desk. "Typical. Everyone too busy for the constabulary."

The helpful element in both women's voicemail: surnames included.

Lana Demarest, Antoinette Bowman. That led to a fruitful DMV search.

Lana Elaine Demarest, thirty-nine, lived on the 500 block of Crescent Drive in Beverly Hills. Antoinette Marie Bowman, forty-five, on La Mesa Drive in Santa Monica.

The internet revealed Demarest to be a pediatric dentist practicing on Twenty-Sixth Street, near the

Brentwood Country Mart. Smiling headshot, vividly colored website replete with cartoon animals.

Bowman, located on a business-link site, self-described as an entrepreneur. Milo looked up business licenses and found ownership of seven gas stations in Hollywood and Mid-Wilshire, and a tow yard in Silverlake.

Logging onto the county assessor pulled up no other real estate for Dr. Demarest but multiple holdings for Ms. Bowman. Eight multi-unit apartment buildings and three strip malls, all east of La Brea.

He said, "Property tycoon. Wonder if she met Meagin through Doug."

I said, "Could be, but there are no kids involved so it's unlikely Dr. Demarest did. Neither of them sound like people with a lot of spare time. Is there a pattern for when they talked to Meagin?"

He checked. "Good guess, always evenings."

"Two friends in a big city," I said. "Neither of whom she could hang with extensively. But maybe they were there the night she met Doug."

"Be nice," he said. "Not that it would get me closer to who killed her."

He looked at his watch. "Nearing six, maybe getting cold-called by the cops will get them curious—or worried enough to get back to me."

By the time I left his office at six fifteen, that hadn't happened.

◆

Tuesday morning at ten, he phoned and said, "They both just got back to me. Like it was coordinated. Demarest cried, Bowman cursed. When I asked to meet, Demarest said she'd have to check her schedule and Bowman said she'd let me know and hung up. I figured they were both putting me off but minutes later Bowman phoned and said they could both be available at twelve thirty in Demarest's office, which is closed between noon and two. Maybe we can score some free floss. Can you make it?"

"Wouldn't miss it."

Dr. Lana Demarest practiced "gentle pedodontics" out of a brick-and-gray-aluminum two-story building just north and across the street from the Country Mart. Ample parking in a rear open lot. An elevator covering three floors responded to Milo's button-push with a labored, belch-like noise. We took the stairs to Demarest's office on the second story.

Offices on the left side of a narrow hallway, windows on the right. Three other D.D.S.'s and a dental lab. Everyone out to lunch. Demarest's door was closed but unlocked.

A Technicolor waiting room was redolent of mint. Kids' magazines were stacked on brightly colored tables. Sesame Street murals on the walls.

One woman sat in a peacock-blue vinyl chair. One stood by her side.

The sitter got up. "Lieutenant? Lana." Brief handshakes. Soft skin.

Dr. Lana Demarest had left her pink nylon tunic on over gray slacks and sneakers. Barely over five feet tall, she was round-faced, freckled, and pretty under a luxuriant pile of wavy amber hair. Her voice was soft, melodic, nonthreatening. Ideal for someone probing the teeth and gums of children.

Deep-blue eyes were red-rimmed. She tried to smile past obvious grief.

Milo said, "Thanks for meeting with us, Doctor. This is Alex Delaware."

The woman near the chair hadn't been addressed but she was the one to respond.

"Of course we'd want to help."

She came toward us, stopped just short of collision. Beige cashmere top, indigo stovepipe jeans, chocolate boots with two-inch heels that elevated her to five-ten.

Toni Bowman was built like a fashion model, causing the top to drape perfectly. A long bronzed face under cropped, black hair was aged hard. Once-supple wood petrified by time.

Another pair of blue eyes, lighter than Demarest's, verging on colorless. Searching eyes, unmarked by any obvious sign of lamentation.

Toni Bowman looked angry.

I thought: **That could be useful.**

13

The four of us convened in Demarest's corn-yellow consulting room. Larger than Milo's office but not by much. Demarest sat behind a small desk, the rest of us faced her. On the wall behind the desk were diplomas and certificates and a collection of color shots of her with a bald, bespectacled man and three blond, round-faced children.

Toni Bowman moved her chair as far as possible from us and angled it. Wanting a good view of the intruders.

Milo said, "Again, so sorry to have to give you such terrible news."

"It was a shock," said Lana Demarest. "It still is. Unbelievable."

Toni Bowman nodded but the movement seemed

to lack conviction. As if unsurprised. She said, "Do you have any idea who did it?"

"Not yet, we're at the early stages."

"Not yet? You're optimistic."

Milo smiled.

Bowman said, "Hope you're right. We're assuming you found us on Meg's phone."

"We did."

Lana Demarest said, "Can you tell us what happened?"

"Meagin was shot to death in the backyard of a man named Giovanni Aggiunta. He was also killed."

"Oh my God." Demarest looked at Bowman.

Bowman said, "Did it have to do with Meagin or with him?"

Milo said, "You knew him."

"We knew **of** him—correction, we had seen him. Once and only to say hello."

"You saw him with Meagin?"

"At the spa. We went into the sauna, Meg was there with him and he left. But you could tell there was something going on between them."

"How?"

Toni Bowman smiled. "The look that passed between them."

Milo took out his pad. "Which spa, please?"

"Agua Fria Day Spa on Montana. That's where we met Meagin. In the sauna. She loved the sauna."

"How long ago?"

"A while back." Bowman looked at Demarest. Uncertainty had softened her face.

Demarest said, "Well, we only started going there around a year ago, right?"

Bowman said, "That's true. So it couldn't have been much longer than that."

"Maybe seven months," said Demarest. "Can't quantify beyond that, sorry."

Milo said, "And you saw Gio Aggiunta when?"

"Hmm," said Bowman. "That was maybe . . . three months ago?"

Demarest said, "That sounds about right."

Bowman said, "I had a feeling he'd be a problem but not anything like this."

"How so?" said Milo.

"Some people, you just can tell. The way he carried himself. The looks he and Meagin gave. He impressed me as lots of flash but no substance. My husband's handsome but he's **made** of something. He's a neurosurgeon. Dr. Emil Bowman, he helps people in pain."

Demarest said, "My husband's a physician and a biochemist. That's how Toni and I got to know each other. At a medical retreat."

Bowman said, "We kidded her about him. Who're you trying to fool. She giggled and said it was just a fling. We didn't judge. That's not our responsibility."

Milo said, "What else did she say about him?"

"Nothing. It was just that one time."

I said, "You two knew each other before you met Meagin at the spa."

"Well before," said Bowman. "We both lead busy lives so we'd begun going to the spa to unwind."

"Meagin's lifestyle was different."

"Meagin," she said, sighing. Pale eyes fluttered as moisture collected in their corners. She reached into her purse, drew out a cloth hankie, and dabbed. You don't see many of those anymore. Milo always keeps a couple in his pocket. Linen, monogrammed set, a gift from the man he'd lived with for years.

Like yawns, sighs can be contagious. Lana Demarest caught the bug and let out a soft breath. "Yes, Meagin lived differently than us."

Toni Bowman said, "She was so bright, what a waste. That's what happens when you marry that kind of money."

I said, "Doug."

"Doug," she echoed. "According to Meagin, he made **sixty** million dollars last year. Even if that was an exaggeration, the total had to be astronomic. And that crazy house. As if they were English aristocracy."

Lana Demarest shook her head. "Hard to conceive living there."

Milo said, "You've been there."

"No, but Meagin showed us pictures. Thought it was funny."

"Living there."

"Living with all that gingerbread and unused space. She said Doug would eventually sell it for a huge profit."

Toni Bowman said, "Mind you, I have nothing against making money. That's what I do, it enables Emil to keep helping people in pain and without worrying about finances. I just think marrying into money at that level can get in the way."

Milo said, "Of . . ."

"Self-development, exercising your brain. Fulfilling your potential. Meagin was bright. Okay, she wasn't educated, big deal, you can get past that. Sure it's harder but you can do it. Meagin had plenty of potential but no avenue to develop it."

Demarest said, "We didn't judge but we did try to give her a little warning. Like are you sure?"

Bowman said, "Emphasis on 'try.' She giggled some more and changed the subject so obviously we dropped it. You can't just come out and preach to a friend because you run the risk of blowing up the relationship."

I said, "You valued your friendship with Meagin."

"She was great," said Demarest. "Kind, sweet, gentle. And yes, bright. She didn't deserve this, not one bit."

Bowman said, "Not one fucking bit."

The women looked at each other. Both began

crying softly, Bowman wielding her handkerchief, Demarest reaching into a multicolored box on her desk and pulling out a parrot-green tissue.

Bowman stopped first. Back to anger. "Maybe we **should've** preached. Who the hell knows?"

Demarest said, "We discussed it between us, Toni."

"I know."

Milo said, "Discussed what?"

Demarest said, "A much younger guy, how that could be a problem because maturity takes longer to develop in men."

"And sometimes never does," said Bowman. "Get someone with the wrong type of mother and you end up with an eternal baby. My husband has always been mature. Even if he wasn't twenty years older than me—even if he was **younger** than me—he'd be a grown-up."

Demarest said, "My husband is five years older than me and we're finally synchronized."

Bowman said, "Men are like vegetables, they need seasoning. I said that to Meagin. She said, 'Thanks but I've had enough of older men.' Then she pointed out Doug was younger, too. So obviously, that had become her thing."

I said, "Had she talked about issues with older men before?"

Twin head shakes.

"Had she been married before?"

"No idea," said Bowman. "She never really told us much about herself."

The Midwest.

Demarest smiled. "Not for lack of gentle prying on our part."

Bowman said, "Look where that got her."

I said, "What was Meagin's attitude about Doug making so much money?"

"Same as with the house," said Bowman. "Amused. Like it was absurd."

Demarest said, "Like what can you actually do with all that?"

Milo said, "She knew he was rich when she married him."

"But not when she met him," said Bowman. "She told us she thought he was some kind of gofer. Money wasn't her focus."

"What was?"

She turned and looked me over. "This is sounding more like therapy than an investigation."

I said, "They're not unrelated."

"Is that so? I suppose I can see that."

Demarest said, "From what I could tell her focus was feeling free." She glanced at Bowman.

Bowman said, "Absolutely. But isn't that any sane person's goal?"

Demarest said, "She joked about it. Trying on cougar fur. I laughed." Downcast, as if confessing a sin.

Bowman said, "I laughed, too. When your friend jokes, you laugh."

I said, "Doug was also much younger than Meagin. Eleven years between them."

"Really?" said Demarest. "I assumed less . . ."

Bowman said, "We both did. Wow. What would that make him—thirty?"

"Twenty-nine."

"A baby. Unbelievable, all that money at that age. Meagin said he was a bit younger, I was figuring a couple of years. Until she said that, I'd imagined some white-haired golf-playing dude. Twenty-nine. **Wow**. We really **didn't** know her."

Milo said, "Did she ever tell you how she met Doug?"

"Some sort of pickup," said Bowman. "She brushed that off, too. Maybe she was into the Madame X thing. Maybe she felt it gave her allure, I don't know. Not that she'd need it, she had a fantastic body and a face like an actress."

Milo said, "Did she ever get into her and Doug's relationship?"

"You suspect he did it."

"Not at all. At this point we don't think anything."

"If you're asking if she complained about him, she didn't. But Meagin never complained about anything. Like being alone in that house, I asked her wasn't it spooky or at least lonely. She just laughed."

Demarest said, "The truth is, she didn't say much, period."

"Yeah, she was the quiet one," said Bowman. "Which was fine. When we got together it was to relax, not to get into heavy stuff."

Milo said, "Where did you hang out besides the day spa?"

"Nowhere besides the day spa. For Lani and myself it's precious downtime. Every morning we're up early for work."

I said, "So Meagin never said anything about her background?"

"Nope, just that one crack about no more older guys. And she wasn't playing games by holding back."

"What kind of games?"

"You know," she said. "Those people who work on getting you curious so they can feel important when you ask questions? Then they parcel out information and basically take control."

"Like celebrities," said Demarest. "Toni's right, there was nothing attention-seeking about Meagin. Just the opposite, she preferred to stay in the background. Even when we ordered drinks at the juice bar, she'd be the last one and say, 'I'll have what she's having.'"

Bowman's pale eyes widened. "You know, that's true, never thought about it. She rarely—never, actually—took the initiative. I guess that made her an easy-wear friend."

"Thanks for the information," said Milo. "Anything else you want to say?"

Simultaneous no's.

I said, "When Meagin first met Doug she was with a group of women. Any idea who they might be?"

Lana Demarest said, "Sorry, no."

Toni Bowman said, "You're thinking someone she opened up to more?"

I said, "No, just trying to learn as much as we can."

"Well, obviously we're not going to be any big help with that. The only thing I can add is my first impression of **him.** One of those Euro-trashers who come over here to absorb Hollywood glamour or whatever. Big automatic smile as he left the sauna. **Signorinas** this, **signorinas** that. I think he actually bowed."

She looked at Lana Demarest.

Demarest said, "I believe he did. My first impression was I kind of felt sorry for him. Trying too hard. To me that says you're not confident."

I said, "Was Meagin confident?"

"Seemed to be. I guess that's part of what made her so appealing."

Bowman said, "Exactly, no bullshit, what you see is what you get. You're right on the money, Lani. Now I want to ask a question. Why wouldn't you think Doug was behind it? Being that rich he'd have an ego the size of Asia. He finds out Meagin's cheating on him? Why wouldn't he consider her a squatter and evict her?"

Demarest said, "Interesting analogy."

Bowman smiled. "Stick to the familiar. You really don't think so, Lieutenant?"

Milo said, "What I said before is true."

"Yeah, yeah, just starting out. Yes, an open mind is good but not so much that your brains drop out."

Milo laughed.

That threw Toni Bowman. "Okay, sorry if I'm coming across too strong. Or flip. That's not how I feel. For some reason, learning what happened to Meagin is making me feel like I should be constantly apologizing. And that sucks. But don't tell me I have nothing to apologize for. I'll get there on my own."

14

We sat in the unmarked as Milo checked his messages. Only one but it arced his eyebrows. "Alicia got nothing much at the boutique so she recanvassed and found a neighbor who'd seen a small black car driving around the neighborhood around midnight."

He called back.

"L.T."

"God will forever bless you, kid."

Alicia said, "Can I get a footnote in your Bible? First off the shoe store. Gio's been there exactly once in two years and didn't do much but flirt with the owner. She's old enough to be his mother, thought it was amusing, figured him for the family wastrel. And she has absolutely no idea who'd want to shoot him. The car isn't much, either, just what I messaged. Small, black or dark, no make, too dark for the neighbor to see the tags. Not that she'd try."

"Who's the neighbor?"

"Eighty-year-old woman living a quarter mile north with two giant dogs. It's their barking that got her looking. She said they stayed tense and she got suspicious because it was a no-big-deal compact and the only time you see cheap cars in that zip code is when maids drive them or get dropped off or picked up."

"Unlikely at that hour," said Milo. "Was she suspicious enough to call it in?"

"No way," said Alicia. "Politically incorrect, she didn't want to be 'classist.' She does have a point, what would the complaint be? Insufficient sticker shock?"

"True. Okay, thanks for persisting. If Moe and Sean are still free, let's aim for a meeting this afternoon—say by four."

"I'll get my lasso and rope them in."

He sat back in the driver's seat, gripped the steering wheel, released it and pulled out a panatella that he rolled between sausage fingers.

"Gotta say Ms. Toni and Dr. Lana surprised me. I was expecting ladies who lunch and got a couple who probably don't take much time for lunch. Like Demarest said, best to keep an open mind. Did anything you just hear unlock portals in your brain?"

I said, "More support for Meagin being socially isolated, probably intentionally. The only friends we've found know nothing about her. Like Doug, they accepted her as she was because she made herself easy-wear."

"Sitting back, smiling, ordering whatever juice someone else was having."

"The other thing is her comment about having enough of older men."

"Bad experiences," he said. "Maybe violent experiences."

"Inflicted by someone who decided to reenter her life."

"Yeah . . . lots more to learn about her."

I said, "About Gio, as well."

"You still think he coulda been the primary?"

"I wouldn't count it out. A young, good-looking guy with an appealing accent and plenty of spare time, flirts instinctively, uses the spa and likely other locales to hit on women?"

"Lots of potential jealous guys out there," he said. "Yeah, even if he favored Meagin his place still coulda been the Airbnb of romance. And I still haven't heard from his family."

He looked at his Timex. "Meeting at four leaves plenty of time to visit the spa."

I said, "You up for an herbal wrap?"

"Only if it's edible."

◆

From the street, no way to tell what went on behind Agua Fria's façade. No signage beyond a discreet **AFR** and small, blue-steel address numerals.

The building was surfaced with thin, horizontal slats of oiled cedar. Miniature bamboo sprouted from gray stone planters. A tiny black camera perched just above the foliage on the left side researched the street.

Twice as wide as any of the neighboring high-end clothing stores, cafés, restaurants, and designer coffee outlets.

Elegant street, nearly all the foot traffic female, lithe and leisurely.

Santa Monica, good intentions gone awry, has long offered services that have turned it into a magnet for the homeless. But this part of Santa Monica had somehow avoided tents, overflowing shopping carts, manic rants, human excrement turning sidewalks into fetid obstacle courses, and any other symptom of no-good-deed-goes-unpunished.

Milo said, "Maybe they bribe them to go to Pico," and tried to nudge the door open. Then he noticed a tiny black button to the right, just above bamboo fronds.

If you need to ask . . .

Five stabs were met with silence. After the sixth, a male voice said, "Yes?"

False curiosity; the camera had swiveled toward us and Milo had offered it a clear view of his badge.

"Police. Could we please come in?"

A beat. "May I ask about what?"

"A client."

A beat. "May I ask who?"

"Better to talk inside, sir."

Two beats. "Hold on."

No click to signal entry. Instead the door swung open and a man stepped out and used his body to prop it ajar.

Bald, stocky, fiftyish, spray-tanned, he wore a black collarless shirt over cream linen pants and sandals.

Black name tag, white lettering. **Mikel.**

Milo introduced us.

Mikel seemed perplexed as he evaluated the information. Like an antiquated computer straining under the weight of a data storm.

"Okay," he finally said. "So who are we talking about?"

"Meagin March and Gio Aggiunta."

"Both of them? You said a client."

Milo said, "Amend that to clients."

"I don't understand."

"The two of them are dead, sir. Murdered."

Mikel's mouth dropped open, revealing small white teeth and a large red tongue. His eyes popped and pigment began squirming beneath the spray tan, creating odd swirls of pallor and flush. As if he'd been dipped in raspberry swirl ice cream.

"How's that possible?"

"Unfortunately it happened, Mr. . . ."

"Dally. Mikel Dally. I'm the manager. You're serious—yes, of course you are. Insane. This is such a shock. How did it happen?"

"That's what we're trying to figure out."

"Well, it has nothing to do with us," said Dally. "That I can assure you."

"We've been told Meagin and Gio met here."

Dally slapped his arms across his chest. "I have no way to confirm or deny that."

Noise from within the spa caused him to turn. Someone talking.

He cocked his head toward the opening. "What? Oh shit. Hold on." To us: "There's a leak in one of the whirlpools, I've got to attend to it."

He rushed inside, leaving the door to swing shut. Milo caught it and we stepped into a low-volume, surround-sound concert. Flutes, whale chirps, tubular bells, back to flutes.

I'd expected something airy, sleek, and geometrical. This waiting space was clearly the former living room of an older house. One of the few properties from the twenties not destroyed to make way for the commercial strip that was now Montana. Exuberant moldings, textured dun stucco walls, a carved wood ceiling painted in the neo-Spanish style of pre-Depression L.A.

The air was cool and fragrant. The dominant

aromas eucalyptus and rose petals. Then an after-tinge of oregano that brought pizza to mind.

Milo had caught that, too. His nostrils expanded and contracted.

We approached a high, carved wooden station where a young woman wearing a black shirt like Mikel Dally's sat. A plaque on the wall behind her informed visitors that the spa had been blessed by Tibetan monks from the Gardenia Monastery in Lhasa in order to install an aura of serenity. A second placard, in smaller print, offered reassurance that all products utilized were cruelty-free. The largest board hung directly behind her and listed services offered.

Detoxifying scalp massage; neuro-mapped reflexology foot massage; Bulgarian black mud wrap; almond butter crème emolument for stimulating the lymphatic system; nontoxic manicure, pedicure, and palmar caress package; aromatic Icelandic sauna; eternally eddying rock whirlpool.

Three-figure prices for each item. Four figures for the "diurnal package."

On the far wall, a teak door centered by an elephant carved in relief was marked **Blessed Entrance.**

The receptionist, young, apple-cheeked, ginger-haired, looked terrified. **Sophie.**

Milo smiled at her and pointed to the board.

"Sounds like good stuff, maybe a nice reward for when I solve the case and can chill out."

No sign of comprehension. He leaned in close. "Hi . . . Sophie. I'm Milo and this is Alex."

She said, "Um, Mikel should be back soon."

"Great. Don't know if you heard but we're here about Meagin March and Gio Aggiunta."

"Oh," she said. "Her I know, him . . . uh-uh."

"Giovanni Aggiunta."

Blank stare.

She said, "Mikel looked really upset."

Milo said, "Maybe Gio wasn't here as often as Meagin but he was definitely here."

"I've only worked here for like six weeks."

"Ah. You didn't hear what I told Mikel outside?"

Head shake. "But it made him really upset."

"Understandable. Okay, Sophie, I'm sorry to bring really bad news. Unfortunately that's pretty typical because I'm a homicide detective."

"Someone got killed?"

"Unfortunately, they both did. Meagin and Gio."

"Ohmigod. Meagin? Really?"

"Sorry, yes."

"Crazy," she said, chin crumpling, eyes welling up, head shaking. "She was . . . so nice. **Nice.** All the time. Always nice."

"How often did she come to the spa?"

"From when I was here? Maybe . . . four times?"

"So nearly every week."

"I guess."

"Like I said, sorry but our job is figuring it out."

Sophie's chin quivered. "I can't believe this. I can't believe it."

"It is hard to believe, Sophie. So you saw Meagin four times but never Gio."

"I don't even know who he is."

"Her boyfriend. They met here."

"That happens," she said, looking down.

He showed her a photo. She shook her head.

"So," he said, "people meet here."

"It's relaxed, so . . ."

"What percentage of your clients are women?"

"I have no idea."

"Most?"

"Yeah . . . Meagin and a guy, ohmigod, what happened?"

"Good question, Sophie. Did you ever observe anyone have any conflict with Meagin?"

"No, no, never. She was nice."

The elephant door swung open and Mikel Dally stomped forward, wiping his hands with a black rag. Glaring. Surprised we were still here.

"Look, guys, I've got a situation. Serious clog, going to take a while to sort. I've got nothing to tell you and that's the God's honest truth. Soph, give these gentlemen complimentary A.F.'s and see them **out.**"

Milo said, "Here's my card."

"Sure, sure." Dally stuffed it into his pocket,

turned and shoved the elephant, offering a glimpse of an inner wall covered with wildly patterned madras cloth interspersed with brass bells. In his haste, he brushed against some of the bells, creating a reproachful clink before vanishing.

Sophie reached under the counter and retrieved two glass bottles filled with cantaloupe-colored liquid.

More tiny lettering. **Agua Fria Custom Blended Herb Chai.**

"Usually," she said, "we take a deposit but it's okay. For the glass. We recycle."

Milo handed her a five.

"No, I can't. It's only a dollar each."

"Keep the change."

Sophie sighed. "Meagin was like that, too. The service providers get tipped but I don't. She tipped me anyway."

"Nice woman."

"**So** nice. I can't believe what you're telling me, she didn't deserve it . . . sorry, Mikel wants me to see you out."

"Sure," said Milo. "So there's nothing you can tell us."

The question perplexed her.

"Anything, Sophie, that could help us catch whoever killed such a nice person."

"I wish," said Sophie, stashing the five in a pocket and stepping out from behind the counter. "I really, really wish."

We followed her to the main door and Milo opened it before she had a chance. Traffic on Montana seemed to have intensified. Daylight felt brighter.

Sophie said, "This is cray-cray insane. She was here last week so so happy. I can't believe it."

Milo said, "Here's my card. If you think of anything."

"I'll take it," she said. "But I won't think."

We got back in the unmarked.

Milo said, "Monks from Tibet. Wonder what that cost. If it happened."

I said, "Maybe Lhasa, Ohio."

"There's such a place?"

"No idea."

He laughed, retuned quickly to serious. "If we just learned something, I missed it."

"Nothing new but confirmation," I said.

"Of what?"

"Predominantly female clientele, plenty of opportunity for a man on the prowl. The prices ensure a well-heeled clientele."

"Yeah, I saw that." He whistled. "Happy hunting ground, no obligations. Which takes me back to plenty of potentially pissed-off husbands and boyfriends besides Doug so maybe Meagin **wasn't** the primary."

He started the car, had made it halfway to the station when a text beeped.

He sped up and handed me the phone.

I said, "Claudio Aggiunta, Gio's brother. He's in town, wants to meet A-sap at your 'precinct.'"

"Text him back."

Immediate response.

I said, "Being driven over from the Peninsula."

"Good, we'll get there first."

15

We stood outside the station as Milo worked his phone, researching Claudio Aggiunta. Senior vice president of the shoe company, in charge of European and Asian sales.

I said, "The bulk of their market."

Milo said, "Important guy, so the brains in the family . . . looks like an older version of Gio." He showed me a headshot of a gray-haired man with a lean, seamed face and piercing blue eyes. A couple of additional clicks. "Here's one of his wife, looks like Sophia Loren . . . four cute kids . . . wanna go out on a limb and say he's the good son?"

Before I could answer, a black BMW 7 pulled up and a chauffeur rushed around to open the rear passenger door.

In real life, Claudio Aggiunta was short—five-five or so—with a fuller face than in his corporate photo. Since posing, he'd grown a full gray beard and let his hair grow longer. Eyeglasses in tiny gold frames perched atop a generous nose.

No **spezzato** here; steel-gray suit, blue-checked shirt, black alligator loafers. The blue eyes were less arresting in person, dull and sagging under heavy lids, bottomed by dark pouches. More than just acute stress. Someone frequently under pressure.

Milo said, "Mr. Aggiunta? Milo Sturgis. This is Alex Delaware."

"Claudio, thank you for responding so quickly." Soft voice, barely accented.

"So sorry to meet you under these circumstances, sir."

"Thank you."

Brief nod. Briefer handshakes.

No one spoke until we entered the elevator and Claudio Aggiunta said, "When we received your message and found out you solve murders, we knew the worst. Then we called your coroner and they confirmed it. They would not give us details, said to call you. So . . ." Resigned shrug.

The elevator dislodged us and Milo led the way to one of the smaller interview rooms. Square table, three folding chairs, hostile lighting that seemed to chill the space.

Stark space, sour-smelling and drab. No sign Claudio Aggiunta noticed. He stood there, arms hanging limply, until Milo motioned him to a chair.

He said, "My parents are suffering—very bad trauma."

"Understandable," said Milo. "Again, so sorry."

Two smallish hands rose and waved. "**Extreme** trauma. My wife and my sisters and all our children are with them. I am the least useful in such a situation so I booked a flight as soon as I could."

"Would you like some coffee, sir? Water? Something to eat?"

Claudio Aggiunta touched his gut. "No, thank you, Lieutenant. The time change . . . the situation. Could you please tell me what happened to Gio?"

"He was found shot to death in the backyard of his house on Sunday morning. It probably happened several hours before, in the darkness."

"Guns," said Claudio Aggiunta. "A robbery? One of those American things we hear about?"

Milo said, "Nothing appears to have been taken, so not likely, sir. There was a second victim found with your brother."

"Who?"

"A woman named Meagin March."

Claudio Aggiunta's head shakes were rapid but restrained. Running on reserves and striving to conserve movement. "Who is this person?"

"Someone Gio was intimate with."

Aggiunta's eyes narrowed and his mouth set, rippling his beard. "And? What else about her?"

"She was married."

No reaction. "Was she older than Gio?"

"She was, sir. Was that Gio's pattern?"

"As far as I know it was," said Claudio Aggiunta. "Over the past seven years it was. Does that sound odd? The fact that I am able to put a number on it?"

Milo said, "It is pretty precise."

"I can be precise because it was a precise event, Lieutenant. Seven years ago, Gio was rejected by a younger woman. He was twenty-two, studying architecture in Pisa, she was eighteen, the daughter of a family close to our family. The two of them were like this"—hooking one index finger around the other—"since they were children. Playing together, always together. The plan was they would marry and raise a family. I am not referring to an arranged marriage, we are not barbarians. Gio and Donatella **told** us that would be their destiny. Then Gio went to Pisa and Donatella remained in Firenze to finish **scuola superiore**—what you would call high school. Two months later, she met another guy and told Gio it was over. His reaction was severe."

A long, deep breath seemed to cave his chest before he exhaled audibly. "Gio took sleeping pills, he was hospitalized, it was a terrible time for the family. He recovered but Donatella was not impressed. She married the other guy soon after. It caused a split in our families. After that, Gio said he'd only be attracted to mature women."

Milo said, "This other family, how far did the hostility—"

Claudio waved that away. "No, no, no, not possible, like us they are not barbarians. And we repaired the split. Quickly. Donatella's family blamed her, they were on our side. We do not hold on to anger. Donatella was young. One cannot plan someone else's life. Gio claimed to understand."

I said, "Claimed."

"How can one be sure what goes on in here?" Patting his own heart. Exactly where his brother had been shot.

"In the end, Donatella's life was not happy. Her marriage was a disaster. What you would call domestic violence. She tried to reconnect to Gio but he had no interest. She moved to Iceland. Works in a hotel. I think."

Another wave. "So nothing to do with her or her family is an issue. They are fine people."

"I'm sure they are," said Milo, opening his pad. "But if you could give me their name?"

Claudio glared. "We do not want you disturbing them. There is no reason."

"I won't contact them unless my investigation points me that way."

"It will not," said Claudio.

Milo said nothing.

"Fine, fine, Lieutenant. I am confident so I **will** tell you: Barone. They are in the leather business. Suppliers of skins and hides. Our families have worked together for generations. Other than Donatella it is only the parents and they are elderly."

Milo scrawled. "So after Donatella, Gio was attracted to older women."

"Yes," said Claudio. "Unfortunately, there were other changes, as well. He dropped out of school and traveled around the world. With no plans. With a backpack. China, Tibet, Nepal, Bhutan, Egypt, Jordan, Israel, Morocco, Tunisia. For three years we heard little from him, then he returned and announced that he wanted to get serious and join the family business."

Long sigh.

I said, "That didn't work out."

"We tried. Everyone tried—Gio tried the hardest."

"But . . ."

"He had no genuine interest in shoes. In anything, really." Placing his hands together, he lowered his head. A sinner in a booth, preparing to offer confession.

No atonement followed. Instead, he looked up at the ceiling, then to the right. Another pat of his chest. "Talking about this pains my heart. It feels disloyal. Discussing my brother when he is—please excuse me."

He rose to his feet, hurried to the door, and

stepped out, leaving it open. Giving us a clear view, as he stood in the hallway and cried into his hands. Then he drew himself up but instead of returning walked to the right.

Milo got up and had a look. Returned and said, "Poor guy's pacing," and sat back down.

A few minutes later, Claudio Aggiunta reentered wearing the stiff mien of someone straining for undeserved calm.

He returned to his chair. "Excuse me. This is very difficult. Very bizarre. One day I'm in Firenze talking to clients, the next I am here . . . doing I don't know what. But it is much better than my parents being here. My mother has high blood pressure and my father's arthritis is severe."

Milo and I nodded.

"So," said Claudio. "We must talk about it. Gio's lack of interest in business. In academics, as well. The truth is we had a sad situation with Gio. Learning problems from when he was a small boy, he was taken to specialists, received no benefit. Mathematics was okay but reading was difficult. So how did he get into architectural school?" Sad smile. "What do you think, Lieutenant?"

Milo said, "Family connections."

"My mother's eldest brother, Gianfranco, is a noted architectural historian and a professor at the faculty. Is that fair?" Elaborate shrug. "Is anything fair?"

I said, "Joining the family business didn't go smoothly."

"It didn't go at all—sorry, I forget your name?"

"Alex."

"It was a total failure, Alex. No fighting, no **tempesta.** Everyone remained quiet, my mother especially. She was afraid Gio would disappear again. So the family supported him and he took long walks and raced his bicycle and bought a Ferrari Dino that he drove on the track and destroyed. He did more travel but not for long periods and not in distant places. Spain, Switzerland, France, Monaco. A week or two, then he'd return."

He threw up his hands. "Sometimes he'd return with a woman. An older woman. The oldest was gray-haired. A contessa from Bologna, without money. Beautiful but almost as old as our mother. No one said anything to Gio but among us, we were . . . we didn't understand. How old was **this** woman—the one he was found with?"

Milo said, "Forty-one."

"Her husband is the killer?"

"We don't know yet."

"It is not logical? A married woman? The rage of a destroyed ego?"

His voice had tightened. Constricted by the noose of memory.

I said, "Had that happened before to Gio?"

He looked down again. "There were a few . . .

inconveniences, but no, no, never any violence, never."

We waited.

Claudio Aggiunta said, "There is no connection between Gio's history in Italy, I assure you. All those situations were resolved."

Milo said, "How many situations are we talking about?"

"Not many . . . three."

"How were they resolved?"

"What do you think, Lieutenant?" Claudio rubbed his fingers together.

Milo said, "Three husbands were paid not to hurt Gio."

"No, no, it wasn't about hurting Gio, we are not primitive peasants, Lieutenant. It was about preserving family reputation. Civilized discussions were held, reparations were determined, Gio pledged to stop. My sister Isabella called it ransom money and the rest of us agreed but it was the only way. Why allow matters to get complicated when there's a solution? After the third time, we suggested to Gio that he come here and he agreed."

I said, "To work in the family business."

"Work is a complicated concept, no? Most of us must work, some of us are lucky to enjoy it. We tried to set up a situation where Gio would enjoy it."

Milo said, "How so?"

"We allowed him time to develop."

That was nonsense and he knew it. Color spread across his cheeks. Another glance to the right took a while to reverse.

Milo said, "Makes sense. So what, exactly, was his job?"

"The official title was West Coast sales manager. We have not penetrated the California market as much as we'd like. Better in New York but America, in general, has been difficult. Our shoes take time to produce and the American way is **al più presto**—as soon as possible. We would like to make an adaptation. Perhaps to partner with an American manufacturer."

Milo said, "Gio was sent to explore that in L.A."

"Gio was learning about L.A."

"The house he was living in—"

"We took care of that," said Claudio Aggiunta. "Also his car." Single head shake. "He wanted another Ferrari, we settled on a Maserati with a smaller engine . . . we took care of everything. His expenses, his allowance. We were happy to do it. Now . . ." His face crumpled. "What else can I tell you?"

"Anything you think would be helpful."

"I know nothing that would be helpful, Lieutenant. Every year I live I seem to know less about everything."

He grimaced. "I was assigned the arrangements. For bringing Gio back. What must I do?"

Milo, long accustomed to guiding family

members through the process of body retrieval, explained slowly, clearly, gently. Then he handed over a list of county phone numbers he'd compiled and run off in multiples. Serious stack. The entire contents of a bottom desk drawer.

Claudio Aggiunta scanned but his eyes clouded. "A process. When will my brother be . . . free?"

"There are still things to investigate, sir, so not immediately. More likely in a few days. If you need to return home, we can help you handle the transfer with phone calls and email. You should probably also talk to the Italian consulate."

Aggiunta worked his phone. "It's in Century City. Looks not far from here . . . okay, I will do what I need to do. Of course, I would prefer to bring Gio home now. To present my parents with . . . how many days is a few?"

"I wish I could be precise, sir."

Aggiunta thought about that. "Perhaps I will fly to New York. There are business matters to be managed . . . does that sound cold? It is not. I need to be busy, Lieutenant. To think about simple things."

"That makes total sense, sir."

"You are kind, thank you. You will keep me informed?"

"I will, sir."

Aggiunta looked at him. "I believe you will."

Another brief handshake was followed by a return to the elevator.

Claudio Aggiunta said, "Am I allowed to ride down by myself?"

"You are."

"Then I would prefer to do that. Thank you for your time, Lieutenant. And Alex."

16

The elevator door closed on Claudio Aggiunta. Milo said, "Class act."

I said, "Carrying a big load."

"He does the all work so Gio's free to enroll in Playboy One oh One."

"Gio may have been outwardly carefree but there was a sad side to him. Growing up as the non-achiever, then he gets dumped by an eighteen-year-old and reacts by attempting suicide and dropping out of school. That says low resilience. He disappears for three years and returns focused exclusively on older women. Which has a rigid, almost frantic quality to it. Though it did make him an ideal match for Meagin."

"She's got problems with older men so she aims young, he's just the opposite," he said. "The perfect monsoon. Which slams me right back to which one of them was the target. Here I was getting confident about Meagin and Doug, but with Gio's history of pissing off husbands, who knows?"

"Pissing off husbands and getting bailed out. The family saw it, accurately, as ransom money. After the third time they'd had enough and sent him away."

"Out of sight, out of mind."

"But with no family connections in L.A.," I said, "he'd be vulnerable. And maybe unaware of his vulnerability."

"Why?"

"Because he's floated through life maybe without doing a lot of thinking. Severe learning disabilities sometimes come with low impulse control. Cracking up one Ferrari and expecting another says in Gio's case it did. Toss in a lifetime of being cushioned and you may not end up with strong self-preservation instincts."

"All his bills taken care of, nice house, nice car, no need to work," he said. "Yeah, I can see it."

"Twenty-nine," I said, "but not an adult."

We headed back to his office.

He said, "Gotta get phone records and find out who else he hooked up with. The gal at the Bel-Air had no details but maybe someone at the other hotels will so I'll send the kids out to snoop."

◆

Nearly an hour remained before the four p.m. meeting. Milo used the time to check with the crime lab about the bullet recovered from Meagin March. Scowling and muttering, "Probably haven't even looked at it," as the phone rang.

Unwarranted pessimism but no satisfaction. The .38 slug had been analyzed but had failed to match ammunition from any other crime on record.

His next call was to the coroner, where he spoke to the day-shift crypt manager, Jorge Braunbauer. No decision yet on autopsies of either victim.

Milo said, "What's your best guess?"

"They probably won't get the scalpel," said Braunbauer, "because COD is obvious and nothing weird came up on either of their X-rays."

Milo said, "When's serology coming back?"

"Not sure, we're jacked and on the form it says you told our guys they were drinking booze."

"What I said was the appearance of drinking."

"Okay."

"Do me a favor, Jorge, get the bloods back, then we'll talk about the scalpels."

"I don't think talking's going to help, Milo. We've got eight bodies from a massive pileup on the 101 including two kids plus a multiple-gang O.K. Corral thing in Willowbrook where the trajectory tapes look like spaghetti."

"A traffic accident and a low-life shoot-out trumps a whodunit double homicide?"

Jorge said, "Death is death."

Milo hung up and examined Meagin's and Gio's photos. "Coupla fit, healthy types, he's probably right. Okay, let's find out who both of you beauties have schmoozed with in times gone by."

Two different phone carriers. Slow going at both when he gave them the subpoena numbers.

Rather than watch Milo fidget and tap his feet and rub his face while on hold, I stepped out into the hall and checked my messages.

One new custody eval referral, from Julie Beck, a judge I'd worked with before and liked. Her message: "All yours, Alex. If you want it."

I reached her in chambers. "That sounds ominous."

She said, "I like you so I'm warning you. These are two of the most unpleasant people who've ever crossed my threshold. Massive money on both sides, you'd think they could each just walk away and continue being rich. Instead, they keep getting stratospherically arrogant and kicking up the anger level."

I said, "Pit-bull attorneys?"

"No, actually okay attorneys. High-powered but smart enough not to be unnecessarily stupid. Unfortunately, they seem to be withering and one's already talking about bailing. So the dogs of war may eventually come snorting in. Now, in terms of positives, I made it clear that you'll be paid up front and I suggest that you price yourself generously because once the process gets going, I can see the principals welshing."

"Sounds like a whole lot of fun," I said. "How old's the child?"

"Fifteen-year-old boy."

The wishes of adolescents are taken seriously in family court so I rarely work with them.

I said, "What does he have to say about custody?"

"Haven't heard him say a thing," she said. "If I had to guess, it would be 'Someone take me. Please.'"

"Neither of them wants custody?"

"That's what it looks like."

"God, that's sad."

"He's been in boarding school since the age of nine, is currently at some preppy place in Massachusetts and scheduled to stay there during the entire summer session. From what I can gather, his parents, if you can call them that, pushed the empty-nest thing as soon as they could. Now both of them have new love interests, neither of whom has any interest in poor Derek."

"What is it you think I can do, Julie?"

"I don't have a clue. But someone should do something."

"Let me think about it."

"No problem, Alex, it's not going to be imminent, I just wanted to get my ducks in a row. And just for the record, I didn't ask someone else before you. When it gets complicated, I've found you ideal for the situation."

I laughed.

She said, "Seriously, I appreciate your ability to contextualize and this case will require it. Anyway, sorry if I've wasted your time."

"Never, Julie."

She said, "There you go. Gallant. Another reason I warned you."

When I returned to Milo's office he was still on the phone. Straining at Mr. Friendly but slipping steadily.

He saw me and jabbed a middle finger up at the ceiling.

I left the building to get some air, strolled up Butler Avenue and phoned Robin and told her I'd be back by six or so.

She said, "Fits my schedule."

"How's the Torres?"

"Beginning to reclaim its gorgeousness. What've you been up to, hon?"

"Not much on the case and just heard something pathetic from my other world."

I told her about the unwanted boy.

She said, "You are breaking my heart. What does this judge think you can do?"

"She has no idea."

"Well," she said, "if anyone can, it'll be you."

A kid easy to give up on.

That's when I decided to take the consult.

17

By ten to four, Milo had wrested listless agreement from the phone carriers to look out for his subpoenas.

"For what it's worth," he said, as we left for the meeting.

I said, "How far back do their logs go?"

"For Meagin a little under two years, before that she used another carrier, they have no idea who. Not worth chasing down, dead data gets destroyed. Gio's American account goes back seventeen months."

"Soon after he arrived in L.A."

"Before that, it was probably an Italian carrier, good luck getting through that fog. And, again, not worth the effort."

He stopped. "Unless some enraged hubby from the Old Country was still waging a vendetta."

I said, "If Claudio knew about that, he'd have told us."

"Good point. So forget think globally, act locally. I've got enough to deal with on this continent."

Milo had scheduled the meeting in a familiar venue: a large interview room adjacent to the space where we'd just spoken to Claudio Aggiunta.

A whiteboard on wheels was equipped with a pointer and a blue marker. A pair of rectangular folding tables had been pressed together and set up with four chairs. He'd transferred the coffee urn from the smaller room but when the three young detectives arrived together they bypassed caffeine and took seats behind the tables. Eyes aimed at the board, obedient pupils.

Alicia Bogomil, hard-bodied and clean-jawed, wore a snug denim jacket, black slacks, and low-heeled Chelsea boots. This week's hairdo was shoulder-length, softly shagged and side-parted. Brown-black on top, electric blue at the tips.

Moses Reed, blond, crew-cut, pink-complexioned and baby-faced, had shifted gears clothing-wise. As long as I'd known Moe, he'd contended with conventional garments that fought his power lifter's body, the result suggesting imminent explosion. Today he wore a pale-blue polo shirt and athletic-cut, black stretch chinos.

Sean Binchy—tall, rangy, and freckled, ginger hair spiked and neatly trimmed—was the sole holdout for Old School Investigator. Black suit, gray shirt, gray-and-black tie. Mirror-polished Doc Martens the sole memento from his time as a ska-punk bassist.

He ended up next to me, said, "Hey, Doc," and smiled. A few years ago, I'd saved his life. We'd finally gotten past that.

Milo strode to the board and said, "In answer to your next question, everything's gonna be on the final."

Small smiles but tense posture. The routine anxiety of detectives new to a case.

Bright eyes remained fixed on Milo, eager for enlightenment.

Nowhere else to look because this was a sad board: empty white space broken only by enlarged photos of two victims and a few crime scene photos that conveyed little.

He pointed to Meagin March, then Gio Aggiunta, and summed up what he'd learned over the past two days. No one took notes. Likely because Alicia knew everything and had passed it along.

Milo said, "Questions."

Reed said, "Any hunch about which one was the primary?"

"Wish there was. I was set on her because she was married and her husband's an odd one. But what I learned about Gio back in Italy makes me wonder."

"If not her husband, maybe someone else's."

"Exactly. Alex has confirmed that he took other women to the Bel-Air and the calls I have had a chance to look at say other Five-Stars were also his hunting grounds."

Sean said, "Any I.D. on the women at the Bel-Air, Doc?"

I shook my head. "The hostess was hazy on details."

Moe said, "You made a special trip or just happened to be there?"

"The latter."

Milo suppressed a smile. "In any event, maybe someone at the Waldorf or the Peninsula or wherever will remember more."

Sean said, "Maybe we should also check hotels that don't show up in his call history. Places he could've dropped in on without planning."

Alicia said, "Happy hunting grounds. He does sound like a guy who did nothing but party."

"Good point," said Milo. "Along those lines, he also called restaurants so let's start with everyplace in the call history and if nothing shows up there, we can branch out."

Moe said, "Five-Stars, we're talking rich folk. You think some waiter's going to give up a name?"

"Let's hope," said Milo. "Yeah, it's thin soup but until the total call history comes in, I don't see any other way to go."

He waited. Silence.

"Anything else?"

Alicia said, "A hotel might give up his older women but what about her younger men?"

Milo said, "Good point. We're also looking for any other guys she dated, especially older ones."

"Problematic coots," said Alicia.

Sean said, "Do we know if she was married before?"

Milo said, "Not in California, as far as I can tell. Gio arrived here seventeen months ago, not sure about Meagin but she's only been married a year and a half."

Alicia sat up straighter. "This may be out of left field, Loo, if she did arrive around the same time as Gio, could they have known each other before?"

"Not unless she lived in Italy."

"Which I'll check. Any chance of a personal look-see in Florence?"

Everyone laughed. Milo's lips twisted. He cracked his knuckles. "I'll take on the paperwork aspect, you guys handle the hotels and the eateries. Hell, have a snack on me."

"Just a snack?" said Alicia.

"Now you're pushing it. Fine, bring me serious info and have a T-bone on me. Or whatever your pleasure is."

18

The following day, a courier from L.A. County Superior Court, Family Division, delivered a legal-sized envelope to my door.

Inside was a handwritten note on Julie Beck's from-the-desk-of stationery: **Here it is, Alex. Thanks. J.**

"It" was a two-page summary of **Ruffalo vs. Ruffalo,** current addresses in Brentwood, Cancún, New York City, Aspen, Vermont. He, a financier specializing in "entertainment start-ups and artistic development," she an "activist and advocate." A few years back Milo and I had met a guy named Ruffalo . . . Charles. Naive money guy living with a hooker who'd been raped. This guy was Brian Ruffalo. Anything but naive. Maybe the tough older brother? Or just coincidence.

I googled, found no link, read on.

The primary conflict was supposedly money, specifically the division of "substantial" assets claimed to have been "primarily generated" by each litigant. He, due to being an "active venture capitalist," she, from a "prominent family" and asserted to have "seeded" every one of his endeavors.

Nothing about Derek Ruffalo until a two-line paragraph at the end containing the boy's name, sex, and age and the fact that his custody status "remains undetermined."

A boy about whom I knew nothing, but I'd found myself thinking about him and that led to wondering what I could do for him. I put the documents back in the envelope, left it on my desk, and moved on to a stack of reports in progress. Cases where I'd been useful.

Wondering about the boy reentered my head when I woke at three a.m. I tried to convince myself that with more information I'd figure something out. It took me a while to slide back into sleep.

Four hours later, as if the thought stream had nagged at me while my brain cycled, I woke up with a sense of futility.

Time to put it aside until he showed up. Just as I filed the envelope, Robin came in with Blanche.

"You around for breakfast, handsome?"

"You bet." We kissed. "Omelets?"

"Sounds good. Our girl here will enjoy a few eggy bits."

We ate and drank coffee in the kitchen.

Robin said, "So what's up?"

"About what?"

She placed her hand on mine and smiled. "You've been a bit thoughtful."

That's tactful for spacy. "Sorry."

"Nothing to apologize for, I didn't say neglectful, just . . . contemplative."

I said, "When did you buy the Dictionary of Euphemisms?"

She laughed. "There's my guy." A couple of sips. "Am I reading it wrong?"

"You never do. Been thinking about that poor kid no one wants. Can't figure out any solution."

"Maybe there is none."

"Exactly."

Neither of us spoke for a while. Then Robin said, "You had a shitty childhood and mine wasn't award-winning. We turned out okay."

"So hope for the best."

"Don't you always tell me not to take on problems I didn't cause?"

I nodded. Poured a second cup for her, a third for me.

She said, "No obvious solution is what Milo's

faced with when he calls you in. And those seem to work out."

All those years with my best friend and I'd never thought about that.

"You're right."

"Think of all the times you've helped him. If anyone can help this kid, it's you."

Same vote of confidence I'd gotten from Julie Beck. Coming from the woman I loved, it had more currency but I still saw no obvious solution.

Let it go, wait and see.

I kissed her again, longer, deeper.

She said, "Looks like euphemisms pay off."

At two p.m. I drove to the Aggiunta/March murder house. The street was quiet but for one gardener watering a blood-red azalea hedge several properties north.

After dark this would be a ghost town. Nice for someone who craved bucolic privacy. Even better for someone out to end life.

The yellow tape had been removed and the driveway the killer had used to gain entry was now blocked by a chain-link rent-a-fence.

Barn door, horse.

I drove a few aimless blocks before heading toward grander digs.

A bit more activity in the estate section of Bel Air. Multiple gardeners, delivery trucks, and uniformed maids strolling, leashed to dogs.

At the house the Marches hadn't bothered to pretend was home, a maid with no canine in tow walked along the stone wall engaged with her phone. When she reached the edge of the property, she reversed and continued, still talking.

The older domestic—Irma Ruiz.

I pulled up alongside her and rolled down the passenger window. She gave a start, turned, muttered something to the phone and slipped it into her pocket.

"Hi, Ms. Ruiz."

"Hi." She forced a smile with vibrating lips. Wide eyes blinked rapidly before settling on a point well to my left.

I said, "Everything okay?"

"You need to come in?"

"Not right now, thanks."

My answer revved up her anxiety. **Then why are you here!**

I said, "Is Mr. March home?"

"No, no, sir."

"Any idea where he is?"

"No."

"He didn't say where he was going?"

"A car pick him up."

"To go to the airport?"

Nod.

"When was this?"

"Seven in the morning."

"Any idea where Mr. March was flying?"

She hesitated. "I hear Ohio."

"Which city?"

Head shake.

"Okay, thanks—is there anything else you want to tell me?"

"No, no," she said. "No. I got to go back to work."

She lifted a remote control from the same pocket that had captured the phone, pressed a button, and squeezed through the opening gate as soon as space permitted.

I called Milo. "Doug March left this morning for Ohio."

"How do you know?"

I told him.

He said, "Wife's dead a few days and he's back to business just like he told us. She have anything else to say?"

"No but she was antsy from the moment she saw me."

"Think she knows something?"

"Could be or she's just affected by Meagin's death. Also, living in that house with just one other person could feel creepy."

"The more meat, the more worms, huh?"

"Where'd that come from?"

"Jewish proverb," he said. "Rick's grandfather's favorite. Okay, I'll eventually do a recontact.

Meanwhile, Sean found someone who actually dated Gio. So to speak. She's on her way to the station. Wanna meet her?"

"So to speak?"

He explained.

I said, "On my way over."

19

Rhonda Mae "call me Rikki" Montel was fifty years old and pneumatically curvy, with huge but hard brown eyes topped by heavily blued lids and fronted by stick-on lashes a quarter inch long. Her deeply tanned face suggested genetic beauty on its way to defeat by gravity. A shaggy black do reached nearly to her waistline.

She wore a second-skin beige knit dress that exposed lean, sinewy legs with pronounced calf muscles. She was pacing when we entered, red-soled, red leather shoes with five-inch heels turning her walk to a totter. Five rings on her left hand, six bracelets around her right arm that provided a sleigh-bell soundtrack.

Per Milo she'd been "an unhappy customer" when confronted by Sean at the Waldorf bar. Pointed out enthusiastically by a bartender after viewing Gio Aggiunta's photo and being informed of his murder.

Before making the I.D., the barkeep, a young woman named Katy Gantry, had scooted back into a far corner. Putting maximum distance between her and the corner table where Rhonda Montel sat studying a magazine and sipping from an old-fashioned glass.

When Sean came over, Gantry said, "She's dangerous? I mean we know she's trouble but I never thought it would get to **that**."

Sean said, "What kind of trouble?"

"You know."

"She gets rowdy?"

"Uh-uh, just the opposite. She's super quiet, behaves herself too good for us to do anything. But we all know what she's up to."

"Which is . . ."

Gantry stared at him. "You really don't know? Hootchie mama, call girl, whatever you want to call it. She's in and out of here all the time, mostly later but sometimes this early. We'd love to lose her but she pays for her own drinks and food and like I said, she's quiet. But it's obvious what she's up to. She sits and waits and pretends to read **Elle** or one of those stupid throwaways. But she's always ready to make eye contact. And sometimes—you know—it works."

"She picks up a guy."

"But never the same guy twice. **Except** for him. That's why I **remember** him. Just from what I saw, she nailed him at least . . . three times. Maybe four. And that's just me, other bartenders could probably tell you more."

Sean glanced at the other person working the bar. Young Black guy, arranging bottles precisely.

Katy Gantry said, "Uh-uh, Jamal just started here."

Sean tapped Gio Aggiunta's photo. "So he was a regular."

"Not like some, the ones who are here all the time. More like once in a while. Great tipper. Very polite."

"When's the last time you saw him and that lady together?"

"Lady." Gantry smirked and began wiping down a section of spotless bar-top. "Maybe . . . I don't know, a while? A month? Honestly, I don't know. But I did see them go off together three times at least. That's why when you showed me—oh, geez, **is** she dangerous?"

"No," said Sean. "Just a person of interest. Do you know her name?"

"I know what's on her credit card," said Gantry. "Hold on." She worked an iPad hooked up to the register. "Rhonda Mae Montel, Amex Platinum. Like I said, she pays her own way."

Sean copied the info into his pad, thanked her, sat

down nursing his Sprite, and did his own research, benefiting from the less-than-usual name.

Rhonda Montel, three months past her fiftieth birthday—from here, he had to say, she looked younger—had two active warrants, both for failure to appear. No soliciting arrests, no one prosecuted that anymore. A pair of long-standing traffic fines.

Good enough.

He walked up, waited until she put down her cocktail. She smiled up at him so sweetly he almost felt guilty. Showing his badge, he told her she was under arrest and asked her to stand. Please.

False lashes fluttered. A little-girl voice said, "You've got to be kidding me."

"Wish I was, ma'am."

Her voice lowered to a sibilant, alto whisper. "This is fucking stupid and you know it, Junior."

Sean smiled.

Rhonda Montel said, "Oh, don't do **that**. Don't make fun of me. Little **boy**."

An hour and a half later, processed but released back to Sean, she sat in the room where Claudio Aggiunta had been interviewed, crossing and recrossing her legs, each movement raising the hem of her dress.

If that was for Sean's benefit, she was wasting her time. He'd positioned himself across the room and was working his phone.

When Milo and I came in, Rhonda Montel checked us both out, began to favor me with a smile then changed her mind and swung blue lids over to Milo.

A nose for authority.

Milo introduced us.

Montel said, "Call me Rikki, Tall Stuff. Maybe you can tell the kid here he's barking up the wrong tree."

Sean smiled.

She said, "Traffic bullshit? With all the crimes you don't solve, you hassle me on that?"

Milo said, "This can all go away, Rikki, if you cooperate."

Montel licked her lips. "I always cooperate. What's your pleasure?"

He showed her Gio Aggiunta's photo.

She said, "Him? He's in trouble? That's a surprise, there was nothing shady about him that I ever vibed on. And trust me, you get shadies even at the 'Dorf. Go upstairs to the roof deck, it's wall-to-wall shady." She stuck out her tongue. Conducted a long, slow lip-tour.

Milo said, "Tell us what you know about him, Rikki."

She grinned. "What I know isn't going to make it into your files or whatever you call them."

We waited.

She said, "Fine. I met him at the 'Dorf maybe . . . a year and a half ago? He was cute, came on like he loved himself. Smooth, you know? Knows he's cute. I was up front."

"About . . ."

She folded her arms across her chest. "What do you think?"

"All business."

"I'm a businesswoman. A lot of times guys get offended, thinking it's all about their charm. Giovanni didn't. He was like, 'Hey, done that before in Italy, this could be fun.' We . . . negotiated, then we walked up the block and he rented a room at the Hilton. Ground floor, tacky." Another grin. "I think at that point tacky was what he was after. Which is fine, I aim to please."

"Did that become your usual place?"

"After that he trusted me and we partied at his pad. Up in Bel Air, we swam in his pool. Not a great house, I've seen better, but we had fun. He liked to call me Mama. Guys call you all sorts of things, that was harmless."

"When's the last time you saw him?"

"Hmm," she said. "Long time. Couple of months? Maybe longer?"

"How many times did you party?"

"Like I keep count?"

Milo said, "Take a guess."

"Why?"

"Humor me, Rikki."

"What'd he do?"

"How many times?"

"Six? Mostly in the beginning. Just a couple at

the end, by then I was . . . I had other arrangements but he showed up and it was like old times, so why not? Okay? Got enough giggles for your locker room? What'd he do?"

Milo said, "He died."

Rhonda Montel slammed her hand to her mouth. She pitched forward, caught herself. Lowered the hand and said, "No."

"I'm afraid yes, Rikki."

"Shit. Such a nice guy. A sweet guy, he was always out to . . . he was sweet and nice. Who would do that?"

"It's what we're trying to find out, Rikki."

"Well you won't find out from me," she said. "Like I said, it's been months. It's not like I was obsessive-possessive. We were always cool, sometimes I'm available, sometimes you're available. It's not like the movies. We're not out to find Mr. Right."

Milo said, "Business."

"Makes the world go 'round." She patted the top of her hair, drew the long fringe forward and fingercombed it, like a groom tending to a horse's tail. "Someone did him? Insane."

"Do you know any other girls he dated?"

"No, no, no," she said, wagging a finger.

"No, what?"

"Don't want to go there."

"Go where?"

"Getting someone else pulled in here." Stroke, stroke. "You ruined my day, why mess someone else up?"

"Giovanni's last day was worse."

She gave him a long look. "Low blow."

"Rikki, if you know anything that could help—"

"I don't."

"The other women might."

"They don't either. Talk about a **really** wrong tree. The ladies I hang with are good people, no one's weird or violent or crazy and we all have style. Okay? No one would do that. Never, not in our DNA."

Milo's eyes drifted toward me. Rhonda Montel's followed.

I said, "I'm sure you're right but the more information we have the better."

"**You're** the big boss?"

"Nope, you were right the first time."

"So what, he gives you a chance to talk when he runs out of material?"

Milo said, "We're a democracy."

"Bullshit." She laughed. "You're like the army, my dad was in the army, I know the army."

I said, "The other girls Giovanni dated?"

She sat back, pulled off a few more leg-crossings. When she finished, the dress had ridden up nearly to her crotch, exposing a triangle of red silk. She let the view endure for a moment, then stood, tugged, wiggled, and sat back down.

"Kind of drafty in here." Small laugh, raspy and uncertain.

I smiled.

She said, "**That** was a nice reaction even if it was bullshit, at least you know how to treat a lady. Or think you do." Another visual survey. "Not bad on the eyes, either—okay, this is not going to help you but there was four of us, used to hang out. We met in Vegas, we all danced there, decided to move here together a couple years ago. But we never lived together, nothing like that, it wasn't like . . . college. We did our thing, hung out. Okay?"

We waited.

Rhonda Montel exhaled, fluttering enhanced lips. "Two of the girls you can forget from the git-go. One moved like a year ago to New York with an eighty-year-old who keeps her on Fifth Avenue and all she has to do is look good and cook him meatloaf and baked beans."

Her lips folded inward. She looked at the floor. "The other died six months ago. Cancer, real quick, and she never hung with Giovanni. Least that I saw."

I said, "That leaves one."

"The baby," she said. "Same deal, nothing for you because she got herself a zillionaire." Another harsh laugh, impossible to read. "We actually watched her do it, it was like one of those nature shows. Started as a joke. A challenge. Nerdy guy all alone at a table, doing paperwork. Who knew he had bucks? She didn't."

"What was the challenge?"

"Hey, look at that one, I could get him like this." Finger-snap. "No you can't, yes I can. We'd all had a bunch of drinks, were taking a night off. So forget her, too, she's probably jetting around somewhere with the zillionaire."

Milo got up and left.

Rhonda Montel said, "Did I offend him or something?"

"Not possible," I said.

That confused her.

Sean smiled.

Milo returned and showed her Meagin March's photo.

She said, "Really? You already know Meg? Why are you guys trying to mindfuck me? You trying to trap me? There's nothing to trap, I don't know shit. And don't tell me she did something bad, no way, not her."

I said, "Did she date Giovanni?"

"Not saying it couldn't happen but I never saw it. If she did, it was when I was on leave."

"From Giovanni?"

"From everyone," she said. "I get busy."

She gave a sly look and uttered the name of an A-list film director.

"Okay? Get the picture? Someone like that wants your time, you give it to him, okay? And trust me, he wanted it until he went to Canada to shoot a picture. So is it possible Meg hooked up with Giovanni? I guess, but who cares, why are you guys wasting your time? No way Meg would hurt him. Hurt anyone, she's a sweetie. Kind of like him, now that I think about it. They probably did a lot of cuddling. He liked to cuddle." She touched her left breast. Unconscious move, evoked by a memory.

Milo leaned forward and looked her in the eye. "Rikki, Meagin was murdered with Giovanni."

Another sudden body slap, this one to her left breast. She clutched fabric. Turned away from Meagin's image and began panting. Standing, she covered her ears, took a few steps, lowered herself heavily.

"You . . . are . . . going to give me . . . a stroke. Or something. A heart attack—I feel like I'm—I feel shitty, really shitty . . . hold on, just hold on."

Shutting her eyes, she tried to deep-breathe herself back to normalcy. Checked her own wrist pulse and said, "It's like a fucking race car, you guys are going to **kill** me."

No one spoke.

Rhonda Montel deep-breathed some more, did another wrist-read. "Now it's a Tesla—don't tell me you were lying about Meg, don't do that. I'm used to lying but don't do that, I don't deserve it."

Milo said, "Wish it wasn't true, Rikki. Can I get you some water?"

"How 'bout vodka? No, no, I'm fine. Not really." A third pulse exam. "Lexus—killed together? At the same time?"

"At his house."

"Don't tell me they were using the pool."

"Not right then."

"But they did use the pool," said Rhonda Montel. "It's a nice pool. I used it. It could've been me."

20

Milo looked at Sean. "Bring her water, Detective Binchy. An energy bar, too."

"Got it, Loot."

Rhonda Montel said, "I told you I was fine."

"Just in case."

"What, you feel guilty for hassling me then freaking me out?"

Milo said, "You just got even more valuable to us."

"Really?" A hard look gave way to a smile.

"Really, Rikki. Whatever you can tell us about Giovanni and Meg will be hugely helpful."

"There's nothing to tell," she said. "Two of the sweetest people. Him, I just knew as a date."

"But you were close to Meagin."

"We liked each other," she said. "There was nothing not to like about her."

"You called her the baby."

"She was younger than the rest of us. But we all liked her."

Milo smiled. "You met her in Vegas."

"We all met in Vegas. The two others—Frankie who's in New York and cooking her little heart out and Cherry who died—they were both showgirls. Tall drinks of water. They got dumped, the way showgirls always do when they have the nerve to develop a wrinkle. That happens, you do what you have to—do **not** judge."

"Wish I could convince you, Rikki. We couldn't care less about anything except murder."

"Murder," she said. "What a fucked-up job you have—anyway, that's it about Vegas. We hung out there then decided to try L.A. My idea because I was born here. Huntington Park. I figured why not try something new and the others agreed."

"Including Meagin."

"Especially Meagin," she said. "She was always about a new adventure. One time, in Vegas, she spent some serious bank on a skydiving lesson. Showed us a video and I nearly puked just looking at her."

"A risk-taker."

"But not when it came to work, she was careful about work, steered clear of anyone who even smelled of creepy. Said she'd had enough of weird."

"How so?"

Rhonda Montel shook her mane. "That's all she said."

Milo waited.

She said, "It's not going to change because you're doing the silent-treatment thing. She never said and no one pushed. None of us liked those stories—ours or anyone else's."

"Got it. What else can you tell us about her, Rikki? Starting with her name before she got married."

"She actually **married** him? Shit. I just thought they were playing house."

"No, they were legally married a year and a half ago."

"Right after she bagged him . . . man, talk about working fast. Her and him matrimonying . . . talk about the odd couple."

"How so?"

"You meet him?"

"We have."

"Then why're you asking? She's gorgeous up the waz, he's a nerd looks like he's got low T—testosterone. Got to tell you, it's a surprise. I'm sure she could've got another rich guy who wasn't a nerd—did she love him? I mean anything's possible, but still . . ."

"Who knows how she felt about him, we can't ask her," said Milo. "But the fact that she was partying with Gio—"

"Means nothing," said Rhonda Montel. "Love is here." Another breast pat. "What happens here"—dropping to her crotch—"is from a whole different nervous system. A guy I know, a brilliant doctor, told me. Wires and glands, it's complicated."

"Learn something new every day," said Milo. "So what was her maiden name, Rikki?"

"In Vegas she went by Jones."

"Meagin Jones."

"Was that real? No idea." Shrug.

Milo said, "I think we both have an idea."

"Yeah, well, can't blame her, lots of weirdos in Vegas. We all had dancing names. Mine was Ravenette, hers was Ash. Coincidence, we thought it was funny, both of us using our hair for the idea. Hers was ash back then, almost white, she ironed it, it hung down her back. Not as long as mine but long."

"Where'd she dance?"

"By the time I knew her she'd stopped so can't give you any names."

"New career," said Milo.

"Don't **judge!**"

He shifted his chair inches from her knees. "Rikki, stop worrying about that. So she was working a casino."

"Bunch of casinos. The good ones. She had the looks and the style for that. Made enough bank to pay off bellmen and whoever."

"The good ones being . . ."

"Caesars, MGM, Bellagio, Venetian, whatever. She never said, all I know is she did well."

"Moving around."

"Why not? Who wants to be a sitting duck?" Her face crumpled. "Don't bullshit me: did she suffer?"

"No. It was quick with no struggle."

"Stabbed or shot?"

"Shot."

Several blinks brought up a rush of tears. Milo handed her a tissue.

"Thank you. It really was quick?"

"Definitely, Rikki. Does that make you think of anything?"

"Like what?"

"Someone who'd do that. Walk in and shoot two people and leave without robbing them?"

"What about whatsisname, Prince Nerd-O?"

"Nothing links him to it, at this time."

"You're saying maybe."

"Why would you suspect Doug?"

"Oh, c'mon. His wife was fucking another guy? A cooler guy. Men are all about wienie-wagging. They start feeling like shit, they take it out on someone."

"Okay," said Milo. "Any other possibilities come to mind besides Doug?"

"Like who?"

"Someone Meagin dated before she got married. A guy who scared her."

"The only things that scared her," said Rhonda Montel, "were in her past."

We sat up straighter.

Milo said, "What about her past, Rikki?"

"Don't know the details, she never said. **Wouldn't** say. Didn't **want** to get into it. The rest of us spoke about shit from our past, that's what friendship is. She didn't like it, would get all nervous, this look would come into her eyes."

"What kind of look?"

"Like something—like some**one** was sneaking up behind her. She'd kind of . . . get closed up and if you tried to talk about it, she'd give this laugh that wasn't funny and say what are you talking about, girls, I'm fine. But I could tell she was lying. I'm basically a lie detector—no, screw that, I'm a psychologist. My profession, you **need** to be a psychologist."

CHAPTER

21

Bottled water that Rhonda Montel drank greedily, supplemented by an energy bar that she nibbled to oblivion, added nothing to her account.

When Milo pressed, there were no tells in her eyes or anywhere else.

He looked at me. I nodded. He stood.

"Really appreciate your help, Rikki, and sorry for the hassle. Detective Binchy will drive you back to the Waldorf."

She said, "Forget that, too many bad vibes today. Take me to the Four Seasons, I need to clean out my head."

Sean approached. She remained in her chair. "What about my warrants?"

Milo said, "I'll see what I can do."

"What does that mean? I'm all good citizen for you and you treat me like a criminal? For fucking traffic bullshit? No way, Jose, don't want anything hanging over my head, some other Dudley Do-Right shows up and interrupts my reading."

"I'll do my best, Rikki."

"What does that mean?"

"Just what I said. Here's my card, you have a problem, call me."

"Yeah, right." She stood and wiggled and tossed her hair.

Sean said, "Ready, ma'am?"

"We taking a horse? You look like you ride rodeo or something. Be nice to see you in boot-cut jeans."

"Thank you, ma'am."

"Ma'am," she said, as if learning a new word. "Maybe I could get used to this place. We could make it a fun place."

After she was gone, Milo and I stayed in the interview room.

He said, "Jones. Creative. Why not go straight to Jane Doe?"

He got up, filled a coffee cup, tasted it, scowled, and set it down.

Pacing a couple of times, he returned to his chair. "Vegas call girl bags tycoon? Looks like Rikki got it wrong, sometimes you can pull off a movie-type triumph." He rubbed his face. "With no happy ending . . . at least I don't have to track down the group

Meagin was with the night she picked up Doug. Guy's sitting there with his beer and his paperwork, has no idea he got targeted by a pro."

I said, "Meagin might have figured it for a one-night stand. Then she learned who she was dealing with and decided to stake a claim."

"Sixty mil a year and clueless about women," he said.

"About relationships, in general. His intelligence may be high but it's narrow."

"Clueless about anything except real estate."

"When you told him about Gio he seemed genuinely surprised—stricken. I can be fooled by good acting but so far I'm not seeing him as someone with theatrical chops. When Meagin was asked about her past, she clammed up and got edgy. But she did let on to her spa friends about bad experiences with older men."

"Someone not naive."

I said, "She moved here from Vegas. It's not hard to imagine."

"Some hard-case parolee—or a casino type."

"Or her problem stretched back prior to Vegas. She was forty-one when she died. Plenty of opportunity for a tough history."

"Unknown suspect from an unknown place murdering a mystery woman? Gee, thanks for clarifying."

He looked at the coffee as if reconsidering. Got to his feet and hitched his belt over his gut and said,

"Okay, let's see what we can learn about whoever she was. Beyond 'Jones.'"

Keywording **meagin march** produced **did you mean megan march?**

Keywording **meagin jones** prompted **did you mean megan jones?**

He muttered, "Screw you, RoboCop, if I meant that I'd say so." But he spent a lot of time trying the more conventional spelling only to learn that none of the women offered up by the search-engine gods was his victim.

"Expected nothing, got nothing," he said. "I guess that's a type of success."

Adding **las vegas** to the search was unsuccessful. Shuffling combinations of **ash jones exotic vegas dancer** and tacking on the names of several casinos was equally futile.

I said, "Maybe she disappeared herself."

Shrugging, he tried a slew of missing persons databases. Another adventure in failure.

Duplicating the entire process with **meg** pulled up tons of data, all garbage. Attempting the same on NCIC returned zero hits. But local arrests can evade the national database as can entire categories of nonviolent crimes so he phoned a homicide D at Las Vegas Metro he'd worked with named Tom Brush and asked him to check Clark County arrest records.

Seconds later, Brush said, "Nope, nothing spelled that way. I do have a Megan Jones busted for meth and simple assault a couple of years ago but she's twenty-four years, two hundred pounds, and has facial tattoos and biker connections."

"Not my gal. Could you try Rhonda Montel?"

"Who's that?" said Brush.

"Known associate of my gal."

"Hold on . . . okay, yup, her I've got, one warrant . . . three years old. But it's penny-ante bullshit: traffic fines."

Milo laughed.

Brush said, "What's funny?"

"She did the same thing, here, Tom."

Brush snorted. "Habitual offender, ooh, call the FBI and get a fancy-ass **pro**-file."

A check of three newspaper databases pulled up nothing. Social Security records were down due to technical difficulties so he shifted to sites that scoured graveyards and funeral records across the country, moved on to county property records.

A second try at Social Security got through. Waste of time.

I said, "Her line of work, she wouldn't need a number."

"But why nothing before then? Teenagers working fast food get numbers."

I said, "Maybe there was no before then."

"Career prostitute?"

"It would fit with a scary past. What if she ran out on a pimp or a violent boyfriend, came to L.A. and went solo along with her friends?"

"The four of them," he said, "total pros. But they're doing a girls' night out when Doug comes in. Meagin likes younger guys so they kid her. She says watch me and picks him up. Then she finds out who he is and takes it to the next level."

He hummed the wedding march.

I said, "Doug's personality would've made him a dream match for Meagin if she'd already been traumatized by a possessive, controlling guy. He's young, inexperienced, distant, and asocial to the point of being uncurious about people. Even better, he was gone nearly all the time, giving her freedom to do what she pleased."

"Woman on the run finds her bliss," he said.

"Until someone caught up with her."

He drove me home and said, "Sure, why not, thanks," when I offered coffee. As it brewed, he sat at the kitchen table, made no move toward the fridge.

Distracted. Defeated.

When I pulled out bread and eggs and milk and began whipping up French toast, he said, "Maybe some of that," but with no passion.

Blanche had been napping in her crate with the door left open. She knows the ropes and as we ate, she lingered near his cuffs and scored occasional tidbits.

When he finished his sixth slice, he sat back, rubbed her head, and said, "Thanks for the blood sugar."

Two cups later: "One thing I figured was taken care of was a nice easy victim I.D. Turns out hers was phony. You really think Doug has no idea about her past?"

I said, "Real estate, real estate, and real estate."

"Guess so . . . he impresses me as one of those kids who got bullied in school, now one of the popular girls finally paid attention. But marrying her still seems crazy careless, Alex. All that money? So maybe he **did** do some research, didn't like what he learned, decided to end the relationship with no way for her to walk away with any of his bucks."

"Either way," I said, "it puts the focus back on Meagin as the primary target."

"Gio was collateral damage."

"That would be my bet."

"So where do I go with it?"

"I'd talk to the people who saw her every day."

"The maids."

"The help sees and hears all sorts of things. And some employers confide in them. Alone in a big house, even a woman escaping her past could've opened up. I just saw Irma Ruiz and she was definitely antsy."

"Making her my target," said Milo. "Let's go."

22

A bell-push at the March estate produced silence. Same for the second time. The third, fourth, and fifth.

I said, "Privacy, the ultimate luxury."

Milo said, "The ultimate pain in the ass for a truth-seeker."

He jabbed two more times. No answer. "She was edgy, huh? Maybe for good reason so she split." Another push. Nothing. "But what about the other one—Adelita? They both cut out?"

"Fear can be contagious."

"If they're scared of a guy with March's resources, hiding out's not gonna cut it for very long." He peered through the gate pickets. "Now what?"

"You could try talking to him," I said. "See how he reacts to his employees being gone."

"If he's what they're scared of, I'm giving him a heads-up."

"Like you said, if he wants to find them, hiding from him will be futile. And letting him know you're aware of their absence could help them."

He thought about that. Pushed the button again. Cursed and yanked out his phone.

Doug March said, "What?"

"How's it going, sir?"

"You're not calling because you care about me. What do you want?"

"You're out of town."

"Columbus, Ohio," said March. "If you must know. The Hotel LeVeque, would you like my room number? My in-room breakfast order?"

"Not necessary, sir."

"Then why bring it up?"

"Sorry if I'm irritating you, Mr. March. I am investigating your wife's murder."

"Any progress on that?"

"Nothing dramatic."

Doug March said, "In other words, you've got nothing. Well, that's not going to change by talking to me. I've told you everything I know about my wife, which is apparently very little. In the last analysis, my ignorance is my own fault. My due diligence on properties is way better than my research on her. Which was nothing."

Prolonged, breathy laugh. The kind of sound effect you'd get at a carnival haunted house.

March said, "My ignorance was fine with her, for obvious reasons. Looking back, she encouraged it. The few times I brought up the past, her family, she'd distract me. Getting what my mom used to call kittenish."

Milo said, "The reason I called is I wanted to talk to your housekeepers. I'm here in front of your house but neither of them answers the gate button."

A beat.

Doug March said, "Without someone around, they're probably slacking off. For all I know, they're swimming in the pool. Hold on."

Half a minute passed before he came back on. "I tried their cellphones, can't get through either. Maybe they went somewhere to stuff their faces. Even though we keep plenty of food around for them."

Milo said, "Could you give me those numbers, please?"

"Hold on. Here we go. The first one's for the old one—Irma. The second's her niece's, don't remember her name." He read off the numbers.

"Thanks. Do you have home addresses for them?"

"Why would I? They live with us," said March.

"You hired them—"

"**She** hired them. One of her few domestic accomplishments, I don't bother with stupid stuff. Okay? Can I attend to business?"

Milo said, "I have to ask: have you thought of anything since we last spoke?"

"I've thought about lots of things," said March. "I'm **always** thinking, my brain's active. But none of it's been about **her**. The less I think about her, the better."

"Okay."

"Do I sound irate, Lieutenant? You bet. The more I thought about what she did, how she played me for an idiot, the more irate I got. At some point I'm going to have to tell my parents and that will not be enjoyable."

"They didn't approve of Meagin."

"Ha. They warned me about her, told me she was too nice. Told me someone who shied away from talking about her past had something to hide. And guess who was right? I do not like the taste of crow, Lieutenant."

Milo said, "Who does?"

"That's neither here nor there," said March. "I am not some clueless moron, I deal with people all the time. Then I go and marry a person who's a flat-out, fucking liar **and** a cheat? So yeah, I'm angry and I don't care if you know that because I had nothing to do with what happened to her. And that Mafia scumbag. Nor do I care to learn about what happened because I'm wiping this phase of my life clean and moving on and the next time, if there is one, I'll be smarter."

Long speech; it left him panting.

Milo said, "Got it, sir."

"Oh, bullshit," said Doug March. "You're just patronizing me like I'm one of your idiot suspects. That's how you make your living. Catching stupid people."

Click.

Milo stared at the phone as if waiting for it to ignite. "No way I can deal with smart people? Was that a dare?"

"More like a tantrum," I said. "If he was guilty, the last thing he'd want to show you was rage."

"Unless he really does think I am that dense. Or he's so weird—what you said, asocial—that he can't handle his rage."

"For all his quirks, I think he's too smart to incriminate himself that blatantly."

He transferred the phone from hand to hand several times. "Maybe you're right and he's just blowing off steam because Meagin made an ass out of him."

"That and what he told us: facing Mater and Pater who warned him against her in the first place. I can see his childhood filled with 'Oh, Douglass, you're such a genius **but** you just don't understand people.' Now the truth of that has smacked him across the face."

"Big-time cognitive dissonance." He grinned. "See, I've been paying attention. Still, he really came across vicious. Told us he's **erased** her, never mentioned her name once. So psychology or not, no way he's off my list."

He tried the maids' numbers, got rings but no voicemail. "Given Dougie's level of anger, maybe they're in there but afraid to talk."

He redialed Doug March. "Like he's gonna answer."

March said, "You again? What?"

"Irma and Adelita still aren't answering their—"

"What do you expect me to do about it?"

"Would there be some way for me to get inside and check on their welfare?"

"Are you nuts?" said March. "You're thinking there's some lunatic running around town wiping out anyone with connections to me? That's idiotic."

"I'm sure it is but—"

"But **nothing.** Even if I wanted to let you in, which I don't, I've got no way to effect that."

"No one at your office has a key?"

Long silence.

"Sir?"

"Didn't think about that," said March, suddenly subdued. As if missing something was painful.

Douglass, you're so smart, but . . .

"Sir?"

"I heard you the first time. Yes, there happens to

be a spare key in the office. A girl who works for me knows where I keep it. You are not to bother her, I'll arrange it."

"Thank you, sir."

"Mind you, I think the whole idea is asinine but if you feel compelled to root around, do it. But only up to a point. She can't stick around long. I need her in the office."

"We'll be quick, sir."

"And," said March, "this is **the** last time I'm going to get involved in your entire mess. Randi will bring a key and the codes. Now it's your turn to do something for me."

"What's that, sir?"

"If there is something . . . unpleasant inside," said Doug March, "clean it up thoroughly before I get back. Which is in two days. A, I don't want to see it, and B, more important, I'm going to be selling the place and need it to be shipshape."

Click.

Milo said, "Mean and crazy. No **way** he's off the list."

23

Cool, pleasant day so we waited outside the gates, occasionally peering through the pickets at the mansion. Milo tried the call button several more times but with no zeal. The two of us shifted yards apart and got on our phones.

One message I wanted to return: Judge Julie Beck. This time I got her bailiff and waited a few minutes before she came on.

"Hi, again, Alex. Two additional facts re: Ruffalo. It's going to be a while before Derek makes it to your office. The prep school's doing some sort of nature thing, hiking, survival, building strong character, whatever."

"Strengthening the resolve of future leaders."

She laughed. "I'm sure that's the rationale but if it was my kid, no way, I don't like outhouses and bears. The main reason I called, and this is incredibly sad, is I just got more paperwork and found out the poor kid was adopted. One of those Russian orphanage deals. So we're talking rejection redux."

I said, "Are either of the parents claiming problems due to the adoption?"

"Product recall?" she said. "Not so far, the egotistical idiots haven't bothered to offer a reason, they just list it as a 'historical factor.' As if it's the court's problem. Sad, no?"

"Beyond sad."

"Alex," she said, "I don't even want to think about how this poor boy will cope. I've got you for that, thank God. You figure something out, it'll be worth whatever you bill. Which I don't need to tell you should be up front and generous. This is going to get ugly."

I hung up, trying not to think about a boy I hadn't met. Approached Milo and heard him say, "Okay, at least the Waldorf worked out, not sure we'd learn anything more from that angle, anyway. Thanks, kiddo."

Pocketing the phone, he checked his Timex, tapped his foot, said, "That was Moses. Whatever time Gio or Meagin spent at other hotels, they weren't noticed."

I said, "Just another romantic couple."

He said, "I'm sure that's how they were feeling when someone visited them on Sunday."

Rising vehicle noise from down the road made

him turn sharply. Gardener's truck with a malfunctioning muffler, the bed laden with mowers, blowers, sacks of soil, plastic trash cans. Brief glance from the baseball-capped driver before it bucked and snorted and continued north.

Milo gave his watch another look. Approached the gate and appeared poised for his twentieth button-jab. Shook his head as if wrestling to control a bad habit and kept walking.

A few minutes later, more automotive noise drew his eyes south. This time more contented feline than rasp.

A shiny, silver Audi Quattro with polished rims drove up, stopped just past the gate, and parked parallel to the stone walls. The purr silenced and a woman got out from the driver's side.

Thirty or so, tall, trim, and Black with tight cornrows, she wore a peach-colored silk pantsuit, blue pumps with moderate heels, and a hesitant smile. After pausing to look at us, she came forward. Jingles from her right hand. Keys and a small gray remote module.

Milo said, "Hi. Lieutenant Sturgis."

"Randi Levine," she said. "Doug asked me to give you these." Nervous glance at the gate. "Do I have to go in?"

"Actually, we'd prefer if you stay right here."

"Great." She handed him the tools of entry. "I will need to wait so I can get everything back. How long do you see it taking?"

"We'll be as quick as possible," said Milo. "What's the alarm code?"

"Oh. Sure." She pulled a yellow Post-it from a pocket and handed it over. "You don't really think something's . . . wrong?"

"Hope not, but it pays to be careful. In light of what happened."

Randi Levine winced.

Milo said, "Doug's told you about it?"

"Just that it happened," she said. "I was concerned. Of course."

"About?"

"How he'd cope with something so horrible. Post-traumatic response, you know?"

Milo nodded. "Has he had any of that before?"

"No, why would he? I'm sure he won't, he's got a way."

"Of?"

"Handling things. He's a very successful man."

"What's his way?"

She worked her lips. "He tends to keep things to himself and works out his own issues. I know people think you always need to express yourself but I disagree. I used to work at Sony, then at Bad Robot, then at Bruckheimer. Everything in the industry is personal. Including things you don't want to be personal."

I said, "Working for Doug is different."

"Totally different," she said. "Good different. Show up on time, get the job done, no egos, no extraneous nonsense, and once he trusts you, he gives you independence. He's gone all the time, needs people he can rely on. After what I went through in the industry, it's a dream job."

She looked at the mansion.

I said, "You've been here before."

"Just to drop off papers. Did what happened— was it here?"

Milo shook his head. "Did you ever meet Ms. March?"

"I haven't. I saw a picture of her, that's all. On Doug's desk, the two of them at some gala. She looked gorgeous." Her voice caught. A woman she'd never encountered but human compassion kicks in easily for those blessed with it. "What a horrible thing to happen."

I said, "What did Doug tell you about it?"

"Nothing. Next to nothing," said Randi Levine. "He's only been in the office once since it happened, yesterday afternoon, prepping for the Apex inspection—that's a project in Columbus, Ohio. I thought **something** might be wrong because he was even quieter than usual. And kind of bent over. Like someone was sitting on his back—forget that. Please. I shouldn't be talking about Doug, period. I'm sure you know all this, anyway."

I said, "Bent over. Affected by what had happened."

"How could he not be? How could anyone not be? I asked him if something was wrong and he came right out and told me what had happened and it blew me to bits. Especially when I saw the tears in his eyes, that's so unlike— oh, shoot, let's stop **talking** about this, Doug wants everything to be discreet. Please don't tell him I said anything, okay? Please."

"Promise," said Milo.

She looked at him doubtfully.

"So he told you what happened."

"Then he said, 'Randi, I don't want to talk about it. Ever.' And went into his private office and shut the door. I went to my desk and ensured that his travel plans were all set."

She looked at the Audi, began tapping a foot.

Milo said, "Anything else you can tell us?"

"Can't see how there would be," said Randi Levine. "You really can't tell me how long it's going to take?"

"Depends on what we find," said Milo.

"Oh God, that sounds ominous," she said. "Well, I hope you find nothing. Okay, I'll just wait in my car and catch up on work."

Unsnapping his gun but leaving it holstered, Milo remoted the gate open then strode past me.

I followed and caught up.

He stopped. "It probably won't take long, wait outside."

"Why?"

"Just to be careful."

"We're not talking about a bad guy lying in wait," I said. "Worst case, there are two corpses in there and my nostrils can handle it."

"Yeah, well, the last time I thought I had everything figured out."

"The last time is irrelevant, no need for superstition." The harshness in my own voice surprised me. Like listening to an evil twin.

He said, "Being careful is superstitious?"

"Finding causation where there is none is the definition of superstitious. Don't worry."

"I always worry."

I walked quickly toward the mansion.

His turn to catch up.

When we reached the front door he said, "You can come in but stand well back and let me do my thing. No debates, okay?"

I said, "Quantify 'well back.'"

"Jesus, what's got into you?"

"The promise of adventure."

"Consider it a broken promise." He unlocked the door. No alarm buzz. Just inside, an alarm company monitor said **Ready To Arm.**

Emptied of people, the marble-floored space felt cold and sepulchral. Like a museum after hours.

The first thing both of us did was sniff the air. Scanning for the cordite bite of recent gunshots or the stomach-turning fetor of death.

None of that, just sterile, odorless air, but in a house this huge that meant nothing. Milo took out his Glock and stomped the floor with a desert boot. Three times. The sound echoed.

He said, "Police," in a loud voice.

Silence.

"Okay," he said, "here's the quantification: you can stand here or get comfy in the living room. Concentrate on producing psychological wisdom while I do the scut work. If there's nothing to report, I'll be back soon enough."

I said, "Okay. Mom."

Muttering and shaking his head, he pointed the gun forward and passed under the right side of the double staircase. Left alone, I circled the center table a few times before making my way to the same seat I'd occupied the day we'd talked to Douglass March.

The path took me past one conspicuous change: the photo of the Marches in full dress was gone. In its place, propped against a lamp, was a framed artist rendering of a residential complex.

Belle-Vieux Gardens. Atlanta, Ga. Venture Quest Properties.

Douglass March embracing true love.

Milo was gone for twenty-two minutes. During that time, I checked and rechecked my phone, then punished myself by scanning national, international, and local events on a "news aggregator" and encountering nothing but the shrill squawks of click-addicted misery pimps. Tired of sitting, I circled the massive room thirty-eight times. Failed to come up with a shred of wisdom, psychological or otherwise.

When Milo returned, he was shaking his head. "Place is crazy-big, checked everywhere including the garage and the pool house. She drove a Porsche

Panamera and his hot wheels are a Mazda SUV with eight hundred miles on it. No sign of struggle anywhere including the maids' room. Irma and Adelita shared it, there are two beds. Both are made up and tucked tight and all their belongings are gone."

"Orderly retreat."

"Hope so for their sake."

I said, "What about Meagin's clothes?"

"Untouched. What **is** different is that little studio of hers. Her easel and supplies are still there but the paintings are in the trash bins outside. Where I spent a pleasant chunk of my time even though no serious smell told me I was wasting my time."

"Could I have a look at the paintings?"

"Why?"

"There's one in particular that I'd like to see." I pulled out my phone and showed him the screen shot I'd taken of the gray-white stalky thing. Ambiguous, maybe unfinished, topped by a starburst, pincer-like extensions at the bottom.

He said, "Oh, yeah, the ugly one. When you snapped it March got miffed and you said art was personal expression or something like that. Why're you still interested?"

I said, "It's different from the others. Exceptions can be interesting. Maybe it meant something to her."

He studied the image. "Don't see what good it can do, but why not? You've been admirably patient."

Six oversized trash bins stood alongside the northern wall of the mansion. Three were green and filled with lawn clippings, the others, black. Two of the black ones were empty, one was packed with three untied industrial-sized silvery plastic bags. Milo having a look.

He said, "Checked out the yard waste, too, nothing but grass clippings down to the bottom."

I pulled out the bags and laid them on the ground. The first two were crammed with the decently rendered but banal oils we'd seen the first time. Stacked but intact.

The last one, retrieved from the bottom, yielded one painting: twelve-by-sixteen canvas covered in shades of gray.

Anything but intact.

The image of the stalky thing had been sliced twice diagonally, from corner to corner. Destroyed by a perfect X.

Milo's eyes had grown wide. "Musta missed it. Guess it meant something to him, too."

He removed the other paintings and restacked them on the ground. Bent and lifted them as a group and held them close to his chest.

"Let's go. Maybe I'll start a gallery."

As we neared the gate, he said, "Art appreciation's fine but back to basics. Irma and Adelita cleared out because they're scared. Which puts it right back on Doug."

"He's the obvious choice," I said.

"But . . ."

"There could've been another lover of Meagin's they'd seen before. Someone she brought to the house."

"Not Gio? One lothario offs another?"

"She's shaping up as someone with lots of secrets."

"Gio she kept at arm's length but Lover Boy Number Two got to use the marital bed?"

"It's possible," I said, "if he was someone with whom she had a longer, more serious relationship."

"She was that blatant in front of the maids?" he said. "Not worried they'd rat her out?"

"Maybe she was confident they'd be on her side. Or she was oblivious to their presence. People can get that way with the help, start treating them like furniture. Alternatively, she paid them off to keep quiet. Then she gets murdered and they start thinking knowledge can be dangerous."

He chewed on that. "Only way to find out is to find **them**." He phoned Alicia and told her to start calling domestic agencies.

That accomplished, we resumed walking. Reached the gate, where Milo laid the paintings down, extracted the clicker, and created our exit route.

Randi Levine got out of her Audi, phone in one hand, small spiral datebook in the other. She looked at the canvases in Milo's arms, raised her eyebrows but said nothing.

He placed the stack in the trunk of the unmarked, returned to Levine, handed over the keys and the remote and thanked her.

"The artwork," she said. "You took it off the walls?"

"Nope, pulled it out of the garbage."

"I don't understand."

"Original works by the late Ms. March. Your boss wasn't appreciative."

"I—okay, fine, whatever you say."

"Thanks for your time."

"Oka-ay."

Seconds after she began driving away, her phone was at her mouth.

I said, "Loyal assistant notifying the boss. He gets sufficiently stirred up, he might call you and give something away."

"You read my mind," he said. "Aka doing your job."

CHAPTER

25

T racing the maids' whereabouts remained Milo's focus when we were back in his office. That changed when he logged onto his email and found an attachment containing Meagin March's phone activity.

Seven months' worth. He printed two copies, gave me one, sat back in his squealing desk chair, and began eyeballing.

I said, "Lots of calls but again, not a single text. Fits someone with secrets."

He said, "She's that hush-hush, why not just use burners?" He frowned. "Yeah, yeah, maybe she did. Okay, let's take a closer look at what she did expose to the world."

Not much more than we already knew.

Meagin March had amassed two hundred and nine days of reach-outs to nail salons, clothing boutiques and luxury department stores, jewelers, the day spa, food deliveries from high-end and health-conscious restaurants.

Nearly all the personal calls were to three numbers, all familiar. Back-and-forths with Lana Demarest and Toni Bowman.

One clarification: calls to and from Gio Aggiunta had begun just over three months ago. Phone contact between the lovers had always been brief, most calls lasting a minute or less.

Setting up jog-over dates, no need for chitchat?

I searched for a day-pattern for the trysts, found none. That made sense; the deciding factor had been Doug March's absence.

I ran through the log twice, searching for evidence of another love interest, and came up empty. A minute later, Milo announced the same conclusion and cursed.

Then he pointed.

I said, "Just about to mention it."

We'd come up with the same question mark, an eight-minute call from Meagin to an 805 number, just over two months ago.

He said, "Long call but only once. Maybe this is the ex she dumped and pissed off. They have a heated discussion, he stews, finally decides to come down here two months later to express his disappointment."

He crossed his fingers and logged onto the reverse directory.

Cellphones have made that a lot less useful. This time it paid off, listing a Ventura County landline.

The auxiliary of St. Jerome's Catholic Church in San Pietro.

He said, "Confessing her sins?"

I said, "Last I heard that had to be in person. You know different?"

"Not since I consulted to the Vatican. Don't know what an auxiliary is, either. Maybe something they put in place after I lapsed."

I said, "Could be a charity group the church runs."

"She wanted to donate?"

"There are plenty of good causes locally, why pick a place fifty miles away? To me an eight-minute call says some sort of personal connection."

He tried the number. Got multiple-choice voicemail presented by a cheerful female voice. First decision: English or Español. Following that, Option 1 was the church's main office. That triggered a new list.

If this is in regard to the schedule of Mass and services, press 1.

If this is in regard to a christening . . .

He said, "How long before God installs a system?" and listened.

Nothing about an auxiliary.

He hung up. "San Pietro isn't big on day spas, it's mostly aggie and oil wells. I was there coupla years ago, some farm dinner fundraiser Rick had to go to. Tables set up in an avocado ranch. I learned that avocado trees don't die. They look like they've had it, then you hack 'em to stumps and they rebloom. I remember thinking if humans could do that, I'd be out of a job."

He looked at me. "You, on the other hand, would be raking it in, helping late bloomers adjust. So what do you think about her calling there? Seeing as it's a church, Angry Ex is looking less likely."

I said, "Maybe she has family there."

"One call in seven months?" he said. "Not exactly a big happy clan."

"Maybe she left the clan and tried reconnecting."

"Midwestern girl packs out to Vegas for excitement that ain't San Pietro?"

"Who knows if that's even true?" I said. "If whoever she called in San Pietro is kin, her roots could be in California. Maybe Vegas attracted her because she'd heard for years how good-looking she was and figured that would carry her a long way. But once she got there, she discovered plenty of competition and at some point she got into escorting. That led her to Rikki Montel and the others and eventually, the four of them decided to try L.A."

He said, "Homecoming."

"Spending serious time in Vegas could mean the older guys she complained about were what you said: big spenders or shady types who got too aggressive. That led her to Doug, at first glance shy and nonthreatening. But he also turned out to be a Mega Type A, so she found herself an easygoing younger lover. With a history of his own that directed him to older women."

"Living ultra-luxe and having a nice dip in the pool at Gio's," he said. "She probably felt she'd won the lottery. But still, why risk it all by cheating?"

"Rikki told us she liked to take risks."

"Skydiving." He sighed. "Bad judgment, bad luck. The kind of person I usually get to meet."

Alicia called. She'd talked to a dozen agencies. No record of either woman being placed. She said, "Want me to keep looking?"

"If you've got time."

"Nothing but, Loo. Until dinner, Al's taking me to Spago."

"In the Rolls?"

"What else? Gets him great valet parking."

"**Bon appétit,** road warrior."

She laughed and hung up.

He said, "Car's worth fifteen G but looks like a million. There's gotta be a moral in that." He rubbed his face. "Where the hell are those maids?"

I said, "If they weren't hired through an agency, maybe it was a personal referral."

"Meaning?"

"Her spa buddies."

◆

On-hold purgatory at Dr. Lana Demarest's dental office was soundtracked by a spiel about baby teeth. When someone finally broke in, it was an answering service operator. Closed for the day.

At Toni Bowman's real estate company, a receptionist listened, and put Milo on hold during four minutes of felonious Beatle adaptation. "Yesterday" and "I'll Follow the Sun" debased by flatulent tuba and trombone and ice-rink Hammond organ.

Milo said, "Sadists," and rubbed his eyes and looked at his Timex.

Finally: "Here you go, sir."

"God bless—"

Toni Bowman said, "You're into the holy roller stuff?"

Milo said, "Whatever helps," and told her what he was after.

She said, "So no progress. Yeah, she asked me for a referral because her genius husband had hired a service who did a lousy job. I talked to my Rosa. She's a gem, I knew anyone she vouched for would be golden."

"Could you please ask Rosa if she has addresses for Ms. Ruiz and Ms. Santiago?"

"Meg hired two people? I only know of one, a friend of Rosa's, no idea what her name is and you'll have to wait to find out. Rosa's on vacation in Mexico for another week."

Milo said, "Long as we're talking, do you know of any connection Meagin had to San Pietro?"

"Where's that?"

"Ventura County."

"She never mentioned it. Why?"

"She phoned up there."

"A lot?"

"Once."

"Sounds like you're grasping at straws," said Toni Bowman.

"Sometimes it comes to that, ma'am. Thanks for your time and when you do have a chance to talk to Rosa, please let me know."

"I'll have a chance in a week," said Toni Bowman. "I have no idea how to reach her in her little village. And don't ask me which one it is, all I know is they keep chickens, she once showed me a photo of chickens."

We both decided to call it a day. I was just out the door when Milo's phone beeped the first four notes of Satie's Gymnopédie No. 1. To me, his ringtones are just as sinful as the assault on Liverpool but they don't seem to bother him.

He looked at the number, motioned me to sit back down, switched to speaker, and said, "Sir."

Douglass March said, "When can I have her jewelry?"

"It's in safekeeping—"

"Where?"

"Our scientific division."

"For what reason? Fingerprints? DNA?"

"Do you need it in a hurry, sir?"

"No, but I see no reason to delay. I'm going to have all her shit appraised at Christie's or Sotheby's then sell it. I've done some research and with inflation looming, prices are rising, and there's one piece I'm fixing to make a serious profit on. Purple diamond necklace, one and a half carats, super-rare. I paid a hundred thou and since then colored stones have skyrocketed."

Each sentence had lowered his volume and pitch, buffering the jagged contours of his words. Calming as he talked about making money.

Then he said, "I need to get **something** out of all this," and the hard edge returned.

Milo said, "I'll have everything inventoried and let you know."

March said, "That's not much of an answer."

"It's my answer," said Milo. "If you have a complaint, my captain is—"

"Oh, don't waste my time by shunting me to another bureaucrat. Everything she owned—is mine, so do what you need to do and get it back to me A-sap."

Click.

Milo stared at the phone. "Gimme a diagnosis."

I said, "F-minus people skills, angry and doesn't care who knows it."

"I was thinking malignant asshole."

"That's another way of putting it."

"But not a psychopath? Not conscious, arrogant, throwing it in my face?"

"You know what I'm going to tell you—"

"Anything's possible. But?"

"To me that came across as a tantrum. One thing he mentioned that was interesting: the purple diamond. I noticed it at the scene because it was small and simple compared with the other pieces. I assumed it was semi-precious, something she'd held on to for sentimental reasons. But now that I think about it, she wore it in the gala photo."

"He's right about it being big-time hoohah."

"Let's see."

Internet research confirmed the rarity of intense pink and purple diamonds. The stones were mined mostly in Australia, occasionally in Siberia or Africa, the color theorized to be the product of extreme pressure.

Milo said, "Should be my birthstone."

Online sites were all over the place value-wise and many came across as scams. Not that any of them actually owned purples; the only images were of pale-pink diamonds many of which were barely pigmented. But still pricey.

I said, "We could try the dealer you used on the Thalia Mars case."

"Remember his name?"

"Not offhand."

He drummed his fingers, began searching years of emails. "This doesn't work, I'll go downstairs and pull the file."

I'm better with faces than with names. Closing my eyes I summoned up a full, pink, white-mustachioed face. Cheerful eyes and voice. Older man, eighty or so, spry, dapper . . . Armenian.

Like the writer.

I said, "Saroyan."

He logged off his mail, looked up the number in his contacts, googled. "Here we go. Harold A. Saroyan, Sargis Premium Jewelers, the downtown Jewelry Mart."

Saroyan's lightly accented voice answered. "Hel-lo. Sargis."

"Mr. Saroyan, it's Lieutenant Sturgis. You may not remember but a few years ago—"

"Of course I remember. I don't get to do such exciting things very often. What do you want me to look at, now?"

"Nothing yet, sir. I'd just like a ballpark appraisal of a one-and-a-half-carat purple diamond."

Saroyan clicked his tongue. "Ah, such a pity."

"What is?"

"The laws of probability say you have a fake, Lieutenant. Maybe, at best, a tasteless chemical enhancement. Did somebody steal it? Or worse, kill for it?"

"No, sir," said Milo. "An owner has requested its return and I wanted to have a—"

"Ballpark estimate," said Saroyan. "Okay, let's go to Dodger Stadium. What shape is the stone?"

Milo looked at me.

I said, "Pear."

"Pear."

"No big difference," said Saroyan. "And the color?"

"Purple, sir. We thought it might be an amethyst."

"And you might be right."

"If it is real—"

"On the slight chance it is real, Lieutenant, we are talking two hundred fifty thousand to three hundred and fifty thousand dollars. Minimum. And the way things are going, that figure will be higher by next year due to inflation."

"Really."

"Really, Lieutenant. But it's more like an infinitesimal chance. The last purple I obtained was six years ago and I worked hard for it, including a trip to Australia. I sold it to a famous person. Six carats. Millions."

"Wow," said Milo.

"I'm glad to hear you say that, Lieutenant. The ability to be amazed is a good thing."

"Happens to me often, sir."

"With murders?"

"With the things people do to each other."

"Ah," said Harold Saroyan. "That sounds more like horror than amazement. If you want me to look at whatever this is, just call me. I will come to you."

"Appreciate that, sir."

"Oh yes, Lieutenant. The last time I worked with you I had a good story for my grandchildren."

Milo thanked him, hung up, scrawled some notes, stretched his legs as far as the mean space permitted. "Two fifty to three fifty and Dougie paid a hundred."

"She scammed him?"

"Given the nature of their relationship, it's possible, no? Notice, he didn't say he bought it, he said he paid for it. What if she came to him, I found something I like, honey. He doles out a hundred. She buys an amethyst and pockets the dough."

"Did she have her own bank account?"

"Don't know yet. Just put in the subpoena but even if I get it, I have no idea where to look."

I said, "Learning she conned him financially as well as romantically isn't going to do much for Doug's disposition."

"Only thing that matters to me is if that led him to shoot two people and I can prove it. Any ideas?"

I shook my head.

"No prob," he said, "it's dinnertime, anyway. Gonna find some slop nearby, then get back here and keep grasping at straws."

"Why don't you come over for dinner?"

"Don't you wanna ask Gorgeous?"

"She loves you."

Despite himself, he smiled. "It's mutual. Thanks for the offer, amigo, but I'm feeling the pull of solitude."

26

I spent the morning writing up my evaluation of a six-year-old girl injured by a bicyclist speeding on a sidewalk in Pacific Palisades. The biker's defense: his activism helped the environment and pedestrians needed to be aware of their surroundings, specifically the child's mother.

No need for me to comment on any of that, just to report on the psychological ramifications of a broken ankle plus significant terror.

I emailed the report to the lawyer who'd hired me, made coffee, and was drinking it when Milo phoned just after one p.m.

"It was a nothing day," he said, sounding strangely cheerful. "Until a few minutes ago when Claudio Aggiunta called. Every year, the family gave Gio a hefty cash allowance. Three hundred thou over and above all the bills they paid for him. The deal was he needed to document everything."

I said, "Probably so they could deduct it as a business expense. Or they just wanted to keep tabs on him."

"Either way, he was compliant, sent everything back to Italy every three months for their accountants to examine. The last batch hasn't been looked at but because of the murder, Claudio just checked. A coupla months ago a hundred G's disappeared with no notation. That spark any free association?"

"The same amount Doug paid for the purple diamond or whatever it is."

"Could be our gal Meagin was an equal-opportunity grifter. Makes sense, given her time in Vegas milking the gig economy."

"It could also explain someone gunning for her."

"Oh yeah," he said. "Rip off one person too many and it's your last scam."

"Gio was wrong place, wrong time, wrong woman."

"It's looking that way, Alex. Poor guy, living the high life, shelling out money he didn't earn to the hottest cougar he'd ever known."

I said, "A hundred thousand for jewelry. Backs up what I said before: more to the relationship than sex."

"Yup, looks like he had feelings for her," he said. "And she led a bad guy to his doorstep. Gonna be tough explaining it to the family. Once I get to the point where I can actually prove something."

"What's next?"

"Finding out exactly what that stone is. Called the lab and Noreen Sharp had fun with me—here you go again, hassling us with bling, why can't you be like the others and just send bullets. I sent Moe over to pick it up, he just got back, they packed it in a big box, triple-sealed. Just opened it and took a peek. You're right, compared with her other diamonds it's dinky. But pretty, at least to my eye. Anyway, Saroyan's on his way. Bringing a grandkid, who am I to deny him?"

I arrived at the station just as a uniformed driver guided Harold Saroyan out of a matte-gray Suburban. The jeweler looked exactly the same as two years ago: five-six, mid-eighties with white hair and a luxuriant white mustache. Turned out impeccably in a cream-colored suit, sky-blue spread-collar shirt, hugely knotted orange silk cravat, and mirror-polished caramel wingtips.

When he'd been safely deposited on the sidewalk, the driver raced around to the street-side door. Not in time; the door flung open and a teenage boy bounded out, heedless of traffic, slouched over to Saroyan, and stood next to him. Wide-eyed.

The boy was fourteen or so, stocky, handsome, with a smooth round face under a nest of brown curls and eyes blurred by thick, black-framed glasses.

His version of dressing for success was a red AC/DC T-shirt, plum-colored board shorts, and orange Nikes.

I made my way over. "Hello, Mr. Saroyan."

Puzzled look for half a sec, then a smile. "Ah, you work with the lieutenant."

"Alex Delaware."

"Yes, of course, Alex." Smooth dissembling, warm smile, warmer handshake. "This is my number one grandson Clifford Avakian."

"Hi, Clifford."

The boy's head dipped. Studying the sidewalk.

Saroyan nudged him. "Clifford?"

"Pleased to meet you."

Throat clear from Grandpa.

A mumbled, adolescent "Sir."

Saroyan nodded approvingly. "Clifford watches police shows. I want to show him reality."

The driver returned to the door that had egested the old man, reached in and extracted a black leather case I'd seen before.

Saroyan said, "Please give it to Clifford, Gerald."

The transfer completed, Gerald said, "Okay if I go and find parking, Mr. S?"

"Please do, thank you, Gerald. Clifford will text you when we're ready to be picked up."

Gerald got back behind the wheel, the Suburban drove south, turned right, and vanished.

I headed for the station's front door ahead of Saroyan and the boy and held it open. No challenge.

The jeweler walked slowly, with stiffness I hadn't seen the first time.

"I'm a little less hare and a little more turtle," he said, lacing his arm through Clifford's free limb. Smiling broadly, in counterpoint to his grandson's grim mien.

"Cheer up, Clifford, this will be educational."

Milo was waiting in the large interview room. Two blank whiteboards, no refreshments, the pair of long tables pushed together, a two-foot-square white cardboard box with the lab's emblem on four sides resting in the center of the right-hand table.

Entering the station and riding up in the elevator had stunned Clifford into silence and he remained that way. Being introduced to Milo lowered his eyes again and parted his lips, as if air supply had dropped and he needed to mouth-breathe.

Saroyan said, "Shake hands with Lieutenant Sturgis, Clifford. If you behave he will not arrest you."

No smile from the boy.

"I'm kidding, Clifford, we kid all the time, no?"

"Yes, Grandpa."

"You and me, we're the best kidders." Gently elbowing the boy's arm. "No?"

"Yes, Grandpa."

Shrugging, Saroyan turned to Milo. "Okay, Lieutenant, let's get to work."

◆

The jeweler sat directly behind the box, motioned for Clifford to settle to his right, then motioned for the black leather case. Unzipping it with slightly palsied hands he drew out a multi-lens loupe and a stereoscopic microscope.

At the same time, Milo reached into the box and drew out a thick wad of white wrapping paper. Once taped, now merely folded back into place. Unfolding, he lifted the necklace and handed it over to Harold Saroyan.

Looking blasé, even bored, Saroyan held the stone up to the light. At several angles. No more ennui, now, just the noncommittal blankness of expert appraisal, as he turned to the loupe and inspected the gem under several strengths of magnification.

Sharp-eyed and silent as the purple pear was transferred to the microscope.

Another full two minutes of minute nudges as he peered through the dual eyepieces.

When Saroyan finally looked up, it was his grandson he turned to. "Clifford, you have just experienced something extraordinary."

"What?"

"This"—holding the stone at arm's length—"is hundreds of thousands of dollars."

"Whoa! No shit!"

"Your language," said Harold Saroyan, "is not the best. But you are excused." He favored us with a denture smile. "No shit, indeed."

◆

Milo allowed Saroyan to rewrap the diamond, then placed it back in the box.

Saroyan said, "I trust you have a safe, here."

Milo said, "We can keep it secure but I want it back at the lab and logged at true value." He texted Moe Reed, who arrived moments later and took the box.

"Retape it, it's three hundred G's," said Milo. "And take Sean with you. Have him notify Noreen."

Unfazed, Reed nodded and left with the box.

Harold Saroyan said, "That's a tough-looking boy, makes a good impression. I sometimes use guys like that, mostly Israelis. Nevertheless I'm glad they're packing heat." To Clifford: "That's the expression, no? From that videogame you play? Hot . . . something?"

The boy nodded dully.

Milo said, "I've got some questions for you, Mr. Saroyan, but no offense, Clifford doesn't need to hear them. Can I offer him a tour of the station?"

"Sure—that's good, no, Clifford?" said Saroyan. "You can ask all the questions, then tell your friends all the stories."

While he spoke, Milo texted again. The door opened and a young, female uniform came in.

"Sir?"

"Officer Salazar, this is Clifford Avakian, a VIP guest. Could you please give him the grand tour while I talk to his grandfather."

"The grand tour?"

"Not the one we give to bad kids in order to scare them. He's an excellent citizen and has been extremely helpful."

Clifford followed the exchange with jumpy eyes.

Officer J. Salazar smiled at him and said, "Let's go, Mr. Avakian. Would you like something to drink, first?"

"Um, sure."

"Coke okay?"

"Uh-huh." Surreptitiously examining Salazar's chest.

She pointed to the door, let Clifford open it, and followed him out.

Harold Saroyan said, "He really is a good boy. So what can I help you with?"

Milo and I pulled up chairs opposite him. "What I'm going to tell you is part of an ongoing investigation. I know you'll be discreet."

"I am Mr. Discreet, Lieutenant. In my business, indiscretion will finish you."

"I can see that. Okay. The necklace was found at a murder scene, along with several other pieces of diamond jewelry owned by the female victim."

"The female victim," said Saroyan. "There was a male victim, too?"

"Yes, sir. Yesterday, the woman's husband called and asked for return of all the jewelry. He specified the necklace. Said he'd paid a hundred thousand dollars for it."

"How long ago?"

"Half a year."

"Ridiculous," said Saroyan. "Not that recently, for something of that quality." He shook his head. "The color, the depth, the richness. It is on a par with that six-carat stone I sold to the famous person. Much smaller, of course, and value goes up exponentially with size. But still, no way he got it for less than two, two fifty."

"Which leads me to my next point. When we assumed the stone was fake, we figured the woman had deceived her husband by having him pay a hundred thousand for what was really an amethyst and pocketing most of the money."

Saroyan said, "An amethyst that size and color? Feh. I give it to you for free. No way anyone sold a diamond like that for a hundred, not going to happen . . ." His mouth screwed up tight. "Maybe if it was stolen goods. Something palmed off by a crook or a crooked pawnbroker."

Milo said, "Making matters more interesting, today we heard from relatives of the male victim that a hundred thousand dollars had vanished from his account."

"The lover," said Saroyan. A smile spread slowly. "Ah, I see. She got them to split it. Okay, two hundred, a bargain but within possibility, that I can see." He fingered the orange tie. "You think she did it to make them more likely to pay?"

"That's what comes to mind."

"Or," I said, "to convince each of them they'd bought it for her. That way, she could wear it when she was with both of them."

Milo and Saroyan stared at me.

Saroyan said, "You think in an interesting way, Alex. So we are talking a very crafty woman. But not crafty enough? The husband found out, decided to avenge himself? Then why leave the diamond at the scene?"

"The husband didn't shoot her, sir. Sorry, I can't say more."

"Okay, a hit man," said Saroyan. "But still, why leave it?"

I said, "If he knew he'd be getting it anyway, there'd be no reason to complicate matters."

"Ah . . . intriguing. When you solve it, please let me know, Lieutenant, so I can have a new story."

A fingertip tapped the smile. "But for now, discretion."

Milo said, "Thank you, sir. So you find two hundred thousand a credible purchase price?"

"It would be a bargain price, Lieutenant, but not crazy, like one hundred," said Saroyan. "And again, if there was a cloud over it—anything that put pressure on the deal—that could cheapen it. Or, I suppose, even if not, depending on the circumstance."

"What circumstance would that be?"

"The right time, the right seller, the right buyer," said Saroyan. "Like the planets moving together.

Buyers sometimes talk big then they try to make complicated deals. Someone with ready cash could benefit. But only at two hundred, not one hundred."

"Got it," said Milo. "So if I wanted to purchase a rare purple diamond and get someone to play along with my hundred-thousand story, where would I go?"

"How broad of a geography do you want?"

"There's no evidence this woman traveled recently so let's start with locally."

"Hmm," said Saroyan. "Obviously, you couldn't go to Tiffany or Graff or any of the big shots . . . okay two names of small shots come up in my head but I can't promise. One, Melulian, has an office in La Jolla. He does very nice rubies and sapphires but last I heard he wasn't well, heart attack. His sons have no interest in the business, one's a doctor, the other's a . . ." He waved a hand. "Forgive me, when I turned ninety I began to wander mentally . . . may I ask where this woman lived?"

"Bel Air."

"Okay, that fits better with the other guy. He's in Beverly Hills but not on Rodeo, off the main drag on the far west side of Little Santa Monica Boulevard. Bobby Kilic."

He spelled it, looking up at the ceiling. "Turkish with an Irish mother. Looks like a surfer."

"You've dealt with him."

"Never," said Saroyan. "You hear stories—just like this one. A lot of people don't deal with him but rich people who don't know better? Why not. And sometimes I hear he does get a great stone. Like a big fancy intense yellow, seven carats. From Africa, from what they tell me, but maybe he also went to Australia for a purple, I don't know. Or Siberia." New smile, wider. "In the winter."

"Bobby Kilic." Milo scrawled.

"Please do not quote me, Lieutenant. Armenians don't do well with Turks."

"Discretion runs both ways, sir. What's the name of Kilic's business?"

"Nonpareil Elite Jewelers." Saroyan huffed. "You see what I mean."

"What's that, sir?"

"Overdoing it." Saroyan tugged his tie knot tighter. "Like your woman victim."

We found Clifford and Officer Salazar in the snack room eating chocolate chip cookies and drinking Coke. Chatting about something and ceasing when they saw us. Clifford sported brown stains where he might one day grow a mustache.

Salazar said, "We were just finishing. I was about to ask Cliff here if he wanted to be a cop."

Clifford nodded.

Saroyan said, "Interesting." He handed the boy a napkin and pointed to his own upper lip. "Let's go back to Glendale, we will talk in the car."

Milo settled back at his desk. "That thing about

Turks and Armenians. Maybe Saroyan wants to get even but let's check out this Kilic."

"That thing" was genocide. A million Armenians slaughtered by the Ottomans less than thirty years before the Holocaust. The world doing nothing, giving Hitler confidence.

I said, "That would be pretty low-level revenge."

"Yeah, you're right, the old guy's been right on, so far. Speaking of old, when he turned ninety? Wonder how far past that he is. I was figuring eighties."

"Me, too."

He logged on. "Nonpareil Elite Jewelers—okay, here he is with a bunch of Hollywood types . . . looks like that's all he posts, kissy-face selfies, no actual jewelry."

We studied a dozen shots of a grinning improbably blond man in his forties with matching stubble and a pair of small gold hoops glinting from his left ear. Broadly smiling, setting off competing glimmer from his teeth.

Bobby Kilic, always in a slim-cut black suit and white T-shirt, looked chummy with a host of familiar faces. Maybe the celebs figured they'd gotten deep discounts. Or their business managers got billed and they could pretend they'd scored free bling.

Milo said, "Let's try to surprise this entrepreneur."

27

Burton Way, named for Burton Green, the developer largely responsible for creating Beverly Hills, had become South Santa Monica Boulevard decades ago. Now referred to as Little Santa Monica by the locals, it's a commercial street barely wide enough for the four lanes allocated by the city, paralleling its larger northern sibling and confusing tourists.

Bistros, cafés, indie boutiques, and a few monobrands predominate, visits to the latter requiring net worth well short of that required for the Rodeo Drive excursions Meagin March had enjoyed. The street throbs with all-day bustle despite the low probability of finding a parking space.

At the western end of Little Santa Monica, once you get past the Peninsula hotel, the action slows, vacant storefronts begin popping up, and the B.H.–L.A. border is heralded by the black-glass towers of Century City looming with unmistakable malice.

Watch out or we'll eat you then spit out the bones.

Nonpareil Elite Jewelers sat at the end of the block, bordered by a service alley in need of paving.

No self-promotion, just a narrow, iron-grated window in an older brick building devoid of architectural intent. Small-letter signage in gilt near the top of the window. Illegible from the street.

I said, "Maybe one of those if-you-have-to-ask deals."

Milo said, "With Bobby's hoohah connections, maybe it doesn't matter." He pulled into a loading zone half a dozen slots west, put his LAPD placard on the dash, and got out.

Up close, the window gilt was chipped and the grates implied not open for business. So did the locked front door and the lack of response to Milo's bell-push.

"Okay, I'll have to call him."

I said, "Tell him you're on the Oscars fashion committee and need adornment."

He laughed. "Yeah, that's me, fashion."

We headed back to the car. Instead of continuing, I stopped and pointed to the alley.

He said, "Why not."

◆

Grubby asphalt, weeds poking from fissures. No windows on the west side of the building. Not a bad idea for a place selling big-ticket gems.

Behind the building, a three-slot parking area backed by a dumpster was one-third occupied.

Black Mercedes S coupe, wheels the same color, interior blood red. A man leaned against the car, facing away from us, smoking a joint, oblivious to our approach.

A level of awareness not recommended for a guy selling big-ticket gems.

Bobby Kilic had dispensed with his black suit jacket, wore a white V-necked tee over black jeans. His torso was narrow and soft-looking. Older-looking than his photos had suggested, with a Mediterranean complexion further browned by the sun, looseness under sagging eyes, and relenting jowls.

He took a deep drag of cannabis, held the smoke in for a long time, looked up at the sky and exhaled. Nothing emerged. As he raised the cigarette to his lips, Milo said, "Good afternoon."

Kilic startled, dropped the joint, turned sharply and put his hand in his pocket.

From what I could see, the pants were too tight to hide a gun bulge. But you never know what can happen when people get surprised and Milo's own hand had slipped into his jacket.

We didn't move.

Kilic stared at us, removed his hand, and backed away. Then he took a second to stare ruefully at wasted weed smoldering on the ground.

Milo flashed his badge. "L.A. police, Mr. Kilic, didn't mean to alarm you."

"Alarm me? You nearly gave me a fucking heart attack." Hoarse voice. Levantine features but an Irish brogue.

"We had no idea we'd actually find you back here," said Milo. "You're not in any sort of trouble, we'd just like a few minutes of your time."

Bobby Kilic drew himself up. Stooped low, picked up the still-active joint, studied it, said, "What the ef," and dropped it back down. "Don't think about a littering ticket, guys, this is private property. What do you want to talk about?"

"Meagin March."

"Meg? What about her?"

"She's been murdered."

Splotches of pallor rose to the surface of Kilic's solar-enhanced skin. "No way. You're shitting me. Can't be."

"I'm afraid it can be, sir."

"Meg? How the—who the—you're telling me this just happened? I didn't hear about it, I hear about things, I always hear."

"Last Sunday," said Milo.

"Who the fuck did it?" Clenching both hands. "Some homeless lowlife? Some gang-banging home invader? Don't tell me it was at her house, she said she was **über**-protected there, felt safe even though her husband was gone all the time."

"Can't get into the details, sir, but it didn't happen at her house."

"Where, then? Where?" said Bobby Kilic. "Where, c'mon? I live in the hills, if it's the hills I need to know."

"At the home of a friend. Gio Aggiunta."

Blank look. That told me plenty about the purple diamond transaction.

Kilic said, "He—whoever the fuck he is—he killed her?"

"No, he was also killed."

"A double homicide? Here in Beverly Hills?"

"In Bel Air," said Milo. "We're L.A. police."

"Oh," said Kilic. "Yeah, you said, I wasn't focusing." Crooked smile. "Taking a relax break, you know? Trying to think positive thoughts. Murder. Now, **that's** fucked up."

Another look at the joint. He winked and smiled. "Got to say it's weird, being able to smoke up in front of the cops. Long time coming. Bet you guys indulge yourselves."

We said nothing.

Kilic's smile crumbled. "Meg. Dead. Fucking obscene. So what do you want from me?"

"We've heard you sold her a purple diamond."

Kilic's face closed up like a flower exposed to frost. "Did you."

"It's not true?"

"Who told you that?"

"Not important. Did you sell it to her?"

"It was an **über**-clean stone," said Kilic. "One point five eight carats, went all the way to fucking Sydney, Australia, to score it. Plus other stuff, but nothing as good, not close."

"Any of the other stuff go to Meagin?"

"No, but I'd sold her regular diamonds, great stones. Always gave her a good price. Gave her a good price on that one because she made it easy. Paid right away, the checks always cleared. And she was the coolest person. One of the coolest I've dealt with."

"Easygoing."

"Decisive. She liked something, she bought it, there was none of this let-me-think-about-it bullshit, then you don't hear from them. Then you do and it's gone and they get pissed off."

"Did Meg pay for the purple diamond with a check?"

"Purple fancy **intense**," said Kilic. "Never saw anything like it. Once in a lifetime you see something like that. Barely made a profit at the price I gave her."

"What price was that?"

Kilic's eyelids lowered, hooding bloodshot sclera and mustard-colored irises. The pale spots created by initial shock had deepened to olive green, like a chameleon adapting to its surroundings. The more time I spent with him, the more lizard-like he seemed.

He folded his arms across his chest. "Why do you need to know that?"

"We're learning as much as we can about Meagin in order to find out who brutalized her."

"Bruta— she was raped?"

"Can't get into details, Mr. Kilic. So what was the price of the stone?"

"What have you been told?"

"Two hundred thousand dollars."

"Have you also been told it was a bargain?"

"We have."

"So you know. That I helped her."

I said, "We also know you gave her two separate invoices for a hundred each. How come?"

Milo's green eyes sparked. Bobby Kilic's mustard pebbles, dull by comparison, did a slow slide to the left.

"What's the difference?" he said.

"Both receipts are dated identically so it wasn't a matter of paying in installments."

Silence.

Milo said, "How come, Mr. Kilic?"

Kilic breathed in. Began coughing and loosened his arms and used one fist to pound his chest. "I don't see what this has to do with any murder."

"The relevance, sir, is what it tells us about

Meagin's relationships. Speaking of which, what do you know about that?"

"**Nothing**. I don't get into that with clients."

"Never?"

"If they talk I listen," said Kilic. "Then I forget. I don't ask. Besides, Meagin didn't talk."

"But she wanted two receipts."

Another inhalation, more coughing that ended up sounding theatrical.

We stood there.

Bobby Kilic said, "It was nothing evil, just strategy."

"For?"

"Convincing the husband he got a huge bargain, she said he was money-obsessed, got off on getting deals."

"That," I said, "would explain one receipt for half the price, not two."

"Okay, okay, okay, fine, okay." Kilic stepped to the side and dragged one foot next to the other. Solo rumba. He reversed it. "Okay, she wanted to impress someone else. No big deal."

"About getting a bargain."

"Yeah."

"Who?"

"She didn't say."

"What did she say **about** him?"

"Nothing," said Kilic.

We waited.

"What I assumed," said Kilic, "was someone she was also . . . messing with."

"A lover."

"I don't know what it was. There's all kinds of messing."

I said, "Serious enough messing to get him to spend a hundred thou."

"To some people, that's nothing," said Bobby Kilic. "To a lot of my clients it's nothing."

"What about to you?" said Milo.

"To me? Depends what day you get me. The day I sold that intense purple, a hundred K was no big deal because it was less than I paid for it."

A beat. "But it was still a bargain for Meg. It made her happy. That's what I do. Make people happy and bank a few bucks for myself. You want to tell me I did something wrong, read me the law on what it was."

Milo said, "No one's saying you did anything wrong, sir. Which is why frankly we're not getting your attitude. If you admired Meagin like you just said, we'd expect cooperation."

"That's what I just gave you. Cooperation. It's not complicated, I sold her a stone at a great price—she bargained me down, I wanted two forty, she wanted one eighty, she'd bought other pieces from me and I figured I was still doing okay even with fucking Qantas for sixteen hours. So I made her happy and settled on two hundred and if she wanted two pieces of paper what the fuck did I care? Now you're telling me someone killed her and I'm **unhappy**. Going to have an unhappy day and an unhappy night and who knows for how long it's going to be unhappy."

A few more questions left us with nothing more. Kilic's demeanor—fatigued, not cagey—led Milo to thank him and hand over a card.

Kilic reached into the same pocket and drew out something wrapped in red foil. Chocolate truffle that he unwrapped with a flourish, announcing, "Chemically active goodness, burnt caramel, coated with Maldon sea salt."

Maintaining eye contact, he dropped the foil to the ground, popped the chocolate into his mouth, and said, "Yum."

But his heart wasn't in it and as we left he'd slumped and was shaking his head mournfully.

As we retraced our steps down the alley, Milo said, "Dope's legal in B.H., but smoking anything—tobacco, dope—isn't. Coulda called the locals."

I said, "Like they'd care."

"True. No problem for me, the stuff should never have been illegal in the first place. Not that I indulge."

"Anymore."

"We all have an anymore, right? Then you gotta concentrate on keeping the brain in decent order."

We got back in the car, he U-turned and drove east.

"Two receipts," he said. "Very elegant the way you sprang that on him."

"Lucky guess."

"I'd been wondering when to bring it up then you pounced." He turned one hand into a claw. "Good timing, it opened him up. Too bad it doesn't tell us what we didn't already suspect. Some schemer, our Meg. Whatever her real name is. I'm starting to think nothing I know about her is real."

A block later, in the midst of a Beverly Hills shopping jam, he said, "Calls her friends, her guy on the side, and a church. Hey, maybe she used to be a nun."

I said, "Anything's possible."

"I was kidding."

I was too preoccupied to answer. Googling **st. jerome's church san pietro.**

I said, "Oh boy."

"What?"

"Find a spot and pull over."

He turned left on Rodeo, driving away from the famous three blocks and toward the residences in the flats north of Big Santa Monica. Lucking out with a green light, he continued for half a block before parking.

"What?"

I showed him. "One of six hits, they all say the same thing."

He took my phone, read, cursed loud and long.

28

Two days after the murders of Meagin March and Gio Aggiunta, a homicide had taken place in the parking lot of St. Jerome's Church in San Pietro.

The victim, shot after dark, hadn't been discovered until the following morning, sprawled near the rear door of a bungalow adjoining the church. What the third account termed "the auxiliary."

The initial story had been posted by the San Pietro Police Department then reiterated by a couple of local news blogs. No further details until later in the day when a second police release named the victim as Richard Brett Barlett, thirty-eight, an administrative clerk at the church.

Since then, no new developments.

Milo said, "She calls the guy two months ago, he gets killed right after she does."

I said, "If Barlett was an ex, that makes it sound less like a big-money Vegas guy focused exclusively on her and more like a stalker going after men associated with her. And that could mean Gio was more than collateral damage. Obliterating him was part of the plan, which is why the shooter waited until the two of them were together."

"Poor Mr. Aggiunta, poor Mr. Barlett," he said. "And God knows who else . . . okay, let's find out about victim number three."

He phoned the San Pietro police and got connected quickly to a detective named Samuel Cifuentes.

"L.A.? What can I do for you?"

"You had a homicide two days ago, victim named Barlett. Was he shot in the heart with a .38, no casings at the scene?"

Silence.

Then: "Your name again, please."

"Lieutenant. Milo. Sturgis. Here's my number, feel free to verify."

"I will," said Cifuentes.

Three minutes of dead air before he came back on.

"Okay, Lieutenant. Sorry, you never know who's out there. Yes, that's exactly what happened. You know because you had the same?"

Milo filled him in.

"A double," said Sam Cifuentes. "Never had one of those."

Milo said, "Reason I linked it to Barlett is his name came up on my female victim's phone log. One call, coupla months ago. Made me wonder if he was one of her boyfriends."

"That I doubt. From what I've been told Richard might've been gay."

"Might've?"

"It's not like down where you are, our gays aren't always open. Maybe he was hiding something or he was just one of those celibates. Like Father Hernandez."

"No dates with women or men," said Milo.

"Not that anyone's seen or heard about," said Cifuentes. "I didn't know him but my wife did, she goes to church and she says he was quiet, peaceful, and what she called delicate. Either way, I can't see him going hot and heavy with some rich lady in Beverly Hills."

"Bel Air, but I get your point," said Milo. "Any motives you've come up with?"

"I wish. We're not like you, people getting killed all over the place. The whole of last year we had two murders. Both cantina things on the South Side, drunk offenders who stuck around, one idiot had a knife in his lap, the other it was a pool cue right on the floor next to him."

"Got the picture."

"Our entire department," said Cifuentes, "is thirty-two officers, which is down two from last year because of budget. The investigation unit is four detectives and we do everything. Mostly burglary, auto theft and shoplifting, a few simple assaults."

"No whodunits."

"Thank God," said Cifuentes. "Until now." He laughed. "Hell, maybe God got mad because not enough of us **go** to church. So this could be related to yours, huh?"

"Don't see how it can't be. What else do you know about Barlett?"

"That's it. First couple of days were spent making sure the scene got processed right. I'm pretty confident it did but unfortunately, no forensics came up. No DNA, no tire tracks, the church has no cameras. No sign of forced entry to the auxiliary, poor guy was shot between the building and his car. No sign of a struggle, just one shot to the chest, very clean. I'm figuring someone waited for him and nailed him while he was walking to the car."

"What time of day?"

"After dark," said Cifuentes. "All the Ventura County coroner could do was estimate. Probably tennish, elevenish, midnightish."

Milo said, "Barlett worked that late?"

"Father Hernandez told me he made his own hours. He's that kind of guy, Father. Easygoing. If he wasn't, attendance would be even lower."

"The church is struggling?"

"Too much God competition," said Cifuentes. "For Catholics, there's a bigger fancier place a few miles up, plus a Baptist church and bunch of others, don't know the denominations offhand. Then there's all these smaller Pentecostals operating out of houses that the Salvadorans and the Guatemalans like."

"What did Barlett do at the church?"

"Clerk-type stuff according to Father and my wife confirms it. She says Richard was nice but kept to himself. Like I said, delicate."

"Effeminate."

"Hah. Are we allowed to say that?" said Cifuentes.

"Between us we are," said Milo. "Your wife thinks he was gay."

"So does one of our officers, she prays at St. Jerome's almost as often as Ramona. First thing she said when she found out about Richard, was it a gay thing, did it happen in Ojai or something. I told her it was at the church and she was freaked out. We've never had a problem there, no one lifting the collection plate, no silver or anything else missing. People respect the church. You really think this could be tied in to yours?"

"I really do."

"Great," said Cifuentes. "So how about I pay you—what's the word, I **commission** you to take over."

Milo said, "What's your offer?"

Cifuentes laughed. "Not going to lie, I'm not thrilled to catch this one. Which isn't to say I won't work it, I will, I'll work it hard. Started to do that the moment I got to the scene. Just spent some time at Barlett's place. Basically a cabin on an orange grove, looks like it was once a storage shed or something. Landlord's a rich grower lives mostly in Tahoe, goes to the church when she's in town, Father got Richard the rental. Which wasn't exactly big-ticket, I found some rent receipts, he was paying three hundred a month and could come and go as he pleased. Only people he'd come into contact with would be seasonal pickers, a few permanent ranch hands, and the manager, who I also know, very stand-up lady, she was out of town. Good luck getting anything out of the seasonals and none of the hands had a thing to say about Richard. He kept to himself, never had a visitor they saw."

"Anything interesting on his phone?"

"If only. It was in his pocket at the scene, I went over what was on it. Not much to go over, called no one, didn't get called so I guess he really was a loner. He called your victim two months ago? Must've deleted."

"She called him."

"Only that once," said Cifuentes.

"That's all I've got in seven months of log," said Milo. "Before that, she had another carrier impossible to identify. Be nice if Richard's records go back further."

"He had a year's worth and it boiled down to basically three, four calls to the church. I got a real hermit feel from his place."

"Nothing interesting there."

"I wish. We're talking like a twelve-by-twelve room, plywood on the walls, a john, and a crappy little kitchen-type dealie with a camping fridge and a hotplate. Nope, nothing personal in there, not even a snapshot, just cutouts from calendars on the walls. My thought was this guy's living more like a priest than Father Hernandez. A monk, actually."

"Bad victim," said Milo.

"How so?"

"No attachments, no leads."

"Ah," said Cifuentes. "Guess so. Haven't had time to think about it much. Like I said, murder isn't our thing, we recover a stolen car stereo, we throw a party."

"Is it worth my time to come up and look at the crime scene?"

"Feel free but what you're gonna see is a parking lot that's cleaner than it was before the shooting. Minute the tape was down, church ladies were scrubbing."

"Maybe we'll pass," said Milo.

"That would be me," said Sam Cifuentes. "We'll talk if there's something to talk about, right?"

"Right."

29

E ven before Milo's left hand hung up, his right was tapping his keyboard.

He logged onto NCIC, then L.A. and Ventura County's criminal databases. Nothing on Richard Brett Barlett. The internet was similarly stingy but for the reports of the murder we'd already read.

He swiveled around. "Lives like a monk. How does a guy like that figure into Meagin's world?"

I said, "Maybe a relative? A close one, seeing as he's one of the few people she called."

"Three years younger than her . . . guess he could be a kid brother but then why did she call him only once?"

I shrugged. "You could try seeing if Barlett was her maiden name."

"You mean Jones wasn't? I'm shocked."

◆

He searched for **meagin barlett,** found nothing, paired the surname with **megan, meagan, meg.** That produced several social media hits, none the woman we were interested in. Combining her name and its permutations with **richard brett** pulled up a lot of noise that took a while to plod through and ended up useless.

He said, "A church guy and a former call girl? Sounds like a bad movie."

"Maybe Barlett wasn't always a church guy."

"What then?"

"He went monastic to atone for his past."

"Not a criminal past."

"Nothing illegal about gambling in Vegas," I said. "What if he'd once been a card ace?"

"Poker shark morphs into church clerk?"

"It happens."

"That also sounds like a movie, Alex. Guy living at the tables, that would be an addiction, right? The only reason I can see for a big lifestyle change would be going broke, not some moral brainstorm. And if that was the case, what are the odds—pardon the expression—of it lasting?"

I thought about that. "Okay, maybe he wasn't a green-felt guy. Or he was and there's a middle ground: He relapsed while working at the church and kept the fact secret. That could also explain living simply. The casinos got most of his money."

"Filing papers for the diocese by day and playing at night. You know what that sounds like."

"Potential for embezzlement."

"Cifuentes said people respect the church, but who the hell knows. Okay, let's go local, that's where a backslider would start."

He turned back to his keyboard. "Closest place to the church is . . . the Players Casino, Ventura . . . and here's another, looks bigger, run by the Chumash in Santa Barbara."

The next twenty minutes were spent asking for and finally connecting to managers at both casinos who could give him answers.

No record of Richard Brett Barlett receiving lines of credit or racking up debts at either gambling house. The same was true for expulsions, banishment, any sort of security issue.

Both Sonia Hidalgo at Players and Harvey Morega at the Santa Barbara casino pointed out that someone habituated to low-minimum slots could go unnoticed.

Milo said, "Silent majority."

"You got that," said Morega. "If they don't cause problems. Or win big."

"Not a lot of those."

"That's the point, Lieutenant. Quiet and steady is what keeps us humming."

Next step: pulling up Richard Brett Barlett's DMV data.

Five-ten, one forty-eight, brn, brn, clean record, corrective lenses required. Barlett's face was pale, narrow, and hollow-cheeked topped by unruly wavy hair, horizontally banded by steel-rimmed eyeglasses and bottomed by a patchy dark beard.

I avoid reading too much into official photos but it was hard not to see these eyes as sad.

Milo said, "No resemblance to our gal that I can see. You?"

I shook my head.

He moved on to Barlett's driving record. "Not even a speeding ticket. Let's see what Meagin's social circle has to say."

This time, Dr. Lana Demarest was in her office and got on the line.

She said, "Richard who?"

"Barlett." Milo spelled the name.

"No, sorry, doesn't ring a bell. Who is he?"

"Someone Meagin called a couple of months ago."

"Months? How many times?"

"Once, Doctor."

"Oh," said Demarest. "That doesn't sound like much of a clue."

Toni Bowman said, "I **told** you a week."

"I'm calling about another matter, ma'am."

"Now what?"

Milo explained.

She said, "I have absolutely no idea who this person is. And frankly, it sounds like you're desperate."

One last try: Rhonda "Rikki" Montel's cellphone. Mumbling, "Like she's gonna answer."

She did, sounding cheerful but slurred. Steady bass beat in the background dusted with conversational hum.

"Who is this? Oh, you. You solved it?"

Milo explained.

She said, "Never heard of him. One time? Sounds like a pocket call."

Click.

He sat back and laughed.

I said, "You didn't tell them Barlett had been murdered."

"Wouldn'ta changed anything, either they know him or they don't."

He stood, stretched, winced. "Go home, that's what I'm doing."

We left the station together, entered the staff lot and drifted apart as we headed to our cars.

I was ten yards away when he called out my name.

I pivoted, saw him standing by his back bumper, waving his phone, and jogged back.

"That was Cifuentes. He reached the orange grove manager and she said Barlett had a visitor a few weeks ago, three, four, probably but she's not sure exactly when. She didn't see the driver, just the car. Wanna guess?"

I said, "Black compact."

"Parked in front of Barlett's cabin. She has no idea

if anything negative went on and Barlett wouldn'ta told her, they didn't have that kind of relationship."

"How long did the visit last?"

"No idea, she just saw the car and thought it was unusual because during the five years Barlett had been living there, she'd never known him to have a visitor. She also can't say when it left because her exit from the grove takes her in the opposite direction."

I said, "The bad guy visits Barlett but leaves him alive. Then he murders Meagin and Gio and comes back because Barlett could I.D. him."

"That's what I'm thinking. Some bastard with a grudge who also knew Barlett."

I said, "Maybe it was Barlett who told him where to find Meagin."

"Talk about snitches ending up in ditches," he said. "I'm still going home but tomorrow the kids and I are gonna do a wider canvass of Gio's and Meagin's neighborhoods, see if anyone else saw the car, maybe some nervous security-conscious type noticed more details."

"Fear, the great motivator."

"Pays my salary."

"Sometimes mine, as well."

30

I phoned Robin from the road, gave her my ETA, asked if I should pick up something for dinner.

She said, "Perfect timing, I defrosted steaks, you can get your grill on and make me that tequila Manhattan you came up with a few weeks ago. My contribution will be coleslaw, two gorgeous artichokes I scored this morning, braised carrots with that za'atar thing you like, and sautéed mushrooms."

"Sounds labor-intensive for you."

"Not if you do the steaks and the booze. I'm also in charge of the treats for the other woman in your life, talk about saintly."

After dinner, we shifted outdoors and lounged on the front terrace looking at trees and night sky and listening to the occasional hoots of owls preparing to dine. Blanche curled between us, recumbent but wide awake and hoping for more tidbits.

Robin obliged by crumbling bits of a chewy thing that claims to help dogs develop strong joints. Whether or not it's true, Blanche loves them. Then again, she's not picky. As bulldog flews vibrated, the two of us tuned in to the quiet and made our way slowly through second **añejo** Manhattans. The key, according to a barkeep I know, is chocolate bitters.

Years of treating patients has made me tolerant of silence but Robin's naturally quiet nature gave her the edge and, as usual, I was the first to speak.

"How's the Torres going?"

"Wonderful. It's a work of art."

"Speaking of art, what do you think it means when a painter creates something totally different from their other work?"

"Hmm. They could be trying to stretch creatively. Or to shift gears completely. Jackson Pollock started off as a realist." She smiled. "If it's old and you ask an art expert, they'll try to tag anything different as a fake."

"No appreciation for creativity?"

"Not unless they've actually created something other than academic articles. I always get a kick when I see some specialist squinting at brushstrokes or underpainting and drawing huge conclusions. Artists aren't automatons and art's not just about producing, it's about diverging."

She sipped, placed her hand on my knee. "That was pretty puffed up."

I kissed her cheek. "Could it also mean the artist had come up with something personally meaningful?"

"Sure, that would be the motivation. This sudden interest, why do I think it relates to something nasty? Who's the artist in question?"

"The female victim was an amateur painter. She left behind a few canvases in her home studio, mostly bland, genre stuff. Her husband found out she'd cheated on him and we found everything dumped in the trash, intact. Except for one painting that looked divergent to me. That, he sliced up."

"Pretty hateful. He's the main suspect?"

"If he was involved, he hired someone, but even that's not clear."

"Sliced," she said.

"Corner to corner." I pantomimed the X.

"Sounds like obliteration," she said. "But no damage to the others?"

"No, he just tossed them."

"So obviously that one meant something to **him.**"

"Whatever the case, Milo's not impressed."

"Milo," she said, "is a saint among saints but when he's doing his bloodhound thing, it can be hard to budge him away from the main scent. Especially when he's frustrated."

She reached down and ruffled Blanche's neck. "Unlike this wolf descendant who can always be distracted by momentary pleasure." Crumble, drop, slosh.

Robin added, "What's different about the slashed one?"

"The others were full of color and there was no doubt what they depicted. This one was gray, black, white, abstract, and sketchy. Maybe that's all it was, a sketch, and I'm overthinking."

We held hands, sipped. Robin put her head on my shoulder. "You don't have to ask."

"Ask what?"

"For me to take a look at the screen shot in your phone."

I stared at her.

"Oh, c'mon, we're not in Sherlock territory. Actually, I must have a look. You've gotten me curious."

I retrieved my phone from my office, had the image loaded by the time I got back.

She said, "That's a ghost orchid."

"A flower?"

"Yes, indeed. I know because I read a book about orchids a few years back, got curious and looked it up."

"The journalist you said wasn't mean."

"Susan Orlean," she said. "Very light touch. As opposed to."

I studied the gray rectangle. "Don't see anything floral about it."

"You and everyone else, darling. It's not exactly your cheerful sprig in a vase. What can you tell me about her?"

"Not much." I summed up the little I knew.

She said, "Manipulative, illusive, and downright deceptive if she needed to be. Okay, makes sense."

"What does?"

"Her identifying with the ghost orchid. It's a **very** strange flower, Alex. Blooms infrequently, has stalky scales instead of leaves and this twiggy deal here for a stem that's so thin it's nearly invisible. More to the point, it doesn't root in soil, just attaches itself to tree trunks and dangles. Gives nothing back to the tree, so it's basically a parasite, though it does no harm."

"Where does it grow?"

"Remote pockets of the Florida swamps. People looking for it have walked right by. As if it's determined to hide."

"Illusive and rootless," I said.

"Sounds like your poor woman, no? Not that botany's going to help you find out who killed her—let's go inside, I don't want to get too drowsy."

I knew better than to say, **For what?**

The following morning, after a two-mile run that barely hurt and a shower, I ate toast and drank coffee and deliberated telling Milo about the ghost orchid.

Botany won't help.

If he was in a decent mood, he'd thank me and move on. If not, he'd grunt absently, thank me, and move on.

So put it aside for now. I spent a while doing my own reading about the flower, starting with the Orlean book then checking to see if anything new had surfaced on the Web since its publication.

It hadn't. Nor had Robin omitted anything of substance.

That left me with a painting that had meant something to Meagin. And maybe to Doug.

An art chat between the two of them seemed unlikely. Despite Meagin's evasiveness, had she told him something personal about the painting that made him determined to destroy it?

Had she somehow identified with a strange, parasitic organism and let that slip? Or was I way off and it had been something trivial.

Look, honey, isn't this a great little weird thing. I'm going to paint it.

Sure, whatever.

A third possibility: the link being more concrete. And that led me to geography.

I paired Meagin's name with **florida swamp** and found a huge state park called the Fakahatchee Strand where a decades-old ghost orchid had been discovered a few years back.

Coming up empty, I redirected the search to the town nearest the park, a former logging town called Copeland. Nothing. I cast the net wider: **meagin southwest florida.** Earned myself big bites of air sandwich.

That was likely to continue because why would a woman vanish in order to reinvent and leave her given name intact.

Detective rule number one: without knowing your victim, your chance of solving a murder is dismal.

No sense reminding my friend.

◆

I took a coffee break then got to work on a nearly completed report, interrupted myself by answering the phone because of the caller.

Judge Julie Beck said, "Morning, hope it's not too early."

"Been up for a while."

"Good," she said. "New development on Ruffalo hates Ruffalo: neither of them wants Derek evaluated."

"Why?"

"The one thing they agree on is any emotional analysis would be irrelevant. Which would be the end of it if I was willing to sign off but they got the wrong judge."

A beat. "Now I'm going to tell you something off the record, Alex: I have credible information about the **real** reason they're trying to prevent an eval. Once they cash out, neither of them has the slightest intention of ever doing any parenting of this poor boy. They don't want anything on the record that will get in the way of ditching him. Let alone paying his bills."

"Ditching him how?"

"Best guess some sort of fraud claim about the adoption. The big bad Russians and all that. Meanwhile, the poor kid goes to foster care and all the wonderfulness that entails."

"Unbelievable," I said. "Credible information as in one of the lawyers doesn't like it."

"Off the record? Neither of them likes it. As I told you the first time, these are decent people, have kids of their own and do **not** want to be parties to abusive abandonment. One has adopted kids, that's really given her a reality check."

"Sounds like the worst abuse could be leaving Derek with either Ruffalo."

"Of course," she said. "He clearly needs to get away from them but not the way they want to do it, basically throwing him away. Not if I can help it. I'm going to do my darndest to see that there's a generous, long-term care plan in place. As in trust fund, these idiots can afford it. It's nuts, right? Usually people drive us crazy because they see the kids as property and stake claims. These bastards can't wait to get rid of their child."

"Good for you, Julie."

"I may not be able to pull it off but I'm going to try, starting with tabling any requests to bifurcate money and custody. The big risk is the evil ones try to get a different judge and the lawyers end up wussing out. But so far, I'm not getting that feeling from them. So you're still in?"

"Of course. What do you need me to do?"

"Nothing right now but be available when the time comes for the evaluation. Your input will be vital. Not just for the emotional stuff, also actuarially.

I want this boy's living expenses comprehensively taken care of and one of the biggest-ticket items will be education. You'll give him an IQ test and if he scores average, we'll go for funding through a bachelor's degree. If you tell me he's smart—and from what I hear from the attorneys, both of whom have talked to his prep school, he's super-smart—we'll make sure he can go to med school, get a Ph.D., whatever."

"How about a postdoc?"

She laughed. "Sure, why not? Notice I didn't say law school, Alex, because cases like this remind me the law truly is an ass."

Milo called at two p.m.

"Just had another charming chat with Dougie. What an asshole, he's still bitching about the jewelry. I informed him he'd get it when he got it and if he had a complaint, file it with Nguyen. Whose name I spelled for him. Then I phoned John and he said, 'What a dick, like I'd take his call.' The only other thing to report is Moe did find another neighbor who saw a little dark car that night. Nervous woman, lives midway between Gio's and Meagin's. She was walking her pooch and it zoomed by, going south."

I said, "Away from Gio's. What time?"

"Within the range of the shootings."

"The bad guy leaving."

"If it's anything, it's that, Alex. Unfortunately, she had nothing on make, model, or tags. Car was moving too fast, that's why she noticed it in the first place. The kids are still out there doorbelling, maybe we'll get lucky."

"Bel Air folk have security cameras."

"They do, indeed," he said. "Conspicuously displayed with impressively hostile signs. It's amazing how many of them are self-deleting or focused on walls and gates but not the road. Or total fakes. The tough thing is a southern getaway would lead straight down on Hilgard, past the U. campus. Zero cameras the whole way and then who knows where he goes. And if he turns east or west, he's zipping past miles of residential with most of the properties set back or behind hedges, so forget surveillance. Where are the dingy commercial stretches when you need them?"

"Maybe there are some in San Pietro. Not at the church but near it."

"Good thinking, but been there, done that. Cifuentes said the church is in an agricultural area, any interest would be poachers not monitoring traffic. So surveillance would be internal, on the grounds of the ranches. In terms of the town's streets, he has no idea how many cameras there are and no way he can spend the time to find out. Can't say I blame him. He's a good guy but clearly would love to punt to me. Anything on your end?"

I said, "The gray painting—"

"Oh yeah, that also came up with the obnoxious Mr. March—God, I **wish** I could pin this one on him. I asked him why he'd dumped all her stuff and why that one in particular deserved a razor. He explodes, gives me mega-attitude about going through his trash without a warrant. I cut him off and educate him about trash and he says it was still intrusive. I repeat the question, he says I don't have to explain myself to you. I say any reason you shouldn't? That threw him, he starts sputtering. Then he says if you **must** know I dumped that shit because it **was** shit. Not only did she lack talent she had no taste and the proof is **that** one. The ugliest one of all but her favorite, she showed it off to me like she was especially proud of it. He also said he'd told her he liked it. Back when he didn't hate her guts."

"Flaunting his hatred."

"He's either the most arrogant murderer I've ever come into contact with or he's not worried because he's innocent. Anyway, that was my lesson in lack of art appreciation."

"I found out what the spiky thing is."

"Oh yeah, what?"

"A flower called the ghost orchid." I filled him in. "It's localized to Florida so maybe that's where she's from but I couldn't find any sign of it."

I expected him to bypass psychology and go straight to geography.

He said, "Ghost orchid, huh? Maybe she saw herself as some sort of phantom?"

I have sold you short, my friend.

I said, "That would be my guess."

"Running from something," he said. "Then it caught up with her."

32

No contact the next day until he phoned at six p.m.

I said, "Busy day?"

"Not with detecting, helped Claudio make arrangements for Gio's body. Talk about contrast with Doug, the guy couldn't be nicer. Asked if I'd learned anything and totally broke down when I told him I was leaning toward wrong place, wrong time. Between some coroner's paperwork getting lost, the hassles of air-shipping a body overseas, he was having trouble negotiating."

"Prominent family, no help from the Italian consulate?"

"You'd think, right? Buncha stiffs over there, they told him they needed official consent from the crypt and when he tried to get that, the crypt said foreign arrangements were complicated, he should get an international lawyer. So I paid them a visit and showed them a bullshit consent form I drafted in my office, filled out a notebook's worth of nonsense, and stayed there until they rubber-stamped it. No openings on Alitalia for three days, but he's booked on the fourth and so is the coffin."

"Beyond the call of duty."

"Like I said, he's a nice guy. Clearly the one the family turns to when things get complicated."

"He have anything else to say about his brother?"

"That assumes I asked him when my focus was on altruistic civil service."

"Same question."

He laughed. "Yeah, I worked a few questions in but the only thing he added was that Gio once mentioned another woman he dated here named Lulu. No details other than it was right after he arrived, so maybe before he hooked up with Meagin. Or he was juggling both of them. But seeing as Gio's looking more and more like collateral damage, don't see the point of pursuing it."

"Makes sense."

He said, "Meaning I should follow up, anyway."

"Up to you."

"Meaning definitely. Fine, but not now, too bushed. Maybe tomorrow unless a miracle occurs and I get an actual lead."

◆

On Monday, I woke up at six forty-five, was at my desk an hour later, and found a text from Milo sent seven minutes ago.

Call me.

I said, "Per your instruction. Good morning."

He said, "The Lulu thing stuck in my head. No doubt because you planted it there."

"I said it was up to you."

"But the way you said it. Anyway, I managed to reach Rikki Montel and she said, 'Oh, yeah, Lulu, saw her with him a few times at the Four Seasons.'"

"Another aging pro?"

"Nope, some sort of executive, Rikki thought she mentioned working in Santa Monica."

"How did the two of them meet?"

"Gio introduced them at the Waldorf and Rikki sat down to have a drink. Rikki liked her because Lulu was successful but didn't snob her out. She never learned a last name but I did a bunch of homework last night and found a hotshot named Lulu whose real name is Evelyn Mastrecht. Chief managing officer of a business software company on Twenty-Sixth Street."

I said, "Not far from the day spa."

"Gio's happy hunting grounds," he said. "Anyway I called her, she'd just gotten back from a business trip to Singapore and hadn't heard about Gio. She broke down and said, sure, no problem talking but it had to be early because she's flying to Santa Clara for lunch. Got her to pencil me in at eight thirty. You available?"

"Where on Twenty-Sixth?"

"You don't need the address, I'll pick you up at ten after."

33

Evelyn "Lulu" Mastrecht did what CMOs do at a company called Visuant Solutions, headquartered in a five-story, pink marble building just north of Olympic. A massive parking area was announced by a **Valet Only** sign backed by half a dozen sky-spraying fountains. The lot was spoon-shaped, with the entrance the stem and the bowl the rounded curb in front of the structure. Chunks of lava rock bordered cobblestone that annoyed the unmarked's suspension. The surrounding landscaping was textbook Hawaiian hotel.

Most of the bowl was a four-deep stack of vehicles overseen by two valets in pink shirts and tan chinos. If you weren't on the periphery, getting free would mean waiting as a giant rebus was solved. Milo slid in at the tail end of the congestion, leaving space between the unmarked and an armada of Teslas and gas-eating Euro prestige.

One of the attendants hurried toward us, shaking his head and wagging a finger. Mid-fifties and showing every second of it, with a pemmican-face shaded by a shaggy, improbably yellow mop. Walking fast but stiff-legged.

Former surfer or still riding the waves despite knotty knees.

He regarded the Impala with the disdain you sometimes see in people who can't afford luxury but have aligned themselves with the power elite.

"Nope, you gotta pull up in front and have us park it."

Milo flashed the badge. "Nope, I gotta stay right here."

The attendant considered a retort but swallowed it. A frown seamed the skin around his lips, like a change purse pulled tight. "Okay, but give me the keys in case I have to move it."

"Sorry, pal, no can do." Clipping the badge to his breast pocket.

"What do you mean—hey—oh yeah, got it. You got lethal stuff in there."

"Let's just say official policy."

"Yeah, yeah, how long you gonna be?"

"Hard to say."

We walked past him. He stood there, looking defeated.

Milo said, "I know, it's sad. C'mon."

◆

We strode past the second attendant, younger, shorter, chubbier. His eyes rounded at the sight of the badge and he saluted as we entered the building. The lobby was a fifty-foot, glass-domed atrium bottomed by black terrazzo. A uniformed guard behind a central station didn't look up. Elevator banks filled both lateral walls.

Four chrome-legged gray faux-suede couches were arranged in a perfect square around nothing. One human being in all that space. A small woman perched on the edge of the leftmost couch who got up and click-clacked toward us on spike heels.

"Lieutenant? Lulu Mastrecht." Throaty voice.

"Thanks for meeting with us, ma'am. This is Alex Delaware."

"Alex." A smile began melting around the edges and ended up wistful. Her hand was firm and soft. Narrow and tiny like the rest of her.

Lulu Mastrecht was around the same age as the parking valet but with smooth, rosy-cheeked skin. Five foot two with the heels, maybe ninety pounds fully dressed, with silver hair cut short and feathered at the front. Her face was heart-shaped, prettied by oversized blue eyes and an undersized, uptilted nose. She'd probably been called cute for most of her life, either loved or despised it. She wore a fitted, royal-blue, mannish shirt over black jeggings, and gold in all the strategic places.

"Do you mind if we speak right here? I like to keep business and personal separate."

"No problem, ma'am."

Lulu Mastrecht returned to where she'd been sitting and we settled to her right.

Close enough for me to see pink rims at the outer edges of her eyes. Among the gold was a broad wedding band studded with emeralds.

She crossed her legs, let a foot dangle. The shoes were white with red soles.

Milo said, "Again, thanks, ma'am."

"Of course. I'm still trying to wrap my head around Gio." Long sigh. Longer, slower head shake. "Such a sweet guy, it makes no sense."

"How did the two of you meet?"

Given the wedding band, a question that could've led to tension. Given the wedding band, why had she agreed to talk?

Lulu Mastrecht's shoulders relaxed, loosened by pleasant memory.

"How did we meet? At the Four Seasons on Doheny. I was there for a business meeting that ended early." Semi-smile. "That's business-speak for it didn't go well. It was too late to come back to the office so I decided to drown my sorrows in the bar. Not my thing, drinking alone, but that night it felt like the right thing to do. The funny thing is, I got strange looks from the host. Finally, I figured out he suspected I was some kind of sex worker."

Full smile. "Pretty crazy, huh, at my age. I chose to take it as a compliment. But I didn't want to give the wrong impression, so I took a corner table, sent a few texts, ordered my drink, kept my head down and logged onto Forbes.com."

"Minding your own business," said Milo.

"Making a point of it," said Lulu Mastrecht. "I.e., ignoring the men who were in there. By my second drink, they must've figured out I was legitimate because they left me alone. I'm midway through it and this young, gorgeous, beautifully dressed guy comes in, looks around, and sits two tables away. I'm thinking, 'Oh boy, he's got the same impression, what is it with this place?' So I ignore him completely, keep reading. A few minutes later, I look up, the way you do, it's natural right? And his eyes are on me. He smiles, which takes me by surprise so I smile back. He summons the waiter, says the next one's on him and moves to the adjacent table. I continued to shine him on but it's hard. Knowing he's there. When the drinks come, he waits a sec, then pulls his chair close and says, 'Ah, you're reading a business article,' in this adorable accent, and tells me he's in business, too—designer shoes. So I'm figuring the hooker thing is out of the way, why not enjoy some attention?"

She shrugged. "We made pleasant conversation, he walked me out, and we parted ways. But yes, I did give him my office number and by the time

I got home and checked for messages, his was one of them. I didn't answer but he called the next day and invited me to dinner. I said no but how about coffee. Which we did in the afternoon at a place I like in Brentwood. It was pleasant, and classy, and again, nothing happened."

A fingertip brushed the fringe of her hair. "The next time, something happened." She leaned forward. "Gio was the most tender man I've ever met. In every regard. Why anyone would want to harm him . . ." Her voice cracked. "I just can't fathom this."

Milo said, "It may have had nothing to do with him, Ms. Mastrecht."

"What do you mean?"

"The primary target might have been someone he was with."

"Oh no, that's horrible. Who?"

"A woman named Meagin March."

"Meg?"

"You know her?"

"I know of her. Gio talked about her. Called her Meagin and Meg."

"The two of you overlapped?"

"Not substantively," said Lulu Mastrecht. "By that I mean I was transitioning away from Gio and she'd just entered the picture."

"Did that create problems?"

"Not at all, Lieutenant. It wasn't some rivalry thing. I called it transitioning because Gio and I didn't have any sort of abrupt breakup. What happened was my husband—we'd been separated, having a rough patch—my husband and I decided to give it another go."

She twisted the wedding band. "That process took a while but when it finally became clear that Ed was serious, I informed Gio it had been great knowing him but it was a phase in my life that had to end. He was totally understanding. Called me **amate**. Took my hand and kissed my **knuckles**."

Her fingers clawed. The ring rotated the other way. "I know what you're thinking. Cheesy. But you had to know Gio. He was sincere. Told me how happy he was for me, how wonderful it had been being with me. That's what I mean. The **sweetest** man."

We nodded.

Her look said she hoped we were also sincere but had her doubts.

I said, "By that time Gio was seeing Meagin March."

"He wasn't sneaking around on me, what we had was open."

"What did Gio tell you about her?"

She lowered her eyes. Beautifully mascaraed lashes fluttered. "Not much, just that she was **vulnerabile**. I said if you know that, don't be a jerk. And we laughed. It was like that with us. Expressing whatever was on our minds. We did a lot of talking, he was so good at talking."

"Did Gio say how Meagin was vulnerable?"

"Just that she'd had a rough life. I didn't ask, he didn't say, we didn't dwell on it."

"Did he tell you she was married?"

"No, but who cares about that type of thing? Especially if she was in my situation. If you want to judge, can't stop you. But from my limited experience Gio didn't try to muscle in or take advantage."

I said, "Where did the two of you generally meet?"

"Not generally, always," she said. "Once more at the Four Seasons, once at the Waldorf, and then always at Gio's place." Rosy cheeks had deepened to coral.

"It was so lovely there," she continued. "Quiet, peaceful, you could forget you were in the city. We loved to swim. And fuck. I'm being open with you because my therapist says I need to work on openness. And I have nothing to hide or be ashamed of. Never sneaked around on Ed when we were together and before we got back together, I told him everything. And he did the same."

Her eyes shifted to the right. Her jaw set. "Ed had a lot more to tell. Now, if there's nothing more, I really do need to prep for my meeting."

Milo said, "Thanks for talking to us. If there's anything else that occurs to you, we'd appreciate hearing about it."

"Before you showed up, I went over everything and no, there's nothing. Will be nothing."

She stood gracefully, waited until we'd done the same, and eyed the left-hand elevator bank. We walked with her. When bronze doors slid open, she held them in place. "Can you tell me where it happened? Was it a robbery on the street?"

Milo said, "It happened at Gio's house."

Lulu Mastrecht gasped. Backed into the elevator and allowed the doors to shut. We watched as her terrified face narrowed then disappeared.

Milo said, "That scared her."

I said, "Thinking it could've been her."

Another layer of chrome had been added to the spoon but an escape route had been set aside for the unmarked.

Milo said, "Thanks, amigo," and handed Surfer Joe a ten.

He said, "Not necessary," as he snatched the bill and jammed it into a pant pocket.

As we drove away, Milo said, "Easygoing guy, our Gio. She breaks up with him but he's cool with it. Probably because he already found her replacement."

"Or," I said, "none of his relationships meant much to him."

"You've changed your mind about him and Meagin getting serious."

"It's feeling that way."

"Meaning there could be others."

"There could be but I doubt it matters. Barlett's murder tells us Meagin was the likely target."

"**Vulnerabile**," he said. "Meaning she coulda told him about whatever it was she was running from. He didn't tell Lulu because if he was loose-lipped about Meagin, she'd know he'd be the same with her."

"Or," I said, "he really was a nice guy."

"**Gallant**," he said. "Goes great with a nice pool in Bel Air."

He took Twenty-Sixth Street and drove east. "Maybe it all has to do with her past but I'm not letting go of Dougie. All that hatred when he talks about her."

I said, "He really did seem surprised to hear about Gio."

"Or so he wants us to think."

"Maybe."

"Mr. March ain't twanging your antenna."

"Find anything connecting him to Richard Barlett and it'll be twanging away."

He chewed his cheek. Said nothing until we were back in his office.

34

Settling behind his desk, Milo phoned Sam Cifuentes.

"Hey, what's up?"

"I was gonna ask you the same thing."

"Oh. Nothing. Your end, too, huh?"

"Just confirmation that my female victim had a tough past. Anything come up like that about Barlett?"

"Nope," said Cifuentes, "and that's the thing. Nothing's come up, period. It's weird. He only got himself a Social Security number when he started working at the church five years ago. Not just Social Security, he's a ghost in any database I can find. Can't even locate a prior address and I looked in a whole bunch of places."

He recited a list.

Milo said, "Nothing I'd add to that, Sam."

"Good to know," said Cifuentes. "I asked Father Hernandez and he said Barlett just walked in one day, told him he had bookkeeping experience, and offered his services at like minimum wage. Church operates on a shoestring, so Father thought not a bad deal. He figured Barlett had maybe been homeless and got it together. If he had, he'd done a great job 'cause he was well groomed and polite, no sign of any mental issues. I'm thinking maybe it was drugs, not necessarily homeless. Some people can get cleaned up, right? Though personally, I haven't seen that with our meth offenders and our crackheads."

"So the guy's a phantom," said Milo. "Same for my victim."

"Really," said Cifuentes. "So maybe they rehabbed together."

Milo looked at me. "You know, Sam, you may have hit on something."

"You think?" said Cifuentes. "So where do we take it?"

"Any local rehab places you could talk to who might remember Barlett? Using his DMV shot, seeing as he coulda changed his name."

"I could try."

"There's a problem?"

"Well, you know, they're big on confidential and all that."

"Sometimes murder trumps that."

"Does it? You'd know, okay I'll try," said Cifuentes. "Your victim have any known substance history?"

"Nothing's come up, so far."

"Want me to show them her DMV, anyway?"

"I'd appreciate it," said Milo. "She was in Vegas right before she came to L.A., probably two years ago. I'll look into their facilities. Gonna text you her picture right now."

"Whatever," said Cifuentes.

"You don't like it, Sam?"

"Not a matter of what I like. With all due respect, I'm not into chasing ghosts."

After sending Meagin's headshot to Cifuentes, Milo sent Barlett's and hers to Alicia, Sean, and Moe and asked them to divide up rehab facilities in Clark County, Nevada.

Alicia and Moe responded with thumbs-up emojis. Sean called.

"Happy to do it, Loot, but there's got to be a lot of them there, Sin City and all that."

"Sin is what pays our salaries, kiddo."

"It sure does, Loot. My mom calls it being an uncivil servant. So no way you want me to narrow it?"

"I wish."

"On it."

Clicking off, Milo wheeled around, half facing me. "If Meagin and Barlett met in rehab, the bad guy coulda also been there. As to why he decided to stalk and shoot them . . ." He shrugged.

I said, "To my mind, the jealous lover thing's still on the table."

"Twelve-step spiced up by the eternal triangle?"

"Mutual addiction's among the worst foundations for a relationship but it happens."

"One phone call in seven months says whatever Meagin and Barlett had, it was over. And she was still in Vegas when he was working at the church. So whatever complication happened was a while back. Which leads me to my next question: why would a jilted lover wait this long to get revenge?"

I said, "Meagin could've done a good job hiding so it took a while to locate her. Or his resentment's been simmering the whole time and as long as he was clean, he could manage it."

"Guy relapsed."

"A return to meth or coke—or even to alcohol— could've topped off his anger with some serious paranoia."

"So I could be looking for an addled and/or addicted ghost who cools down long enough to plan three homicides, shoot precisely, and get away clean."

"His criminal skills could be well seasoned."

"Phantom with a prior history," he said. "Even more wonderful."

35

Time stretched to nine days after Meagin and Gio's murders.

When Milo and the young detectives' contacts with Clark County rehabilitation centers produced nothing, he expanded the search to the entire state of Nevada. Then California, excepting Ventura County, where Sam Cifuentes had paid personal visits to facilities with the same disappointing result. Failure had led Cifuentes's sergeant to direct him to robberies.

Next stop: Arizona. While that was going on, Milo phoned to ask if I had any other ideas. Given the ghost orchid's home in Florida, I suggested they try there.

"Already begun."

That stretched the investigation but turned up nothing.

He switched gears and looked for any murderers across the country featuring the use of a .38 Police and Military revolver and a precise single shot to the heart.

And found something.

Five-year-old unsolved in New Orleans.

That victim, a bartender in the French Quarter named Nicole Fontenot, had been ambushed in a rear parking lot as she left work shortly after two a.m. She'd gone through two boyfriends with substantial felony histories but both were incarcerated at the time of the shooting and no evidence pointed to their associates.

Milo said, "The D on that case retired last year but I reached her and showed her Meagin's and Barlett's DMVs. She'd never heard of them, told me who to call at their records department. Nice fellow, actually apologized in a Cajun accent for no result."

"Any chance of getting a ballistics match?"

"Unfortunately not. The bullet went through Fontenot, hit the side of a metal dumpster, and got too deformed for comparison."

"Same as Meagin and Gio," I said. "Powerful load, relatively up close. And a parking lot behind the bar sounds like Barlett."

"And Louisiana's close to Florida, the way this is going, we'll be playing Game of the States into the next millennium. I've still got a loose end with Irma and Adelita, didn't hear from Toni Bowman so I called. Her maid extended her vacation in Mexico until yesterday. Minute she got back, Toni had her call Irma. Straight to voicemail. The maid did give her an address where she'd driven Irma a couple of times, the two of them weren't close pals, they met in MacArthur Park and chatted from time to time. Studio apartment near the park, I just got back from there. New tenants, manager has no idea where Irma is, she hadn't lived there for a while. Probably after getting the job at the mansion, why pay rent? Now she's gone somewhere else, hopefully not Mexico."

"Hiding," I said. "Ups the chances something she saw or heard at the mansion scared her."

"Exactly, as in something Dougie said or did. What you said before about people treating the help like furniture. We've seen his temper firsthand, he coulda let loose in her presence—hers and Adelita's—and freaked them out."

"Maybe they saw him slash and trash the painting."

"That or worse. The more I think about the guy, the more I'm back to seeing him as my prime suspect. Despite his supposedly being surprised about Meagin's death. So he is an actor. He had the means to hire a pro—maybe some construction guy he's used on jobs, there's always ex-cons on work crews. And no problem making sure he was out of the city when it happened."

"What's his connection to Barlett?"

"Same deal, Barlett was an old flame of Meagin's, Doug found out they'd corresponded and got mad. We learned about Barlett from Meagin's phone, easy enough for Doug to do the same. He phoned me yesterday, still bitching about the jewelry. Called me an obstructionist bureaucrat with no clue how to do my job. Then he repeated it. The word 'clue.' And cackled. **Then** he said he'd be hiring a lawyer to get all the bling back and hung up. He's nuts, Alex. Why obsess on the jewelry? Yeah, we're talking a few hundred thou but for him that's small change."

I said, "Easier to focus upon a side issue than his big problem."

"Which is?"

"Coming to grips with how Meagin manipulated him. Beginning with how she picked him up. Seduced him and got him to marry her without divulging anything personal, then proceeded to cheat on him from the get-go. Getting suckered is totally at odds with his self-image as a savvy businessman and a tough negotiator. Once he finds out she also conned him about the purple diamond so she could wear it for Gio, he could really blow."

"Hmm," he said.

"Tell him and hope he does?"

"Stress makes people screw up. I get him to go all-out volcanic, he could end up saying something

I can use to convince John about a phone warrant on Doug's other phone. Or phones, as the case may be."

"You don't need John for that."

"Technically, no, but he's holding me back, says if I get the info prematurely via a friendly judge, the kind of lawyer Doug's likely to hire could shred it to inadmissibility then move on to a big-time fruit-of-the-poison-tree thing. If Doug actually goes bananas and blabs something incriminating, I'll be on safe ground."

"Before you talk to him, it would be good to know if he's got links to New Orleans?"

"Hmm. Hold on."

Several minutes of dead air.

"Hopes dashed again," he said. "Nothing, at least not professionally. He's never done a project anywhere in Louisiana. So what do you think about feeding him the uncomfortable truth about the necklace?"

"You could try."

"Wanna be there?"

I said, "Never acquired a taste for lava but sure."

An hour later I was in his office as he propped his cell against his monitor, switched to speaker, and made the call.

"You," said Doug March.

Milo mimed a fingers-crossed vampire defense, then told him about the purple diamond.

Silence.

Seconds passed. Milo's eyebrow arched. He picked up a pen and opened his pad.

More silence. The voice that finally came through was tremulous, barely audible.

"Oh no."

"Sir—"

Doug March said, "What an idiot I was. Totally out of my element."

Two exhalations.

Milo looked at me. I mouthed, "Wait," and picked up a stack of Post-its.

Doug March said, "Okay. Now I can see why you held back on the jewelry. You were trying to shield me. Thank you. Sorry. For being a jerk."

Whimper. Whine. The huff-huff of strangled breath followed by muffled sobs.

Milo mouthed, "What the?"

I wrote: **Wait** on a Post-it.

We sat there as March cried. Tried to catch his breath. Coughed. Finally succeeded. "Total. Jerk. Stupid. Sorry."

I wrote: **Limited sympathy.**

Milo said, "It's okay, sir."

"It's not okay," said Doug March. "I need. To learn. This isn't. The. First time."

"You've been married before?"

"No. Girlfriends. College. Got played. Didn't learn." March moaned. "I need to learn. **Need** to."

Milo said, "I'm sure you will."

"Doesn't look like it. Okay. Thanks."

Ask what you want. Use his name.

Milo said, "Do you mind if I ask you a question on a whole other subject, Doug?"

Long sigh. "I did something else stupid?"

"Not at all. Do you know a man named Richard Barlett?"

"He's the one? Who . . ."

"He may be another victim, Doug."

"**Of** the one **who?**"

"It's possible."

"If you're asking," said March, "it's more than possible, you don't do things randomly. I see that now—sorry for what I said this morning, I was totally out of line."

"No big deal, forget it," said Milo. "So you don't know Richard Barlett?"

"Never heard of him. Was he also one of Meagin's . . . distractions?"

"There's no evidence of that."

"But the same person may have killed him."

"Like I said, we're looking into all possibilities. Here's another name: Nicole Fontenot."

"Sounds French."

"From New Orleans. Ever been there?"

"In college," said Doug March. "Spring break between freshman and sophomore."

"So about ten years ago."

"Let's see . . . nine. Thought the place was gross."

"How so?"

"Everyone out to exploit you." March laughed harshly. "Like I'm the expert. Is there something else Meagin did besides the necklace and . . . you know?"

Milo said, "Not that we've found."

"So far," said March.

"So far. In terms of the jewelry—"

"Keep it, Lieutenant. All of it."

"Can't do that, Doug. It's legally yours and you'll get it back."

"Then I'll toss it straight in the trash," said March. "Heh heh, no, I'm not **that** idiotic. But I certainly don't want it near me. What would I do with it? Give it to another woman who'd . . . I'll just give it to some charity."

"That'll be your decision," said Milo.

"Decisions," said Doug March. "I used to think I was good with them."

"Doug, we all make mistakes."

"Mine appear to be major."

"It may seem that way but I've seen really smart people—like you—taken advantage of."

"Appreciate that," said Doug March. "What you're trying to do."

Milo said, "Now I'm going to ask you something that may upset you. If you want to say no, feel free."

"What?" Resignation.

"How many phones do you use?"

"Two."

"Would you have a problem letting me see all your phone records?"

"For what purpose?"

"To eliminate you as a suspect."

March laughed. "I know you've suspected me from the beginning. My mother told me you would. She watches crime shows, says that's what you people always do, go for the husband. She told me plenty of other things, too. E.g., what an idiot I was to marry Meagin without knowing anything about her. Also that she'd warned me and I'd been too headstrong to listen."

"Sounds like a tough conversation."

"I'm used to it, Lieutenant. The only problem I'd have giving you my records is that my business depends on the acquisition of knowledge requiring privacy and confidentiality."

"We've got no interest in your business affairs, Doug. Just in anything that pertains to Meagin's murder."

"Like what?"

"No way to know until we view the records."

Doug March said, "Okay, time to stop being a jerk. If you assure me the data won't leave the station, I'll believe you. I'll have Randi Levine bring a printout over to your office. How far back do you need to go?"

"Say a year."

"A year? I'm really not comfortable with that."

Milo said, "How about Randi brings it over and we examine it in front of her."

"You don't need to take possession?"

"Not if it's business-related, Doug."

Silence.

"Why not," said March. "Extricating myself from this mess is smart. I need to be smart."

Thirty-eight minutes later, Randi Levine was standing in the doorway to Milo's office bearing a tome of printout that she placed on his desk.

Milo said, "Thanks. Coffee or something else to drink?"

She shook her head. "Never been in a police station before. What did this place used to be, a closet?"

He smiled and turned to the printout. Flicked pages. "Lots of calls."

She said, "Six thousand five hundred and fifty-six over the twelve-month period you requested."

Milo said, "You counted."

Randi Levine said, "I'm thorough."

I pushed buttons on my phone.

Milo said, "Appreciate that, but this is way too much to go over while you wait. Please call Doug and ask if I can photocopy."

She said, "He won't like that," but complied. Speed-dialing March, she began explaining, then handed the phone to Milo, who flipped it to speaker.

Doug March said, "You really need to, Lieutenant?"

"Unless you want Ms. Levine to make multiple trips for days."

"There's that much?"

"Six thousand five hundred plus, Doug."

"Wow. Who knew I was that popular." Low laughter. "Sure, what the hell, it's in my best interests. Also, I owe you for being a jerk."

That admission parted Randi Levine's lips and corrugated her forehead. As if straining to make sense of a foreign language. She recovered quickly, stood tall and turned impassive.

Milo said, "Really appreciate it, Doug," and returned the phone to her. She looked everywhere but at us as Milo scooped up the dense wad of paper and sidled past her into the hallway.

"Be back in a sec."

I sat there as Randi Levine continued to avoid eye contact. A minute or so later, she did what everyone does for distraction in the age of questionable information: got back on her phone, pulled up a screen, and began scrolling studiously. My chair put me close enough to catch an oblique glimpse of what occupied her attention. Women posing in bright colors. Fashion website.

I used the time to check for messages. Neither of us had spoken by the time Milo returned with two tomes. He handed one to her.

She logged off and we walked her to the elevator.

As we waited, she said, "I've never heard him like that before."

"Like what?" said Milo.

"Vulnerable."

"He's been through a lot."

"Obviously," said Randi Levine. But her expression said the possibility of change was unnerving.

36

Milo began leafing through Doug March's Oxford English Dictionary of phone communication.

"Six thousand five hundred plus."

I said, "Just under eighteen calls a day. Doesn't seem excessive for a tycoon even if you eliminate weekends."

"You calculated?" He laughed. "Of course you did." He pushed the stack to the side. "Time to be a bad boss."

He texted the young D's to come by if they were in the station. All three were and they arrived together minutes later.

"Here's the deal, kids."

He explained. They remained expressionless.

"Yeah, it's mind-numbing, sorry. But it could turn up something important."

Alicia glanced at the printout. "Are we splitting it three ways or four?"

"Four," said Milo. "God forbid I wouldn't do my share." He looked at me. "Nah, hiring you would be too expensive."

Dividing the printout into rough quarters, he distributed the shares.

Moe Reed said, "Probably a lot of repetition, shouldn't be that big of a deal."

Sean Binchy said, "I was thinking the same thing. And if any of the numbers are landlines, we might be able to reverse-directory."

Alicia nodded.

Milo said, "I don't deserve you."

Our next contact was two days later. Not by phone, he rang my doorbell just after ten a.m. looking haggard and carrying the Meagin March / Gio Aggiunta murder book.

I had a pretty good notion of what haggard meant, said nothing until he'd beelined to the kitchen, rummaged in the fridge, and drew out a bowl of leftover bowtie pasta tossed with peas, onions, and mushrooms.

"You mind? No breakfast, yet."

"All yours. Want me to make you some eggs?"

"Nah, thanks, this'll do."

"I'll heat it up."

"Nah, thanks, cold'll be fine."

◆

Settling at the kitchen table, the murder book at his elbow, he downed several forkfuls, drank the coffee I'd given him, wiped his mouth, rubbed his eyes then the rest of his face, and sat back, flushed and breathing audibly.

I poured my fourth cup of the morning and sat down.

Another dozen mouthfuls, then: "You haven't asked so you figured out why I'm not smiling."

"Nothing interesting in March's call log."

"Business, business, more business," he said. "Airport lounges, hotels, drivers, longer conversations with investors, real estate agents, and contractors. Just bosses, no construction workers. And nothing remotely connected to New Orleans or San Pietro, just in the cities where March owns property or is building. The only personal calls were to Meagin."

"How many?"

"A hundred twenty-three. Don't bother activating your abacus, it's less than two percent."

"A couple of calls a week," I said.

"Subtract travel times, sleep, and when he was home and it still doesn't amount to much. And the conversations were what we saw on her phone, no more than a coupla minutes. 'Hi, hon, how's it going, I'll be home whenever.' Assuming he bothered with 'hon.' And same as Meagin, no texts."

"Same reason," I said. "In his case for business. Any chance he's got another phone?"

"Anything's possible, Alex, but I'm not feeling him as my suspect."

"His reaction to the purple diamond."

"Right from the beginning you figured he was no Olivier. Hearing him being kinda human when I told him about the diamond, I've come around. Why do you think it knocked him so low?"

"Sexual deceit was bad enough but maybe learning she'd bested him monetarily was too much to bear."

"Not only is he socially inept, he's not the financial alpha he thought he was."

I said, "On top of being conned, he probably realized if he'd researched the price of purple diamonds in the first place—the way he does with his projects—he'd have known something was off. His choice was keep raging or admit he'd been taken and try to move on."

"A little self-therapy."

"Maybe hearing from his mother sped up the process."

He laughed. "One place I do **not** want to be for Christmas is Stuffy Manor in Tuxedo Park."

He ate more pasta, pushed the bowl away. "Speaking of denial, I'm probably doing all this psychologizing so I can avoid thinking about my reality."

He ticked his fingers. "No physical evidence, no witnesses, no motive I can prove. Before I came here, I called Toni Bowman again, maybe her maid had heard from Irma. She gave me that you're-an-idiot attitude: wouldn't I tell you if she had? And I'm thinking, maybe not, you're a hard-edged piece of work."

He drew the bowl back and resumed eating. "You make this or Robin?"

"She did."

"Thought so. Very subtle. So. You have any therapy for **moi?**"

"I think putting Gio aside was smart—one less distraction. Ditto for Doug as a suspect. Richard Barlett may very well turn out to be relevant but until you can come up with a solid link to Meagin, I wouldn't spend time on him, either."

"It's all about her."

"It's all about her past," I said. "And I keep coming back to revenge. I'd been thinking of a financial scam but now I'm leaning toward a mixture of money and emotion."

"Like with the diamond."

"Exactly. There was no need to set up a ruse for the money. Doug had already paid for lots of jewelry, he'd have likely agreed to come up with the full cost. My gut tells me she wanted dominance over two men because she'd been severely dominated and manipulated."

"Playing games with the big boys and losing," he said.

"Maybe I'm making too much out of the ghost orchid painting but I think she identified with it.

Not just because she became a phantom. We're talking a plant with no solid roots, parasitic, rare and hard to locate. Is there anything more you can do on the Florida connection?"

"Looked at their missings, including felons on the run. No one who could be her."

The garden door opened. Blanche waddled in first, followed by Robin, smiling and looking energized.

"Babe." She kissed my cheek. "Big Guy." Ditto.

Blanche's nose was working overtime. She scooted next to Milo and rooted for crumbs. No immediate success, so she looked up at him with big, soft, imploring eyes. He dropped a noodle, long past trying to conceal their relationship.

Robin laughed. "What some people won't do for approval."

"Me or her?"

"Both." Her eyes drifted to the murder book. "Am I interrupting a work session?"

Milo said, "Unplanned. I dropped by, he fed me, we're tossing a whole lot of nothing back and forth. Excellent pasta, by the way."

She smiled and bent closer. "These are their names."

Milo looked surprised.

She said, "He's told me the basics, not that. Gio and Meagin. Makes them seem more like people."

Talking to Robin about patients I treat has never been an issue. I don't do it. Ever. Crime cases are different and early on that caused tension between us. My wanting to shield her from ugliness, knowing how sensitive she is. She feeling infantilized and sidelined. We've worked it out. I tell her as much as she wants to know.

Her eyes drifted back to the name tag. "Meagin. Never seen it spelled like that."

I said, "She reinvented herself totally, why not be creative."

"Guess so." She left without comment.

Milo and I looked at each other.

Seconds later, she returned with a sheet of paper and a pencil. "Do you mind?"

Milo said, "Mind what?"

"Indulging me, I'm sure it's nothing."

Sitting down between us, she wrote in her firm artisan's hand:

M E A G I N

Studied the letters, squinted, wrote:

N I G

M E A

Several additional moments of contemplation were accompanied by rapid pencil twirls and an eraser tap of her lower lip.

Then:

E N I G M A

Milo and I stared at the paper.
He shook his head.

I said, "Right in front of us, the whole time."

Robin said, "No big deal. My advantage was coming in fresh. And it probably doesn't mean much."

Milo said, "It helps us understand her. That's always useful."

He leaned over, kissed her hand, took the paper and placed it in the murder book.

"Seeing herself as enigmatic," said Robin. "Painting a ghost orchid. To me that seems more than some cute California reinvention. More like erasing herself and trying to start over. Maybe a woman who's had a really hard life?"

Milo said, "And ended up married to a millionaire."

"And ended up dead."

He flinched and said nothing.

Robin's eyes had misted. I squeezed her hand. Cool to the touch.

"Anyway," she said, "it just looked like an anagram to me. I'll leave you guys to it."

I said, "Woman with a hard life."

"I know the obvious assumption was she was a gold-digging con. Being unfaithful, that thing with the diamond. And maybe I'm just getting mushy-hearted. But I can't help feel she was struggling to make sense of who she was. And remained a puzzle to herself. Then to be murdered like that. It's just . . . even if she wasn't a saint, it's sickening."

She stood, took a can of Pellegrino from the fridge and popped it. "This is what I came in for. Bye."

She headed back to the garden door. This time Blanche followed.

When they were gone, Milo said, "You want to go talk to her?"

"Nope."

"She's okay?"

"She needs her solitude in these situations."

"These, being . . ."

"When she needs her solitude."

"Okay, your call," he said, doubtfully. "Enigma. Hard life. If Robin's right, we could be talking a crime victim."

I said, "That's exactly what I flashed on. Maybe

the victim of an older man, not some mistress who conned a high-roller. And if we're talking years ago, you know where that could lead."

"Child abuse, incest. Whatever evil they haven't put a name on yet." Veins formed in his forehead. He rubbed his face, shot up and paced the kitchen for two circuits. Continued into the living room for the third. When he returned any trace of haggard was gone.

Energized by anger.

"How the hell am I gonna do her justice?"

Supplying an answer would've felt great.

I had nothing to offer.

At three in the morning, woken abruptly from dreamless sleep, I lay on my back, assaulted by question marks.

I turned the case over and over. Kept coming back to a spiky white thing that reduced the concept of a flower to a bizarre abstraction.

A fugitive hiding out among the marsh-nourished trees of a murky swamp.

The botanical **essence** of enigma.

Meagin March had identified with the ghost orchid. Maybe because she'd seen it.

As a child, subjected to terror and cruelty, seizing upon the flower and the stories surrounding it as inspiration. Like most victims, yearning to disappear. And she'd finally succeeded. But she'd never been comfortable laying down roots.

Playing by the rules was out of the question. The rules had failed her when she needed them most.

Nothing counted but survival.

By the age of forty-one, she'd figured she finally had things under control.

Then . . .

Thinking about the way she'd died—along with a man driven by his own issues—made my eyes ache.

I sighed. Letting loose a barely audible outflow of air but Robin stirred.

The person who loved me as no one else ever had. Finely tuned to my emotions. To the world.

It had taken me this long to reach the empathy Robin had achieved within seconds of solving an anagram.

What that said about the difference between us was something I didn't feel like thinking about.

So I did what I always do when introspection looms: focus on a task that drew upon what I'd gone to school for.

A fifteen-year-old boy no one wanted. What would that do to a kid? How should I approach him? What should I refrain from asking?

Would I have anything to offer?

No satisfaction, there, so I switched back to a girl living near a swamp. Maybe no older than the unwanted boy.

Her problem: being wanted **too** much.

I pictured her, lying in the dark, shivering, as she anticipated a hideous, chronic ordeal.

Withering in the aftermath.

Imagining herself an exquisite parasite, a fragile beauty that had survived for millennia because it had learned to subsist on nothing.

The more I thought about it, the more certain I was that the ordeal of the woman who'd come to call herself Meagin March had begun in southwest Florida. Milo's probing had been limited to checking out missing persons databases. But that had been doomed to failure because public scrutiny was the last thing an abusive family would want.

Careful not to wake Robin, I rolled out of bed, opened and shut the door gently, and padded on bare feet cramped by tension up a silent, dark hallway.

38

I settled at my desk, using my Robin and Blanche screensaver as the sole lighting and smiling at it for a few seconds. Then, onward.

Meagin March—I had no other way to think of her—had died at forty-one. If her personal papers could be believed. Even if they couldn't, the age seemed reasonable, so I began with a five-year spread in either direction.

Assuming she'd been abused and that it had taken place when she was a minor, I set twenty to twenty-five years ago as my target range and began searching for crime stories related to the Fakahatchee Strand Preserve. Starting with Copeland, the town listed as the park's home base.

The Copeland of today was rated more violent than ninety-five percent of comparably populated

U.S. communities but back then, things had been a lot quieter.

The closest thing to criminal violence in or near the former logging outpost had taken place twenty-two years ago, miles away at sea, when a commercial grouper fisherman had been stabbed to death by a deckhand. Other than that, published offenses were limited to vandalism, theft, and trespassing, the only other notable corpse that of a Florida panther. Cause of death of the rare creature undetermined because most of the body had been consumed by alligators.

Narrowing the time band to more recent events revealed only a couple of hikers lost in the preserve. Both had been suspected of illegal orchid poaching and when rescued, were suffering from severe malnutrition and dehydration.

A park ranger, unidentified, stated, "If they were up to no good, they got their punishment. If they weren't, they just had bad luck."

I searched a map of southwest Florida for nearby population centers, came up with the city of Naples, forty-four miles northwest and now known for its low crime rate. Directly west of the preserve and slightly closer was Marco Island, the most expensive beach destination in Florida and one of the state's safest locales. Neither produced anything interesting.

After two hours, I logged off, figuring my search

had been a quixotic thing to begin with, fueled by Three A.M. Syndrome.

The kind of iniquity I was looking for—the kind of crushing, inevitable oppression that led a girl to take to the road—flourished in secrecy.

When I returned to the bedroom, Robin, curled up, eyes closed, facing me, said, "Learn anything?"

I laughed.

"Did you, baby?"

"Nothing gets past you."

She smiled. "Yeah, it's a problem."

39

The next day, Judge Julie Beck's clerk called to let me know Derek Ruffalo would be arriving in L.A. in a week for a "seven-day forensic evaluation." I penciled the dates in, did some reading on rejected adoptees, learned nothing encouraging.

When I hadn't heard from Milo by noon, I reached him at his desk and told him of last night's futile search. It felt strangely like confession. If so, he was a compassionate priest.

"I like your thinking, kid, but with the time lapse and what you said about secrecy—not surprised. But thanks anyway."

"Worth following up?"

"By me? What could I add?"

"You've got the contacts."

"Guess I could try to find some cop who'd been working back then. Best case retired, worst case deceased." He chuckled. "Like there's a difference. Okay, I'll see what I can dig up, nothing else is happening."

Just under two hours later, he phoned back.

I said, "You found something."

He said, "Not what we talked about. Got a call-me message from some lawyer named Porras. Before I phoned him, I looked him up. Personal injury practice in Pico Union. Didn't recall slipping and falling or God forbid tripping a citizen, so I didn't call back. But he did, insisted I'd want to talk to him about my murder case. I said c'mon by, there'll be a welcome mat. He said he strongly preferred not to meet at the station, said let's do coffee. Someone that persistent, I get curious. Appointment's in forty, some designer java place he suggested in Brentwood."

"Pico Union to the Westside. Serious drive."

"I'm figuring he's billing by the hour."

Hava Lava Java sat on a block of Wilshire west of Bundy shared by single-floor storefronts, a quarter of them vacant, fronted by homeless people claiming the sidewalk.

Despite heady aromas and a staggering assortment of choices, the coffee joint was empty but for two thin women in jogging suits and baseball caps through which ponytails had been extruded. The hats bore the name of a local prep school, the suits designer logos.

Per usual, Milo and I arrived five minutes early for the meeting with Antonio Porras, eliciting upraised eyebrows from the women. The same kind of look a nerdy kid might get from the spoon-fed student council of the school on the hats.

We ordered tall black coffees, which stimulated puzzlement from the kid behind the counter, took the table farthest from the women, who stared a bit longer, then returned to animated conversation.

I said, "I also looked Porras up. His partner does immigration law. You're hoping he's got a message from Irma Ruiz."

"Saw that, too, but I'd be here anyway because beggars are forbidden from exercising options—yeah, of course, I figured there might be immigration issues."

He drank, grimaced, put his cup down. "Maybe they've got all those flavor options because the basic stuff tastes like wastewater."

I said, "Gonna go back and ask for pumpkin spice?"

"Not unless they're peddling pies."

"Closest thing I saw was zucchini bread."

He was about to reply when his eyes focused over my shoulder and toward the door.

The man who'd entered was forty or so, six-three, pencil-straight and thin with sparse gray-black hair and the watchful yet adventurous eyes of a raven contemplating a swoop into something nasty. He wore a beautifully cut navy-blue suit, an ecru shirt, and a confidently knotted wine-colored tie. Brown suede loafers with brass buckles propelled him toward us. He smiled faintly as he pushed a wheelie bag that matched the shoes.

"Lieutenant? Tony Porras." Smallish, light-brown eyes shifted to me. "You're his sergeant or just a detective?"

Milo said, "Dr. Alex Delaware is our consulting psychologist."

Tony Porras blinked. Amusement fought wariness. That same avian ambivalence. I wondered if balancing his emotions exhausted him by day's end.

"You thought I might be a nut-job?"

"Of course not, sir. Dr. Delaware works with us on certain cases."

"Certain, being . . ."

"Cases we think a psychologist can help with."

"And you think—"

Milo pointed to a chair. "Please. This has nothing to do with you, sir. I could be wrong about why you contacted me and if so, the doctor will be on his way. If I'm right, he'll stay because he's been working on the March/Aggiunta murders."

Tony Porras's head drew back. "Two victims?"

"Yes, sir. Though I'm sure Ms. Ruiz only knew about her employer."

The attorney breathed in deeply. Grimaced as if air intake had been insufficient and sat down. He took in our barely touched cups. "Not decent?"

"Not to our trained palates."

"Darn," said Porras. "It got four stars on Yelp. Okay, fine, we'll proceed. But you understand my caution."

"Not sure I do but I respect it."

"The people I tend to represent often have an unpleasant history with the police."

Milo nodded. Tony Porras gave me a long look until I did the same.

The kind of silent Socratic approach a law professor might use. I wanted to say **Where do you teach?** But the question could do nothing but harm. If I was wrong, I'd look foolish. If correct, Porras would feel psychoanalyzed.

He said, "Okay, you're right, this is about Mrs. Ruiz. She's actually my partner's client."

Teresa Guzman. We both knew the name; we both kept our mouths shut.

Tony Porras said, "Terri—my partner—does immigration law."

Milo said, "Got it. Please assure her we couldn't care less about legal status."

Porras smiled. "You're murder snobs? That's what my uncle calls homicide detectives. He did patrol in Hollenbeck for twenty-eight years."

Milo said, "He got it right."

"If it breathes, they leave," said Porras. "That's how Uncle Ernie pegged it."

"No debate there."

Porras cracked his knuckles and glanced at the board behind the counter. "Nothing's drinkable, huh—okay, enough screwing around. Mrs. Ruiz had something in her possession that she passed along to Ms. Guzman, who consulted me because during the early days of my practice I did some defense work. Not criminal, civil. Let me make it clear: this material was acquired legally by Mrs. Ruiz, via conditional transfer."

"That's a new one on me, Counselor."

"Mrs. Ruiz was given something on the stipulation that she'd maintain possession and do her best to provide security for the object unless and until circumstances dictated that she transfer it."

"Ah," said Milo.

"Yeah, it's legal mumbo jumbo but I need to define parameters. You wouldn't be recording this, would you?"

Milo smiled. "Feel free to pat me down. The doctor, as well."

Porras smiled back. Uneasily, well short of camaraderie. "I'll pass. Sorry if this is coming across paranoid. One thing I've learned practicing law for fourteen years is to be careful."

"Don't blame you," said Milo. "So Irma was given something by Meagin March and instructed to hold on to it unless something bad happened to her. Which turned out to be the case."

Tony Porras's lips tightened. "Before we go further, I need to ensure that the time lapse between that unfortunate event and the present time will not be held against my client."

Milo said, "She has no reason to worry. No one will blame her for being scared."

"As is appropriate," said Porras. A last-word kind of guy. "All right, then, I'm going to transfer the material from my possession to yours after which Mrs. Ruiz's obligation will have been fulfilled."

Reaching down, he unzipped the wheelie bag and drew out a white cardboard box that had likely once held a fresh ream of paper. Grasping the box with both hands, he stood, quickly rezipped the bag, placed the box on the table, and began walking away.

Milo said, "Counselor?"

The women turned and stared.

Tony Porras said, "What?"

"A second." Milo guided Porras out of the coffee shop. The women and I watched an intense sidewalk conversation through the glass.

One of them said, "Lawyers," as if it were a dirty word. Milo, made shabby by contrast to Porras's perfectly put-together look, might've been flattered to be taken as an attorney. Then again, maybe not.

Finally, Porras walked off and Milo returned. He caught the women staring at him and frightened them with a mouthful of teeth.

"C'mon," he said, gloving up and snatching the white box. To the women: "Hope the kids get into good colleges."

At the unmarked, I said, "What was the sidebar about?"

"I told him if what he gave me was relevant to solving the case his client might be subpoenaed to testify so it would be better if he gave me her contact information. He said he was under no obligation and I said that was true, but still, it would be in everyone's interest if she remained available. He refused flat-out, I talked about two victims cut down in the prime, one of them collateral damage. Then about how appreciative we were of Ruiz's coming forth, how she'd be in no danger from immigration or anyone else and that I'd get that in writing. The writing part seemed to impress him but the best I got out of him was he'd think about it."

He hefted the box. Thin shuffling noise, as if full of dry leaves. "Not much inside."

I said, "Enough to terrify Irma Ruiz."

"True," he said. "It's a good sign when witnesses get terrified."

The box rode on the Impala's rear seat, belted securely, like a prisoner. Waiting until we'd returned to the office to open it had been a heroic test of self-control. Milo had remained gloved and handed me a pair.

"Just in case there's some blockbuster Agatha Christie thing in there: the butler did it."

He carried the box to his office.

◆

No tape or any other sealant. He lifted the lid.

Less than a quarter full. Papers and smaller objects that slid around like crumbs in a can.

Both of us had been holding our breath. I felt as if I needed to exhale willfully.

When we saw what was on top, he said, "Interesting."

I said, "I'd start at the bottom."

40

Lowermost in the box was a two-inch-by-three-inch rectangle. One of the sliders.

State of Texas picture identification card issued to Persephone Sue Gilmore, age eighteen.

The picture was the adolescent face of the woman we'd known as Meagin March. Pallid, puffy, the hair long, stringy, medium blond. A few zit spots, but despite all that, markedly pretty.

Uncomfortable being photographed: pale eyes had shifted to the right in response to the flash.

Dated twenty-three years ago. Meagin March had done a lot of dissembling but she'd been truthful about her age. Given that, I wondered if she'd used her real name on the license. Considered the uniqueness of the name and figured she had.

On the I.D. was an address in Midland. Milo looked it up. A long-defunct oil field.

He studied the image some more. "Jumpy eyes. Reminds me of a mugshot."

I said, "If I'm right, she'd been in a type of prison. Persephone was raped by Hades, her uncle. Some say also by Zeus, her father. Give that name to a girl and your intentions are clear."

"Or she called herself that as kind of a victim statement."

"Or that but my guess it's the name she began with."

He thought about that, tensed up and moved on to the next item.

Oklahoma driver's license issued twenty years ago to Martha Erika Johnson. Same face, longer hair, platinum blond now, and complicated by flips and waves. No more pimples but the cheeks had hollowed and the eyes remained wary.

Address in Tulsa. Milo matched it to a truck stop. A call confirmed it had been a truck stop for half a century.

I'd spent the same time checking obituary files, had quickly found a grave for Martha Erika Johnson, age two at the time of her death in Oklahoma City. No hint of cause on a white marble gravestone, just the smiling, engraved face of a chubby-cheeked tot.

Our Little Angel, Taken From Us Far Too Soon.

Identity Theft 101: exploit the dead, the younger the better.

Next: an official United States of America Social Security card issued to Martha Erika Johnson and a pay slip from The Ol' Oak Bucket Family Restaurant in Tulsa.

Then, a surprise: a diploma from Tulsa Community College dated seventeen years ago awarding Martha Erika Johnson an associate in applied sciences with a major in physical therapy assistance.

I said, "With the card, she got a job and enrolled part-time."

Milo said, "Then this—a better job, American success story."

He'd plucked out a plasticized, clip-on badge. Employee I.D. listing Martha E. Johnson as an asst. physical therapist at Bright Life Rehabilitation Center in Boise, Idaho. By the approximate age of twenty-five, she'd cut her hair short and business-like and had tinted it brown. Gone were the facial hollows and the blemishes, in their place, a somewhat blank demeanor barely brightened by a faint, off-center smile.

No more avoiding the camera. Ready to take on scrutiny full-face.

The next bit of bio featured the same visage on an Iowa driver's license issued to Lori Adriana Boone two years later. The DOB listed made her twenty-eight, again accurate.

I ran another death search, found an Ada,

Oklahoma, grave for Lori Adriana Boone, deceased at the age of two. Black granite marker, no heart-wrenching face, just an engraved teddy bear.

Boone née Johnson née Gilmore now sported teased-up honey-blond hair, and assertive, challenging eyes rimmed by shadow and fringed by press-on lashes. Makeup was caked on so heavily an apathetic bureaucratic camera had picked it up. The overall effect: a mask with great bone structure.

Paper-clipped to the Iowa license was a pink pearlescent business card.

American Dreams Gentleman's Club.

Toll-free number, address on North Fifteenth Street in Council Bluffs.

I said, "Finally, the Midwest."

Milo said, "She takes the time to get a serious degree, lands a decent job in Idaho, ends up stripping in Iowa?"

He ran a map search. "Nearly thirteen hundred miles away. You know what I'm feeling."

"Maybe she got in trouble in Boise and lammed. Pilfering from the rehab center, even embezzling."

No arrest records on Martha Erika Johnson popped up on NCIC. If she'd committed an offense, it had been too low-level for the feds to care about.

But serious enough for her to morph to Lori Boone, pack up quickly, and land in yet another state.

Milo cold-called Boise PD, spoke to a series of cops far too young to have any idea. It took a while but he finally connected to a civilian records clerk able to direct him to the open-sesame that unlocked their internet cave.

Two years into her employment at Bright Life, "Erika Johnson" had been arrested for prostitution during a raid by Boise vice cops at Sweet Orchid Massage Therapy, Ltd. Five-hundred-dollar fine, no jail time, supervised visits for a year that never materialized.

I said, "Moonlighting."

He said, "Different type of physical therapy to make more money. If you're right about the Persephone angle, why would she want to go near a place like that?"

"To achieve control."

He thought about that. "Horny guys on the table instead of on her . . . guess so." Long sigh. "Okay, let's see where our poor girl traveled next . . . okay, here we go."

If the records she'd left were complete, Lori Boone had remained uneventfully in Iowa for four and a half years until acquiring a Nevada driver's license as Meagin Jones and listing her age as thirty-three.

Sleek, shoulder-length, red hair styled skillfully. Less conspicuous makeup allowed natural beauty to shine through. Small smile; confident. An eye-catching woman.

Address on Highway 95 in Amargosa Valley.

No deceased child by that name.

Milo said, "Now she's used to being Ms. Enigma, no need for a formal name change."

I said, "Once she switched to dancing and living off tips, no need for documentation."

He typed, stopped, pointed to his screen. "Address matches a place called The Fantasy Farm. Legal brothel in Nye County . . . still in business . . . looks as if it changed hands a few times since then . . . gets high marks for cleanliness, security, good-looking hostesses."

He sat back. "From waiting tables to legit massage to not-so-legit bodywork to stripping, then full-time sex work. Which according to Rikki Montel, she stuck with in Vegas."

He peered at the Nevada license. "So many women enter that world and deteriorate. If this can be believed, she matured and got healthier-looking. Guess taking control can do that to you."

I said, "Emotional and physical control. You know where most of the deterioration comes from."

"Dope and pimps."

"Nothing we've seen or heard says there was ever a substance issue. She also had the physical and intellectual assets to work in a high-end, protected environment."

"Which," he said, lifting the final piece of paper, "she left just after three years."

We'd reached the topmost level of Meagin March's pocket biography. Several sheets of fine print that had led me to suggest we start at the beginning.

◆

At age thirty-six, Meagin Jones had left the brothel, moved to Las Vegas, and leased a house in the Tule Springs neighborhood. The documents she'd held on to listed the rent as twenty-two hundred dollars a month. She'd paid a year in advance and had repeated it for two additional years.

Milo said, "Almost eighty grand. That's serious cash on hand. Why do you think she held on to this?"

I said, "Point of pride. After living frugally at The Fantasy Farm and saving her tips, she'd put herself in a strong financial situation. Someone with a strong sense of self-preservation."

"Too bad that petered out." He looked up the property, found it on Zillow, now for sale for five hundred twenty-six thousand dollars.

Twenty-four hundred square feet of tile-roofed pink stucco in one of the city's safest neighborhoods. Two stories, three bedrooms, three baths, a family room that looked out to a kidney-shaped pool surrounded by a concrete deck.

He groaned and I knew why.

The pool and the decking were freakishly reminiscent of the place where Meagin March and Gio Aggiunta had been slaughtered.

Placing the lease back on top of the stack, he said, "So why'd she leave all this with Irma? It's not like she's telling us who killed her."

I said, "It wasn't about that. She'd been hiding

and dodging her entire adult life, wanted some sort of legacy—letting the world know who she was and how she got there."

"A pocket bio left with a maid? No way this was random, Alex, she musta known her past could catch up with her. Why not come out and say who she was afraid of?"

I said, "Don't know . . . unless at some level she **is** telling us."

I took the box and fished out the Texas I.D. card. **Persephone Gilmore.**

Yet another find-a-grave search revealed no matches. No surprise.

I said, "I'll lay odds this was her real name and she figured someone could trace her past using it."

He chewed on that. "Making me work for it?"

"She operated illegally for most of her adult life, may have developed low regard for law enforcement. But someone who bothered to follow up would be more likely to be thorough."

"Testing the cops? I don't know, Alex . . . okay, nothing else to look at, what's the name of that town near the swamp?"

"Copeland."

Another map search.

He said, "She took an even longer trip the first time out. Over sixteen hundred miles to Midland."

I looked at the map. "Dallas would've been simpler, it's a nearly straight, westerly trip, so she was clearly avoiding it. Same for veering south to

Houston and Austin. Big cities can be easier to hide in but if she was a country girl, she could've found them intimidating. We'll never know why she stopped in Midland or how she got there but back then you could buy bus tickets anonymously so my bet's on Greyhound, hitchhiking, or both. And it's an oil town, trucks coming in and out."

"Hopping semis."

"Doing what it took to escape."

He shook his head. "Eighteen years old and moving halfway across the country."

No surprise to me. I'd made my escape from Missouri to California at sixteen, fleeing the rages of an alcoholic father and a chronically depressed, apathetic mother.

Milo knew about that in general terms but I'd never gotten into the core of the experience. He read something on my face that made him turn away from me and back to the box.

Tapping the top, he said, "Abused so she runs. You think whoever she ran from found her and killed her all these years later? That's . . . oh, man, that's so **evil**."

His hand traveled to his gut and massaged, as if sick to his stomach.

I said, "Maybe it didn't start out as a murder. What if the abuser found out she was rich and tried to take advantage?"

"Blackmail? I raped you twenty years ago so pay me off?"

"Whoever it was could've figured the threat of disrupting her Bel Air life would be enough to motivate payment."

"Whoever it was," he said. Another queasy look. "Bastard shows up and exposes the family history? Yeah, I can see that not going down well in socialite circles. But still, he's putting himself in the crosshairs if she reports him."

I said, "Sexual psychopaths get off on risk and reliving. This is someone he's dominated before. If she told him to get lost, rage might've taken over. Why return empty-handed from the hunt? I'll snag myself a trophy."

The hand on his abdomen clawed. He winced, turned away again to hide his reaction.

I said, "If we're talking a father or an uncle, he could be in his sixties or his seventies but still healthy. Physically. A brother or cousin would be younger."

"Happy family," he said. "So how did whoever the asshole is find her after all these years?"

I said, "Obviously, it took a while and I'm wondering if Richard Barlett had something to do with it. Meagin spoke to him months ago and two days after she died, he was dispatched exactly the same way. If she told Barlett where she was living and he passed it on, he could've signed his own death warrant."

"Why would he rat her out?"

"Only thing I can think of is a connection to the bad guy. A close one. Barlett also changed his name and wiped out his past and he's two years younger than Meagin."

"A brother?" he said. "Two kids escaping the same hell."

"He would've been sixteen when Meagin left, could've gone with her, or waited and done it solo. If they were together, their lives eventually diverged. Meagin grew progressively more confident and developed a steely resolve. Maybe Barlett didn't."

"So he rats her out to a psychopath?"

"Maybe he got conned."

"Whatever . . . the whole thing is vile. She works her entire life to get it together then gets snuffed."

Another wince. Reaching the fury that a lot of homicide detectives achieve as cases clarify.

I sat there, intellectually troubled but not allowing the emotional aspect to occupy my brain. It's a skill I've acquired over a lifetime. At times it's made me a better therapist. Able to focus on people needing help, providing genuine empathy without feeling their pain.

Sometimes I wake up at three a.m.

The man who'd closed over three hundred homicides, and still ached with every new one, got to his feet but made no move to leave. Instead, he used the shift in posture to stretch within the oppressive space.

I continued to sit, thoughts flooding my head.

Knowing what it was like to be trapped. The terror and joy of escape. Things I'd never told anyone and never would.

Thoughts allowed, feelings forbidden.

Milo sat back down, looking drained. "Anything else?"

I said, "Now we've got her real name."

He sighed. "Time to excavate."

41

Milo and I typed away separately.

No **gilmore** references paired with **copeland, fakahatchee,** or **naples fla.**

The usual approach when searching is to keep narrowing focus. I did the opposite, broadening to **gilmore case florida.**

And there it was.

Twenty-four-year-old piece in archives of **The Fort Myers News-Press.** The resort town was nearly a hundred miles from Copeland but legal proceedings had shifted there due to a change-of-venue motion entered by a defense attorney named Meryl Rittenhouse.

Murder-Suicide in Ochopee Tied to Upcoming
Abuse Trial

Samson Rodriguez, Staff Writer

Copeland police report that two bodies
found in an Ochopee mobile home are those
of the defendant in an upcoming child
abuse trial and his common-law wife. Davis
Gilmore, 44, released on bail after being
charged with sexually abusing his 17-year-old
daughter, reportedly fatally shot the victim's
mother and his longtime companion, Sally
Rooney, 39, then himself.

Gilmore, a maintenance worker at the
Fakahatchee Preserve with a history of drunk
and disorderly misdemeanor arrests, was
accused by his daughter of sexual abuse
that stretched back over a decade. The
charges, police say, were supported by physical evidence and resulted in Gilmore's arrest.
Gilmore's trial, which could've landed the
defendant a substantial prison term, was
slated to begin in a week. Prosecutor John
Bolt had protested the decision by Judge
Razzie Clark to grant Gilmore an "inappro-
priately light" bail of $1,000, with a 10% cash
outlay and the remainder guaranteed by a
bondsman.

Judge Clark, agreeing with Defense
Attorney Meryl Rittenhouse that the absence

of violence in Gilmore's past and community ties to the rural Ochopee community made him an unlikely flight risk, had stood fast by his decision. Clark had received the case after Rittenhouse successfully filed for a change of venue, citing undue prejudice in Naples.

Immediately prior to Davis Gilmore's release, the complainant along with two younger brothers, ages 15 and 9, were secreted in an unnamed county facility.

"Lucky for them," said Copeland police chief Oliver Banks. "This guy might not of had much of a record but he was known to have a temper and he was clearly out for blood."

42

I sat as close to Milo's screen as the stingy space permitted and watched as he hunted. Beginning with obituary shopping, because twenty-four years had passed.

Reporter Samson Rodriguez's name pulled up nothing until Milo found him listed as a correspondent for a wire service, now stationed in Bangkok. No personal email listed. Milo sent a message to the service's Asian headquarters, got an automatic away message, and moved on.

Copeland police chief Oliver Banks had passed on eight years ago, age seventy-seven. Predeceased by his wife and two of his eight children. Big church funeral.

Former defense attorney Meryl Rittenhouse had been working as a real estate agent at the time of her death twelve years ago. Age fifty-six, leaving behind a second husband and two children. In lieu of flowers, contributions to the American Cancer Society.

Judge Erasmus "Razzie" Clark's demise was three years prior to Rittenhouse's. Age sixty-four, no survivors listed.

Clark's name also pulled up a twenty-year-old news story in the same Fort Myers paper. He'd been tossed off the bench after being implicated in "multiple illicit affairs leading to charges of favoritism," his sexual partners three attorneys who'd appeared in his court.

Suzanne Volga, Pamela Barker, Meryl Rittenhouse. No mention of the lawyers' fates but Rittenhouse's career shift suggested disbarment.

Keywording **prosecutor john bolt** failed to reveal evidence he was no longer breathing. Nor did it indicate he'd remained an officer of the court in Florida. Pairing his name with **district attorney, magistrate,** or **judge** failed to produce a single word.

But again, spreading the net worked, and **attorney john bolt** pulled up three hits. A bankruptcy specialist in Toms River, New Jersey, a criminal appeals lawyer in Boston, and a man working "of counsel" to a midsized New York firm.

Milo said, "Criminal appeals sounds like a good bet," and called the number. A massive robot-voiced voicemail menu with options for Spanish and Chinese finally connected him to Boston John Bolt's extension. He was midway through his message when a young voice broke in.

"This is John. You're probably looking for my dad."

"Thanks for picking up, Mr. Bolt."

"I wasn't going to answer but it sounded like something Dad would get a kick out of. He's in Manhattan, of counsel to a white-shoe firm. You know what that means?"

"Working there but not a partner."

"You've got it. In Dad's case it means his best friend from law school is a senior partner and was nice enough to give Dad a desk and some pickup work."

"Did your father ever mention the case I'm looking into?"

"How long ago was this?"

"Twenty-four years."

John Bolt the Younger laughed. "I was eight, only thing Dad brought home from the office was donuts. Give him a buzz, you'll probably make his day."

New York John Bolt picked up after one ring.

"Bolt." Raspy voice, Brooklyn accent. Former snowbird returned to his roots.

Milo introduced himself and said, "I'm calling about a case you were involved in a while back. Just talked to your son and—"

"Which son?"

"John Junior."

"Mr. Harvard. What'd he tell you, I'm bored and senile, you'd be doing me a favor?"

Milo laughed. "He didn't mention senile."

"Well, he's right about all of it," said Bolt. "As opposed to his political views. What case?"

"The Davis Gilmore murder-suicide."

"That one."

Milo punched air triumphantly. "You remember it."

"You're lucky. Haven't done criminal work in years, most of my cases were dinky-shit, they blur. But that one sticks out because it was so goddamn ugly. Three kids, probably totally screwed up forever, the wife claimed to know nothing about what the bastard was doing to the daughter. Maybe she was just too damn scared to speak up but we're talking a trailer in the swamp, how the hell do you keep anything private? Anyway, why's it relevant to you?"

"The daughter's one of my cases," said Milo. "Murdered a coupla weeks ago, still unsolved."

Silence.

"Sir?"

"That," said John Bolt, "is disgusting. For her to go through all that and then . . . Jesus, life is **not** fair. You have any idea who did her?"

"Not yet."

"Weeks ago. So a whodunit stinker, my sympathies. Well, I'm afraid I can't help you much, I wasn't involved with the kids, met 'em just once and that didn't include talking. They were shell-shocked, you know? Only reason I would've been involved was if I planned to put them on the stand."

"That wasn't part of the plan."

"Never, no need. He, the father—don't want to honor him with that title, he was a flat-out, mentally fucked-up, psychopathic monster—he was planning to plead out and I was happy to spare the kids a trial. I didn't like the bullshit bail he got but nothing I could do, judge was an asshole. But I figured it wouldn't matter with the kids gone and where the hell is a loser like that going to go? It's not like he had a passport."

Milo said, "We read about the judge."

"Corrupt, stupid enough to screw a bunch of female attorneys and one of them was Gilmore's court-appointed. Very hot-looking number, what was her name . . . Myra? Myrna—no, Merle . . . like the actress. Oberon. Merle the It Girl, totally in cahoots with Clark—the judge. Anyway, the case was going to be settled with a way-too-Mickey-Mouse sentence. If I recall correctly, something along the lines of five years. But I held out for five real years, no early release no matter how well behaved and reformed some prison shrink said the motherfucker was. He heads home, promptly shoots his wife and himself. Go know."

"What happened to the kids?"

"Into the system, no idea," said John Bolt.

"Foster families?"

"That would be my guess. The girl—the victim, her name I remember. Persephone. It's mythical, some girl who got raped by her father. You name a girl that, it's no secret what your intentions are, right? She was a quiet one, close to majority. The boys, there were two of them, were younger so I assume they were in the system for a while. Hey. Just thought of something. We had a social worker handling them, very nice gal. I didn't appreciate her bleeding-heart bullshit when she was trying to convince me some juvenile delinquent criminal deserved compassion instead of punishment but with the Gilmore kids, I was glad she was there. What was her name . . . names, damn, it's like they disappear . . . she was young, couple of years out of social worker school, so she'd be . . . late forties, maybe fifty . . . what the hell was her . . . damn, damn . . . okay, retrieved it from the Alzheimer file. Katherine . . . Kathy. Kathy Bookbinder. I used to tease her about that. Tell her you should be throw-ing the book, not binding it. Kathy Bookbinder, for all I know she's still in Florida."

She wasn't.

Katrine J. Bookbinder, D.S.W., was now a pro-fessor of social work at Chandler University. Small selective institution in Orange, California. I'd lec-tured there a few years ago and said so.

Milo said, "Now you're gonna tell me you know her."

"Nope, but it's an hour's ride with decent traffic, so that's decent karma."

"I will take what I can get."

His fingers pounced on his phone.

A husky voice said, "This is Kathy. It says LAPD on my screen, what's going on? Is there something on campus?"

Milo began to explain.

She said, "Persephone? Oh no. That's horrible. Repellent. My God, poor girl. Woman I guess. That's evil. And here I was thinking this was going to end up a good day."

"Sorry, Doctor."

"No need to apologize, you're doing your job," said Kathy Bookbinder. "But it's been a lifetime since I saw her and she was just a kid. What do you think I can contribute?"

"Anything you can tell me about her and her family situation would be helpful."

"Situation," said Kathy Bookbinder. "Talk about a euphemism. Well, it was a public case, not therapy, so yes, I can tell you what I know. But not over the phone. This is too . . . shocking. Too heavy. I need to compose myself. Can we meet somewhere close to here?"

"Happy to come to your office."

"No, no, I need to get away from campus, under the best of circumstances it's an altered reality . . .

God, my heart's pounding, my first thought was there was an active shooter and I was trapped."

"Has that happened before?"

"Not yet. But we did have a student last month who was actively delusional and needed to be removed. And before that, there was a sexual predator who still hasn't been caught."

"Got it," said Milo. "Again, sorry for alarming you."

"You didn't mean to . . . a margarita sounds like the right medicine, there's a place I go, Rosita's on Glassell Street. But the freeway could be a mess, why don't we do it tomorrow."

"The earlier the better, Dr. Bookbinder. I'll cope with the freeway."

"You're dedicated . . . okay, but at the least it'll be an hour and it could be a whole lot more. I'll straighten up here, notify my husband, go over to Rosita's and get settled. Call me from the road if it's nuts."

43

The freeway wasn't nuts, just slightly neu-rotic, turning a forty-eight-mile trip into a seventy-one-minute stop and go. During that time, Milo made two calls to Katrine Bookbinder. The first time, she was still in her office. By the second, she was at the restaurant nursing "my first dose."

Milo said, "On our way."

She said, "Don't worry, not going anywhere."

Rosita's was a pretty place on a pretty street half a mile from the pretty Chandler campus. Great aro-mas, the gratifying absence of bullfighting posters, serape wall hangings, and dangling sombreros.

The minimalist, tasteful ambience was working; the dining room was nearly full and abuzz with conversation. Or maybe it was just the food. The clientele was students and older people who could be faculty or just older people who liked Mexican cuisine.

No one noticed our entry except a blond woman in a corner booth facing the door. She waved, the hostess saw the gesture, smiled, ushered us through, and said, "Here they are."

The table was set for three. The woman sat with military posture as her fingertips grazed an empty margarita glass. She wore a black cowl-necked sweater and dangling onyx earrings. Fifties, angular and pleasant-looking with tightly curled shoulder-length blond hair and green eyes.

Vivid green, a surprising match to Milo's. Surprising because only two percent of people have pure-green eyes and I'd never seen ocular emeralds like my friend's.

Neither Milo nor Kathy Bookbinder seemed to notice.

She said, "Milo? Kathy." A glance at me.

I said, "Alex."

Her lips twisted. She stared at me, puzzled, but said nothing.

Milo said, "What're you having?"

"My usual. Chile relleno chicken taco combo with black beans."

"Sounds good."

"If that's what you really want." Kathy Bookbinder looked at me again.

I said, "Fajitas sound right."

"An individualist—no offense to you, Lieutenant."

"Milo's fine."

"Milo, then." Yet another examination of my face. "I know you. You spoke here a few years ago. Long-term effects of child abuse. You're a psychologist."

I said, "Alex Delaware."

She repeated my name. "Your talk was excellent."

"Thanks."

Milo began his speech: "Dr. Delaware helps us on certain cases—"

"Good for your department," said Kathy Bookbinder. "Being that forward-thinking." Back to me. "I can see why you'd be on this one."

A waiter came over and took our order. Kathy Bookbinder tapped her glass and said, "Another, please."

"Coming up. What about you gentlemen?"

"Iced tea."

"The same."

When the waiter was gone, she said, "It's only my second dose, Milo. In case you're curious."

"I'm curious by nature but not about that."

Kathy Bookbinder folded her lips inward, let them open slowly and settle as a neutral hyphen. "Tell me about poor Persephone."

He gave her the basics.

She said, "Killed with a lover. She was the main target, not him?"

"Yes."

"Poor guy, guess he just happened to be cheating with the wrong person."

"That's what it looks like."

She looked at me, as if expecting some sort of psychological supplement. I said nothing and she turned back to Milo.

"So. You drove all the way out here. What do you think I can tell you that'll justify the trip?"

Before he could answer, the drinks arrived. Kathy Bookbinder let hers sit there and maintained unwavering eye contact.

He said, "We'd appreciate anything you think might be relevant."

"To a murder that occurred, what . . . twenty-five years later? How about you start by filling in what happened to Persephone as an adult. Because after she ran away, I never heard from or saw her again."

"Away from a foster home?"

"No, she spent one night in a county facility for adolescents with lax security and just walked away. Most of the kids there had committed crimes but a few, like Peri—that's what she called herself—were wards of the court. I made her one—made all three of them wards— because some idiot judge let **him** out on bail. We were worried about their safety so we separated them and sent them to three different cities. Peri ended up in Pensacola because she was the victim of record and deemed the most vulnerable and that was far north. Barlett—the older brother—him we felt comfortable keeping closer so we placed him in—don't hold me to this, it's been ages—I want to say Tampa. The little one was vulnerable for other reasons, clearly a kid with issues, so he went to a psych facility clear across the state near Fort Lauderdale."

She smiled and sipped. "I had no idea my memory was that good."

I said, "Relevance will do that to you."

"I'm relevant?"

I smiled back. "What was Barlett like?"

Dual emeralds glinted, then nearly vanished as she squinted straight at me. Through me. "You think **he** did it?"

"We definitely don't."

Milo said, "A man named Richard Barlett, two years younger than Meagin—Peri—was murdered a couple of days after she was. Can't get into details, but we have reason to believe the killings were related."

Kathy Bookbinder's shoulders rounded and she seemed to compress. "Richard Barlett. Well, that's no stretch, his given name was Barlett Richard Gilmore. Both of them killed? My God, what else haven't you told me?"

Milo said, "Nothing substantive."

Two pairs of green eyes faced their mates. "You can honestly say there are no other victims?"

I thought of New Orleans. If Milo did, he kept it to himself.

He said, "I can, Doctor. What kind of kid was Barlett?"

"Nice, quiet, didn't make much of an impression. What kind of adult did he turn out to be? For that matter, you still haven't answered my question about Peri."

"We know very little about him, other than he lived alone and didn't have much in the way of physical possessions."

"Homeless?"

"No, he worked as a clerk at a church and lived in a shack in an orange grove."

"Hmm," said Kathy Bookbinder. "Guess that makes sense." She scooted closer to us, hand tight around the stem of her margarita glass. "And Peri? Was her life hellish clear up to her death?"

"Not at all," said Milo. "She ended up marrying a rich man and living in Bel Air."

"Bel Air? Wow. And you're sure the husband didn't do it—seeing as she was having an affair?"

"He's pretty much been ruled out."

"If you say so." She fiddled with her drink, then tugged at her curls.

The food arrived. No one ate but we all drank in silence for a while.

She was the first to break. "Can you give me a sense of what she was like beyond Bel Air? Just for my own edification."

Milo looked at me.

I said, "Intelligent, self-possessed, had a few friends but mostly stuck to herself. For recreation, she ran and painted."

"That I remember—art, her liking to draw. Not nasty stuff and I was looking for it, given her experiences. Girlie fantasies—unicorns, that kind of thing. I chose to take it as a good sign but maybe she was just holding it in. My job was like that, doing the dirty work, never really getting to know the kids."

She looked at me hopefully.

I said, "She painted mostly landscapes and still lifes. But also a ghost orchid."

"Really," she said. "Well, that also makes sense. The monster who abused her worked in the swamp where those crazy things grow and he took her in there regularly. Allegedly to help with cleanup. Obviously I suspected it had nothing to do with cleanup but Peri denied he'd abused her there, insisted every attack took place in her bedroom. That's how she nabbed him. She hid a mini-recorder under the bed and gave the cops the tapes. Made a special trip to the Copeland police station, marched in and said she had evidence of a felony. The rest of the family was on some kind of day trip and she'd faked illness. Luckily, the Copeland police chief was a wonderful man who immediately broke into action and protected her. And that's not what I've always seen from law enforcement."

I said, "A bedroom in a double-wide trailer."

She took a long swallow, stared at her food, shook her head. "Exactly. **She** had to know. The enabler."

"Her mother."

"Ms. Rooney," she said. "Some piece of work she was, always playing the I'm-stupid game. I can't prove she knew but of course she did. She wasn't educated but she was wily. Though I imagine the last thing she figured was Davis blowing her head off."

She took two long sips before I said, "What were the younger boy's problems?"

"Rooney? Yes, the same as her last name so you have to figure for all her servile bullshit she had clout in the family. What were his problems? Poor impulse control, temper control, disruptive behavior at school, bad grades. **Horrid** grades so obviously, I suspected some sort of learning disability but I never tested him, my job was finding all three of them refuge. You could try asking for records at the place they sent him to but I doubt you'll get them due to confidentiality issues."

Milo said, "Remember the name?"

"I don't. Just that it was privately contracted and got federal funds."

"Scam or the real deal?"

Kathy Bookbinder said, "As far as I know, the real deal. At least I never heard about any scandals there. But right after I placed the kids, I left clinical work. Tired of being dipped day after day into the toilet of life. I came out here, got my doctorate, and switched to teaching. Got married and had two of my own and thank God, they're great."

She sliced a small wedge of chile relleno, passed it between her lips, chewed slowly as if it took effort. "Now that I've told you about Rooney, do you suspect him? 'Cause I do."

Milo said, "What motive would he have?"

Kathy Bookbinder sat back. "He was close to his father. Super-close, clearly the favorite. And he got treated differently, you could see it in the way the kids were dressed. Peri and Barlett wore what looked like hand-me-downs but little Rooney was always spiffed up. Bizarrely, actually. The family's living in a double-wide and he's got designer jeans and Ralph Lauren polo shirts."

She turned to me. "What is it about some twisted families, Alex? That pathological inequity? Why do they target one kid and deify another?"

I said, "Wish I knew."

She smiled broadly. "At least you're honest. Better than what passes for wisdom nowadays, all those papier-mâché prophets."

She drank some more. "I'd better get more solid stuff in my stomach. If I come home without eating my husband will press pastries on me, he's a chef."

Milo said, "Sounds like a good deal."

"It can be," said Kathy Bookbinder. "Duane takes super-good care of me when I let him. A few years back, cancer had the nerve to impose itself on my body. Nothing really scary, totally taken care of. But you learn to practice what you've preached to patients: live each day. Duane helps me do that."

Her lips folded and unfolded again. Her chin quivered and she tugged at her hair. "I hope poor Peri had a bunch of good days."

44

We sat with Kathy Bookbinder through a first-rate meal. Drifting away from the murders into shop talk. Letting her set the pace and the subject matter, hoping that would elicit new information, but it didn't.

When the check came, she reached for it but lost out to a quicker, larger hand.

"It's really not necessary, Milo."

"It really is, Kathy."

She grinned. "My problem. Relinquishing control. But you know, this has been good. Getting in touch with the bad old days and confirming that I did the right thing by escaping."

We walked her to her car, a small, white Mercedes sedan.

She said, "I do hope you find whoever did it. And tell me once you have. Please."

"Scout's honor," said Milo.

"Duane was an Eagle Scout, that's where he started cooking. I did Brownies but we moved around so much that I dropped it."

I said, "Military dad?"

"And mom. Two colonels. You can imagine why I like control."

We smiled, thanked her, watched her drive off.

Milo said, "She was right. Rooney sounds like a pretty good bet. What do you think?"

"The same thing. If he was that attached to his father, he could've doubted Meagin's accusations and blamed her for his parents' deaths. For the dissolution of his family."

We stood there, breathing in cool, California night-air. The restaurant's door opened periodically, disgorging human movement and happy talk. People for whom dinner was just that.

"Okay," he finally said. "Let's do the big no-no."

"What's that?"

"You piloting so I can play database poker."

Allowing a civilian to take the wheel of a police vehicle is a serious infraction. Over the years, Milo's risked it a few times, but always on short hops.

He said, "What, the iced tea was spiked? Just point the damn car north and don't hit anything."

◆

I like to drive, having regarded it since the age of sixteen as a conduit to freedom. And the hard truth is—one never uttered—I'm a far better driver than Milo, who tends to express frustration with the leaden foot.

I adjusted the Impala's seat, turned the key, cruised out of the lot and headed back to the 405. Milo lit up his phone, hunched over the screen and began clicking away.

Traffic had eased and I was able to sail north at sixty-five mph or close to it. There were stretches when I could've gone faster but the last thing I needed was a highway patrol encounter.

It took less than three miles for Milo to say, "Look at this. Not literally. Rooney Luther Gilmore—age thirty-two, so it's gotta be the right guy . . . though I'm not seeing any family resemblance—anyway, he's got a fourteen-page sheet. Starting when he was eighteen but no doubt there are sealed juvey arrests."

"Where'd he offend?"

"So far I'm just looking at Florida. All over the state . . . okay, here's his first move, he shows up seven years ago in Louisiana. A place called Empire, then Baton Rouge, then New Orleans, gets busted in all three places. Assault in Empire—he knifed someone, claimed self-defense—then shoplifting and battery in Baton Rouge, then . . . aggravated assault pled down to battery in Nawlins."

I said, "Was he still in New Orleans five years ago?"

"Let's see . . . as a matter of fact, he was, another assault, pled down to misdemeanor battery, four days of jail time. Why? Oh. The bartender."

"Nicole Fontenot."

Twisting and stretching, he reached back and retrieved the March/Aggiunta murder book from the rear seat, found what he was looking for, and switched back to the phone.

"Dates match. He beat up a guy in a bar two weeks before Fontenot got shot in the heart. Not the same bar she worked at but on the same street, looks like . . . two doors away."

He sat back. "The favorite child grew up to be a **not**-nice person."

Back in his office, he pulled up the same files he'd viewed on a tiny screen and printed.

As each page entered the bin, I picked it up and read.

Rooney Gilmore's first mugshot, taken in Gainesville, Florida, at age eighteen, showed a chubby, pasty-faced, long-haired adolescent sporting a minimal sprig of sandy fuzz on a less-than-assertive chin.

Sullen expression, flat eyes. Subsequent photos revealed the evolution you often see with career criminals: premature aging and a steady accumulation of crude tattoos. Rooney's expression remained uniform: barely suppressed rage coexisting with theatrical nonchalance.

Like his sister, he'd moved around the country with no apparent geographic order. Staying for a while, as Kathy Bookbinder had recalled, in Florida, then shifting to Louisiana for a twenty-six-month stay. After that the pace picked up and the sojourns were shorter.

Brief stays in Georgia, Alabama, and Tennessee were followed by a two-month return to Florida, this time in Miami. Then frequent back-and-forths between that state and Alabama followed by a stretch in Arkansas.

Each locale had been commemorated by at least one arrest, charges frequently pled down because that's the way the system works. And Rooney's nomadic life offered an additional fringe benefit: law enforcement tends to think locally so by shifting locales criminals avoid piling up too much iniquity in any one jurisdiction.

The youngest Gilmore's most recent booking had been eighteen months ago, possession of metham-phetamine and larceny. Back in the Sunshine State: Tampa.

This mugshot revealed a bloated, sagging face with tendrils of black ink scaling a stumpy neck and sweeping upward to a soft jawline. He'd grown progressively bald and now sported a skinned head. One constant: eyes that continued to lack depth or sparkle. His sentence after pleading to both charges: three weeks in county lockup.

One thing struck me: none of the states where

he'd operated criminally matched any his sister had called home. If he'd been looking for her, he hadn't come close.

Until . . .

I continued reading until something at the bottom of the Tampa bust caught my eye: his vehicle had been confiscated, no explanation offered.

I said, "His last ride of record was an eight-year-old black Honda Civic."

Milo took the sheet. "Meth and larceny and he gets twenty days, unbelievable. Actually, believable. For all we know, official compassion included keeping his wheels safe while he enjoyed the local hospitality."

He ran a search on the Honda, pulled up traffic fines stretching from Kansas to California. Unsafe lane changes, failures to stop, a couple of speeders, but mostly parking tickets.

Each one paid up promptly.

On that trip Rooney Gilmore had displayed clear geographic intention, taking an arrow-straight route that drew him across Missouri, Colorado, and Nevada. No way to know where he'd entered California but he'd been pulled over four months ago in Fresno for a broken taillight. That fine remained unpaid but it hadn't been marked delinquent or stimulated any police action.

Milo said, "So we've got clear verification of his being here." He scrawled in his pad.

I said, "Why no alert on the unpaid fine?"

"Penny ante. Paperwork's probably stuck in some file, still unprocessed."

"Or," I said, "a taillight crack was too ticky-tacky for Fresno to bother with, seeing as he'd paid all his previous tickets."

"Mr. Law-Abiding." His laugh was bitter.

"At first glance," I said. "But not because he reformed. When you've got a goal in mind, keep your head down. His was go west young man and kill your sister."

"And brother."

I said, "Yes but I think Meagin was his main target because in his mind, she'd destroyed his family. His entire life. Come to think of it, that could explain the kill shot: you broke my heart, I'm breaking yours. He'd looked for her for years but couldn't find her. Spending chunks of his life behind bars didn't help. But he did eventually locate Barlett because Barlett wasn't under any deep cover and hadn't done much of a name change. Rooney made his way to San Pietro and announced himself to his brother, made sure to come across nonthreatening, just the long-lost kid brother reaching out. Unfortunately for Meagin, she'd contacted Barlett before then, initiating her own attempt at reunion. That turned out to be a fatal error but given Barlett's easygoing nature, she'd have had no reason to fear him."

"Why would she reach out after all those years?"

"We may never know," I said, "but one possibility is loneliness. The isolation of being in that big house day after day. Also, she'd built up her confidence, finally figured she had it made and could afford to reach out."

"She tells Barlett where she's living and he tells Rooney."

"Maybe not intentionally. Rooney could've found the address in Barlett's cabin. Either way, he had what he wanted, drove to L.A. and began stalking Meagin. Learned her habits and made his move. Unfortunately for Barlett, he'd become a liability and two days later, he paid for it in the worst way."

He checked the page listing the Fresno ticket, placed a nationwide BOLO out on the car and its owner, tagging Rooney Gilmore as a suspect in three homicides, to be considered armed and dangerous. Any watchful cop anywhere in the country spotting the Honda would initiate a felony stop.

"For the cherry on top," he said, "I contact the marshals tomorrow."

He sent Reed, Alicia, and Binchy a one-sentence email informing them of a meeting tomorrow at eight a.m.

No **if you can make it** qualifier.

I said, "Yes, I'll be there."

"Now I can sleep peacefully."

45

Same room, coffee, tea, pastries, none of which had been touched. A single whiteboard sported a blowup of Rooney Gilmore's most recent mugshot next to enlargements of a black Honda Civic matching Gilmore's drive and the actual car's Florida plates and VIN number.

Milo had summed up the revenge theory. A few questions had been asked, a pall had settled followed by glum discussion.

The dominant sentiment among the young D's: disgust at the motive.

Sean said, "Anything on the New Orleans murder?"

Milo said, "I just talked to them, they'll be asking questions at the bars, we'll see if anything comes up. But it's been years so I'm not expecting much."

Alicia said, "Ugly bastard. Talk about a con face. Rich folk are security-obsessed, car like that, guy like that, you'd think more people would've called him in."

Reed said, "If they noticed, sure. But no one's ever out on the streets, there. Even the dog-walkers are mostly maids."

She said, "No soccer moms or kids shooting hoops or selling lemonade."

Sean said, "Plus these folk have multiple homes, so lots of vacants."

Alicia shook her head. "Mausoleum, U.S.A."

I said, "Committing the murders at night also helped him. Once he learned about Meagin's after-dark runs and saw how easy it was to access Gio's house, that likely clinched it."

Sean said, "Poor people. Going for a swim and **that** walks in. Wonder if he said anything to them before he did it."

Milo said, "Once we find him, we'll ask."

He sat down, giving them the chance to talk more. The goal, more therapy than problem solving. Bleeding off some of the gut-grip that arises when you finally develop a suspect but have no idea where to find him.

When silence ensued, he said, "Onward. I'm on shaky grounds making a strong case for your exclusive participation but as long as no one else demands your time, I could use help looking for the

Honda. We talked about his exit route from Bel Air before. Now I'm motivated to do something about it. I'm guessing his most likely route woulda been south but it's just that, a guess. I'm not bothering with Little Holmby, Westwood, or campus, because there are no places there where a transient lowlife would bunk down. We'll start south of Pico, which is basically around here, and continue to Palms, Culver City, and beyond."

Reed said, "Beyond is plenty of lowlife real estate. Imperial Highway, the bad part of Inglewood, those motels near the airport."

Alicia said, "Hot-sheet Hiltons. You want us to cover the same area, do parallel searches?"

"Just you, kiddo," said Milo. "The two of us will keep in touch on a tac line, make sure we're not duplicating. I can't neglect east–west so Sean, take east, Moses, west. Don't read anything into that, it's arbitrary."

Both of the men nodded. Reed looked disappointed.

Milo said, "What?"

"Not going to lie, L.T. From Bel Air to the beach is nonstop seven-figure houses. I like a pleasant drive as much as anyone but I'd rather be useful."

"That's if you take Sunset. Go with Pico and come back on Olympic."

"Got it."

Sean said, "Me, too?"

"No, you stay on Sunset. You can wear a

blindfold through Beverly Hills but once you get into West Hollywood, there'll be plenty to eagle-eye. Especially east of La Brea, plenty of the same kind of roach-palaces all the way to downtown."

Sean said, "On it, Loot." Bright-eyed and ready to go.

Reed tapped his foot. Alicia kept giving the board sour looks.

Milo said, "I know the whole search is iffy at best and with the black-and-whites having the BOLO, you could be thinking, why bother? But just getting the uniforms the info means nothing. Some officers pay attention, others don't. The marshals are a better bet and no one'll be happier than me if they find him. But we're not extraneous because we're focused."

Alicia frowned but said nothing.

Milo said, "This is an open forum. What?"

She said, "Obviously, I'll be giving it my all, L.T., but I'm just wondering why he'd stay in town."

"That's a very good point," said Milo. "But since when do we limit ourselves to sure bets?"

CHAPTER

46

Three days of fruitless searching passed before Sean and Alicia were pulled off and assigned to a street mugging / attempted murder barely on the wrong side of the West L.A.–Venice border. Milo and Reed continued to look for the black Honda, but Milo's captain was making noise about optimal use of Reed's time.

The United States Marshals' Fugitive Task Force, working with the FBI, did a commendable job of communicating with their units nationwide. The FBI also produced three unsolved shoot-to-the-heart deaths other than Nicole Fontenot, coinciding with Rooney Gilmore's travels. Two in Atlanta, one in Biloxi, Mississippi, all associated with armed robberies.

The Biloxi victim was an Ethiopian immigrant working as a convenience store clerk, left on the floor of the business, shot once in the heart, the till empty, CCTV picking up a stocky hooded killer. The Georgia cases were both bartenders, one male, one female, ambushed shortly after closing time and relieved of the night's take. No cameras.

Unlike the California homicides, bullets had been recovered intact, each time tracing to a .38 Smith and Wesson Police and Military revolver. A common weapon and lack of communication among three teams of detectives meant no attempt had been made to match ballistics. A rush job meant the FBI lab might get the results back in a week.

All in all, a well-coordinated effort.

It didn't matter.

Inglewood police officers Armando Casagrande and Karen Brousse were doing their usual midmorning thing: patrolling a particularly annoying stretch of Imperial Highway in their spiffy new Ford Explorer. Annoying because the street was lined with by-the-hour motels and the businesses they attracted and that meant nuisance calls, lots of them. More street psychology than police work.

Casagrande and Brousse didn't mind nuisances. Their previous assignment had been the night shift and they'd contended with tides of serious gang crap and more than their share of maimed and dead bodies. They'd applied for the transfer days apart. Not by chance, they were a secret item and joked that one day they might actually use one of the no-tell motels. If they could bring their own sheets.

One hour in, having just finished 7-Eleven coffees, they received a 415 call to a smoke shop two blocks from where they were chilling in the parking lot. About to read this morning's BOLOs but that was boring and actually going out on a call was a lot more fun so they checked with Dispatch.

Attempted shoplifting and threatening behavior at a smoke shop. Probably another homeless mental case. They knew the store and the only thing you could easily lift were dinky edibles and a few bongs left on the counter.

When they got there, the owner, an emaciated goat-face named Otto Banks, was standing out front, moving his foot up and down and gesticulating with pipe-cleaner arms.

Armando Casagrande said, "Whoa, he should use his own stuff."

Karen Brousse laughed, pulled up to the sidewalk, and asked Banks what the deal was.

"Guy lifted all my pipes and my sweet-treats, just scooped it into his pockets and told me not to report it or he'd blow my fuckin' head off."

That was another level.

Brousse said, "Did he show you a gun?"

"No, but he groped around in his pocket, you know? I'm not taking chances, I let him rip me off and called you. Go get him." Pointing south.

"Description," said Casagrande.

"Fat guy, white, er . . . knit cap, yeah a cap," said Banks.

"Anything else?"

"Inked like a con, stringy beard on his chin. That enough?" Tapping faster.

"How old?"

"I dunno," said Banks. "Forty? Also, he smells bad. Can you just get him? Please?"

"Clothing," said Casagrande.

"Shitty," said Banks. "Smelly green jacket—like a military whatever. Big pockets, he stuffed them, just cleaned me out. Are you gonna go get him or what?"

Brousse said, "Of course, sir. Anything for our citizens."

Smirking. Armando loved her sass.

Brousse pulled back onto Imperial. "The old hand-in-pocket thing. We shoot the fools, turns out it's a toothbrush we're the bad guys. There should be a law against stupid."

Casagrande said, "I hear that."

She loved his agreeability.

They went south, checking the main drag and side streets, on the lookout for a fat white guy with pockets full of jelly candies and dope toys. It didn't take long to spot him, walking stiffly but fast. More stocky than fat. Wide but solid-looking.

Head down, shoulders all bunched up. Black watch cap, olive-green army surplus jacket, soiled gray sweats, combat boots.

Brousse pulled up ten yards behind him, shifted to Park, and checked that her vest was on tight. Armando's, as well.

He said, "Thanks, I'm fine," and got out. "Sir. We need to talk to you."

The guy stopped, rotated slowly. Flashed what he probably thought was a friendly smile that came across confused.

Casagrande muttered, "Definitely another mental case, okay, here we go."

He approached, hand on holster. "How you doing, sir?" Using honey, not vinegar, his natural tendency plus it mostly worked.

The guy nodded and kept smiling. Then he slipped his hand under the jacket and toward his waistband.

Glint of metal.

Casagrande ran back, flung his door open, and crouched behind it. Creating a shield like he'd been trained.

Brousse did the same.

"Oh shit, Karen. He really is packing."

Brousse did her authority-scream: "**Drop the gun drop it drop it drop it drop it!**" while Casagrande called for backup.

She rose from her crouch and peeked through the driver's window. Kept shouting.

The guy seemed unfazed by the noise. Looked at her, shrugged, then let his eyes drop to the handgun he'd retrieved. Uncurling his fingers, he held the weapon in an open palm, as if offering a gift.

"Good," said Brousse. "Now drop it and follow my instructions do it **now**."

The guy nodded and lowered the gun.

Thank God. This would end easy.

Then the guy's smile vanished and his hand closed and his arm flew up and now he was aiming straight at her.

She ducked low. **Ping. Ping.** Metal and plastic vibrated.

Casagrande was off the radio, standing to the right of his door, his service revolver aimed straight at the guy. Who kept firing at Karen.

One more bullet hit her door. Then another. And another before Casagrande shot the guy. Aiming for center body mass like he was trained but missing and hitting him low in the gut. The shooter looked surprised.

Red spread on dirty gray cotton.

But he held on to his weapon and Casagrande, thinking of Karen, elevated his arm in correction and was about to fire again when the guy let the gun roll from his finger and clunk on the sidewalk. He stared at Casagrande, openmouthed, stood there for a second. His knees went first, bending, buckling, collapsing, then the rest of him. He fell on his face, blood spreading around his bulk.

Sirens were wailing. Karen Brousse thought, **When did that start?** She saw the stricken look on Armando's face and motioned him back. Approached the bad guy, her gun gripped in two-handed Weaver stance.

Lots of blood. No movement. The fool's head had landed on its right side, exposing a gaping mouth and five inches of thin, gray-brown beard. Poor Armando, first time he'd fired his weapon, other than at the range where she outshot him every time. Now he'd killed someone. Her baby would have to go through the OIS crap.

What she wanted to do right now was nudge the body with her toe just to make sure he was no longer a threat. But people had massed on the sidewalk across the street and one was phone-filming. If she touched the fool, even delicately, the internet would accuse her of kicking a poor, defenseless victim of police brutality.

No sign of the gun. Probably trapped under him. Why **do** that? For **what**? Jelly beans and bongs?

He looked damn dead but just to be safe she'd warn whoever came over to move him. And now his smell reached her and yeah, he did reek, stale and sour, like someone who'd slept in his clothes for a month. Those tats, definitely prison art. Up and down his neck and what she could see of the backs of his hands. **Love** on one set of knuckles, **Hate** on the other. No imagination.

She'd just turned her back to see how Armando

was doing when four spiffy, black-and-white Explorers sped up and screeched to a halt. Adrenaline was starting to do its thing and she was draining. Let someone else take over.

The fool on the ground groaned.

She wheeled and re-aimed at him. Her heart felt like it had stopped. Then it started thumping like the power hammer in her dad's machine shop.

The guy didn't move. No more sound. Maybe what she'd heard was one of those weird after-death things, gas escaping, whatever.

Then she saw it. Rapid pulse in his inked-up neck. Each beat swelling the belly of a crude, black, snake tattoo. Like the hideous thing had just swallowed a mouse and was digesting. Creepy.

Her own heart raced faster. She stood there, hot, cold, hot, eyes blurring, starting to get nauseous.

But she kept her eyes on the snake as it pulsated. Fool was alive, unbelievable. Probably because Armando had shot low.

If he survived, fool would probably be shitting into a bag for the rest of his life.

Fine with her.

Though it would be paid for by the taxpayers and that sucked.

Crazy world but the one she'd signed up for.

A voice behind her said, "You're covered, Karen."

Three officers, all of whom she knew well but in her state, she had no clue what their names were.

One of them, a small Black woman, took Karen's

arm and guided her back. Name tag: **S. Joyner.** Oh yeah, Stella.

Karen said, "He's still breathing."

Stella Joyner said, "Very funny."

"He is. Look at his neck."

Stella did. Said, "Wow. A few hours ago, we got called to an eighty-year-old woman, home-invaded, beat up, died of a heart attack. And this guy survives."

Karen said, "Life's not fair."

Stella Joyner said, "If it was, we'd be doing something else."

47

An Inglewood captain named Laquitha Morrison was smart enough to remember the BOLO and considerate enough to phone Milo. He was at my house when the call came in, assaulting a triple-decker sandwich and bemoaning the policeman's lot.

"Sturgis."

Morrison introduced herself and said, "We got your multiple murderer, Gilmore."

"Fantastic!"

"But complicated," said Morrison. "He's at Centinela Hospital getting his bowel stitched up."

She told the story.

Milo said, "What kind of gun did he pull?"

"Cheap Polish automatic," said Morrison. "Why?"

"I was hoping for a .38 Police and Military."

"Then you'll be happy—I'm going to call you Milo, okay?"

"You can call me any damn thing you want, thanks so much for cluing me in."

"Didn't want you to hear it on the news," said Laquitha Morrison. "Anyway, we found one of those, too. Thirty-eight revolver. Along with another cheapie .22, a .25, a sawed-off shotgun, three pairs of brass knuckles, one with spikes, and a bunch of knives. All in his motel room. We found the room because he had a three-day receipt in his pocket."

"The car—"

"Black Honda, we found that, too, parked in the lot out in front of the motel."

"Which motel?"

"The King Henry," said Morrison. "Anything but regal. We did a forensic tow. Car was dead, our tow guy said it looked like a blown head gasket."

Milo said, "Breakdown. That's why he stayed in town."

"Lucky for you, Milo."

"Lucky for me you did all the work, Laquitha."

"Aw shucks," she said. "Anything not to get de-funded."

He laughed. "Anything else in the room?"

"Whatever was found we took. You can wait for us to log it or come by."

"The latter," he said. "You've been great, again thanks. You mind if I pay Gilmore a visit?"

"Suit yourself," said Laquitha Morrison. "I'm

concentrating on all the OIS noise that's sure to come. And supporting my people. The officer who shot him is a sensitive sort and people were phone-photoing the scene. Hope some prick doesn't edit and warp."

Milo said, "Gilmore's implicated in my three murders and a good bet on four more. Can't imagine anyone's gonna turn him into a hero."

"In a perfect world, Milo. But you know how it is, reality's a concept, no longer a thing."

48

That afternoon, Milo and I drove to Centinela Hospital, where he used his badge to get us into the ICU.

In the movies, doctors are always warning cops about unduly stressing patients and displaying an overall hostile attitude to law enforcement. A. Singh, M.D., Rooney Gilmore's attending physician, said, "Have your way with him but he's been in and out of consciousness, good luck."

"Prognosis?"

"Hard to say with a bowel wound," she said. "He tolerated surgery okay but you never know how many bad little buggies have leaked out."

"He say anything?"

"Mostly he fought the cuffs and cussed everyone out. He did tell one of the nurses that it was an Isis thing."

"He sees himself as a terrorist?"

"People like that," said Singh, "does it make a difference why they do the things they do?"

She led us to a room in a corner, separated from the others in the ward and tagged with a hand-lettered **IPD/Special Circ.** sign taped to the door.

Milo said, "Special?"

Singh said, "As in dangerous."

She left as we entered.

Rooney Gilmore lay slightly propped on a hospital bed, his left wrist shackled to a side rail bolted into place, his right arm immobilized by an I.V. setup affixed to a bedside stand also attached to the floor. The hospital was in a high-crime area. Lots of Special.

An oxygen tube in his nose failed to improve his color. His vitals peaked and troughed graphically on the monitors, beeping and burping in concert. Slightly elevated blood pressure and pulse, oxygen level ninety-two. Not bad for someone a few hours out of surgery.

The pasty face from his arrest photos had settled to a doughy consistency, slack around the edges. Black tats had faded to charcoal gray. A bald head was inked, as well. Lightning bolts. His beard had been cropped to stubble. His chin displayed razor nicks. Hasty shave in the O.R., eliminating loose hairs, one less hassle for the surgeon.

His eyes were open but glazed. They began blinking manically when he saw us. His pulse and his

BP began rising. One of these days, someone would start using ICU gear as impromptu polygraphs.

Milo said, "Hi, Rooney. Milo Sturgis."

Guttural groan.

"How they treating you?"

"Uck U."

"Not comfortable, huh?"

"Uck. E-U."

Milo leaned in closer. "We know you killed your sister and your brother. What we don't get is why."

Rooney Gilmore's eyes turned to paper cuts. BP and pulse soared, beeps and burps moving past **allegro** to **presto.**

"I-sis," he said.

Milo said, "You're an Isis guy? Not quite sure what that means, Rooney."

The eyes opened again. Emotion fighting fatigue as they widened to the max.

Muddy-brown irises, yellow sclera. Plenty of acreage but no lighting. When I looked close I saw yellow fingers curling at the periphery of his face. Notable jaundice; liver function disrupted.

He said, "Mish . . . in."

"You were on a mission."

Rooney Gilmore tried to nod, achieved only a minuscule downturn of crushed nose that vibrated the oxygen tubes. His lips worked better and he managed a smile. Closed his eyes.

The bulk of his body sank. Settling. BP began

sliding back down. His chest rose and fell slowly. Took on a steady rhythm.

Sleeping. Easy for psychopaths.

Outside of the room, Milo said, "What just happened?"

I said, "He expressed himself and it relaxed him."

"I'm his therapist, huh?"

"You do have the touch."

We left the hospital.

After we got back to my house, he called to see if Gilmore had woken up and said anything.

The nurse he spoke to said, "Just that he hates my guts. It's mutual."

A call two hours later revealed the fact that the patient had spiked a fever.

Milo's next attempt to get information was met by voicemail.

He said, "Nothing more to do, I'm going home."

I walked him down to the Impala, watched him drive away slowly.

Just after eleven p.m., he texted me.

He got sepsis and died.

49

The case received media exposure: TV, print, online digests, a few bloggers rehashing what they'd read. With the news cycle reduced to twenty-four seconds, the story lost currency nearly immediately. No attempt by self-labeled activists to make something of the officer-involved shooting. Maybe for the same reason or because Rooney Gilmore's criminal history made him an inapt victim.

Milo kept me informed with occasional calls but we had no face-to-face contact, swamped as he was with completing the murder book and arranging for the transfer of evidence from Inglewood's jurisdiction to L.A.'s.

The move was a formality because the Honda and everything collected from Rooney Gilmore's filthy room at the King Henry Motor Lodge was destined to end up in the same place no matter who sent it: the county crime lab at Cal State L.A. But rules are rules.

Gilmore's weapons would eventually be shipped to the FBI to see if a match could be made to other crimes. The revolver, specifically, would be compared with the bullets recovered at the three cold robbery-homicides. New Orleans PD, learning of those cases from Moe Reed, theorized that Nicole Fontenot's murder had started out as a robbery but that Gilmore had failed to catch her inside the bar and when she resisted reopening, he'd shot her. But, as their public relations officer was careful to point out in a press release, the truth would likely never be known.

One of the calls Milo did make filled me in on his final chat with Doug March, whom he reached in Columbus, Ohio. March had listened patiently, then said, "I'm finding myself feeling sorry for her. Thank God he didn't kill me. Appreciate your letting me know."

He'd also reached Claudio Aggiunta in Florence who'd alternated between profuse thanks and weeping.

"He was with his parents, lots of tears in the background, that was a tough one."

His next communication was a text asking if I minded calling Kathy Bookbinder. I said sure and reached her in her office at Chandler.

She said, "Yes, I read about it, but thanks. Even though it's what I expected, it made me sad. But also glad that I got out of that cesspool."

Even while contending with small-print torment, Milo made a point of going to the lab, eager to examine the contents of each evidence box as it was opened. What he got for his efforts was rancid clothing, food wrappers, empty beer bottles, a packet of methamphetamine, a bottle of pills that turned out to be codeine, another containing Oxycontin, and a few primitive hand-drawn cartoons of guns, knives, clubs, axes, skulls, and blood drips. The kind of art you get from angry ten-year-old boys.

Finally, at the bottom of the last carton, something he could use.

Two computer-generated maps, one leading to the church where Richard Barlett had worked, the other, dated weeks later, to the mansion occupied by Doug and Meagin March. Crudely drawn skulls and crossbones on each.

A shakily scrawled message on the map to Meagin.

avendge Daddy!!!!

Three days after the story died, Milo received an email that he forwarded to me with the heading **Still tied up. You mind handling this, also?**

The message had been sent by a woman from Gainesville, Florida, named Felice Heidl. I read what she had to say, sent her my number and told her she was free to call.

Two hours later, she did.

"Doctor? This is Felice Heidl."

"Hi. Thanks for getting in touch."

"I figured I should. I didn't figure I'd be talking to a psychologist, but that's great, the cops having someone like you. I guess you'd be the right person to talk to, anyway."

"Anything you want me to pass along to Detective Sturgis, I will."

"I'll leave that up to you."

I said, "What would you like to tell me about Rooney?"

"Rooney," she repeated. "It's been a long time since I fostered him but thinking about it, I can't say I'm shocked. About what happened."

"How long did you foster him?"

"A little over a year," she said. "After they released him from the facility. We were doing that, back then, my husband and I. Taking on high-risk cases. Bill's a pastor, we'd done missionary work in some pretty rough places and thought we were equipped."

She sighed.

I said, "Rooney was a challenge."

"To say the least," she said. "And one I'm afraid we didn't meet very well."

"Tough kid."

"Tough and scary," said Felice Heidl. "Our cat had kittens and he killed two of them. Just went to the den one day and wrung their necks and didn't seem at all upset. He also set fires. Outdoors, at first, but then we barely managed to put one out that he'd set in the kitchen. He wadded up newspaper, soaked it in cooking oil, and lit it on the gas range."

"Scary."

"Terrifying. We'd had our share of kids with tough histories and were well aware of his but still . . . the last straw was one night when he came into the bedroom of another foster, a seven-year-old girl, and tried to rip off her pajamas. We knew then that he had to go so we returned him to the county and I have no idea what happened to him after that. I felt guilty about it for a long, long time. It led me to do some reading about dangerous children—a book called **Savage Spawn**—and poor Rooney ticked all the boxes. I say 'poor' because what control did he have over his childhood? A father like that."

I said, "Did he ever talk about his siblings?"

"Not the brother, just the sister. He called her a whore and a murderer. Said she'd killed his father and his mother, if not for her he'd be hunting and fishing with his dad, life would be perfect. Of course that was a distortion but we didn't feel anything good would come from debating him."

A beat.

"The truth is," said Felice Heidl, "we avoided confrontation because he really, really frightened us. I don't want to be melodramatic but his eyes, they were flat, Doctor. Different. Really different. Anyway, I just thought you should know. Maybe it would help fill in some blanks."

"It does. Thanks for getting in touch, Ms. Heidl."

"I know it doesn't change things . . . he really killed them both? All that irrational hatred, festering all these years?"

"Unfortunately."

Another sigh. "What can you do . . . thanks for listening, Dr. Delaware . . . like I said, I didn't figure I'd be baring my soul to a psychologist. No offense but we tried that for Rooney. Before we gave him back. Used a person on a list the county gave us. He evaluated Rooney and called him a 'fulminating sociopath.' Told us unless Rooney shaped up by age twelve, there was no hope. Rooney was eleven, so talk about time pressure. We asked him—the doctor—what we could do and he looked at us as if we were stupid and said, 'My point is, nothing, really.'"

"What a thing to go through."

"We'd done well with nearly every other child, even those with tough backgrounds. The girl Rooney tried to bother is married, has her own kids, sends us Christmas cards and photos. A lot of the children we had the privilege to work with keep in touch.

But still, the failures get to you. A few years ago, we returned to missionary work."

"Where?"

"Last time was Colombia, our third trip." Soft laughter. "The slums of Cali didn't seem quite so bad."

50

A note from Judge Julie Beck's law clerk informed me that Derek Ruffalo was in town and available for evaluation at my convenience.

The number she included connected me to the law offices of Wendy Sugihara. Her assistant said, "This is Lance. Great to hear from you, Doctor. Anytime you'd like to see Derek would be great. Wendy and Jack Toth will both be bringing him, if that's okay with you."

"Wendy represents—"

"Derek's mother. Jack represents the dad."

I said, "First time for everything."

Lance said, "Everyone's hoping it'll be a **great** first time."

At ten o'clock the following morning, a chauffeured black Escalade pulled up in front of my house. I'd positioned myself five minutes earlier, just close enough to the rail to see the driveway but sufficiently back to avoid attention.

Curious about two opposing lawyers taking the time to serve as escorts. Wanted to collect as much non-rehearsed, nonverbal data as possible.

First to exit the SUV was a thickset gray-blond man in his fifties who hitched his trousers and smoothed his jacket. Seconds later, a teenage boy with straight sandy hair that half shielded his forehead got out of the same door.

Average size for fifteen but equipped with the gangly limbs of someone much taller. Maybe the sign of an impending growth spurt.

The last to appear, from the other side of the ute, was an Asian woman in her forties with wavy light-brown hair. About Robin's height, which put her at five-three on a good day.

Both adults wore gray suits. The boy had on a sky-blue polo shirt, olive-drab cargo pants, and high-top sneakers.

They took turns addressing him. He listened without comment or movement. Not the shine-you-on serenity of an adolescent shutting out grown-up noise. Paying attention.

I stepped forward to the rail and said, "Good morning."

Three faces looked up. Even from a distance, the size and width of Derek Ruffalo's eyes were evident.

Narrow shoulders but good posture. Triangular face bottomed by a square chin.

Wendy Sugihara said, "Dr. Delaware? Glad we're on time. It's quite an excursion up here."

Jack Toth said, "Probably weeds out the serious ones from the flakes."

Derek Ruffalo smiled.

The three of them climbed the stairs. I'd closed the door and stood with my back to it. Still out for any sort of tell, mostly from Derek. He remained calm. A tell of a sort.

Both lawyers gave me their cards. Jack Toth's full name was Janos.

Wendy Sugihara said, "Jack and I are ready to talk to you first and fill you in."

I said, "Maybe later. I'll be seeing Derek first."

She looked at her adversary of record. Nothing adversarial about her expression. Jack Toth's eyebrows were high and quivering.

She said, "It's really better if we start. It'll simplify matters."

Jack Toth said, "Putting it mildly."

I said, "Appreciate that but I'll start with Derek."

I opened the door and ushered them into the living room. I'd arranged a few magazines, bottles of water and glasses, had switched on soft Latin jazz. "Make yourselves comfortable or feel free to leave and come back."

Both lawyers looked grim but they said nothing.

I motioned to Derek and he walked to my side. Lemony aftershave. You don't get that much in teenage boys. Prepped by an adult or precocious?

As we headed up the hallway to my office, Jack Toth said, "How long do you expect to be talking to our boy?"

The word choice made Derek smile wider.

I said, "An hour. I'll text you a quarter hour before."

Derek produced an iPhone from a cargo pocket.

"Better yet, Derek will."

The lawyers looked at each other. Sugihara said, "I've got plenty to do, don't mind working in the car. That okay for you, Jack?"

"Better than just sitting around on my duff," said Toth. To Derek: "You okay, son?"

"Yessir."

"No need to text, just c'mon out when you're done."

I motioned Derek to the battered leather couch and sat opposite him in my equally seasoned armchair. He settled without slump or an anxious perch on the edge of the sofa. Sitting straight but not overly so, both feet flat on the floor, hands resting in his lap.

I'd thought about the appointment for a while, still had no idea how to get into the topic of abandonment.

I said, "Good to meet you."

"Same here." A boy's voice transitioning to manhood. The result was the usual cracks and small squeaks. No self-consciousness about that. A self-possessed fifteen-year-old?

The widely set eyes were dark brown and soft, the square chin spotted with tiny pox-like zits. Similar gravel had been deposited between the eyes and on rosy cheeks. Spots of dark fuzz sprouted above his upper lip.

"Before we start, is there anything you'd like to ask me, Derek?"

"Not really."

I waited.

"Not at all," he said. "I've actually done this before."

"Talked to a psychologist."

"More like a counselor," he said. "At school, when they thought I was going to freak out."

"About what?"

"Why I'm here," he said. "Neither of them wanting me after the divorce."

He sighed, eyes shifting to his lap. But his voice had remained steady. Same for the eyes, when they finally rose and met mine.

I said, "They told you that?"

"They didn't like come out and say it but they wanted me to know that they were going to be traveling a lot. Like all the time. So it wouldn't be in my best interests to be dependent on them."

"Was that a surprise?"

"Not really," he said. "It's been pretty obvious right from the beginning."

"What has?"

"They're not equipped."

"To . . ."

"Be parents." He shifted forward. "They're not bad people. They changed my life. Do you know where I was before they adopted me?"

"An orphanage in Russia."

"In Ukraine. My birth mother was dead and my father was unknown. I was five when they brought me over. I don't remember much except for being cold and hungry. When I got here they were excited."

Several blinks. Momentary frown. Recalling a phase that had passed?

I said, "Excited about adopting you."

"Yes. They told me how smart I was to learn English so fast. I wanted to learn it fast. So I could have a better life. They smiled a lot, there was a lot of smiling, I wasn't used to smiling, no one smiled at the orphanage. They spoiled me."

"With . . ."

"Toys, games, clothes, whatever. I had my own room. A sixty-inch flat-screen with full streaming. I don't care about clothes but they like it so I wore what they got me and got into it. They sent me to private schools. Got me a BMX, then another when I outgrew it, then another even though the second was big enough but they wanted something more deluxe. Whatever I asked for I got. I thought I was in heaven." Fleeting smile. "I kind of was."

I said, "A good life materially."

"Yes. I don't want you to think I don't appreciate it. Appreciate them. I like them. I've always liked them. When either of them was alone with me they were cool."

"Not when they were together."

He shrugged. "They didn't get along. They tried. Let me do what I wanted."

I said, "Was all that freedom good?"

"Why wouldn't it be?"

"Sometimes too much can be frightening."

"Not to me," he said. "It was the best."

"It almost sounds like they were more friends than parents."

He stiffened. "I don't want anyone thinking I came in here to put them down. I never will, they're not bad people, they're just—okay, yeah, they never acted like most parents. But that also gave me more independence."

"Total freedom."

"I mean, I wouldn't say total, Doctor. Like I'm sure if I wanted to drive his Lamborghini it would be no way. But I never asked for crazy stuff."

"Anything safe was okay."

"Please," he said. "I really don't want to put them down."

"Don't mean to push you in that direction. Sorry if I made you feel that way."

"No, I know, you're trying to help me. Sorry for criticizing."

"You didn't, Derek."

"Whatever," he said. "I never gave them a reason not to give me freedom." He folded his arms across his chest.

I said, "You didn't take foolish risks and they respected that."

"Exactly." The arms relaxed. "They knew I'd be smart—they've always said that. You're smart. They tell me that all the time."

"Got it. I hear you get great grades."

"School's not hard."

I smiled.

He said, "Okay, I get a few A's."

"What did they think about that?"

"They said it was cool—I'm not saying they didn't **try** to be parents, Doctor. Keeping a good attitude, they took me on a few trips when it was appropriate. But mostly they traveled separately."

"Without you or without each other?"

"Both."

"Who took care of you when they were gone?"

"Nannies when I was home. The school when I was in school. Everything they could do, they did."

"I understand."

"I hope so," he said. "Like with . . . what's going on. Wendy says they'll be setting me up so I don't have to struggle."

"Financially."

"Yes, a trust fund, whatever that is. Enough to take care of me so I can keep going to school."

I said nothing.

He said, "There's no reason they should force themselves to stay together because of me."

"You feel that's what they've done."

"Yes."

"For how long?"

"For always." His eyes climbed to the ceiling. His hands knitted. "I mean they never **said** it to me."

"But . . ."

"I heard it. When they were fighting."

"You realize," I said, "that doesn't make their bad marriage your fault."

"Well, it kind of does." He smiled. "No, I get it, everyone says that so it's got to be right. I don't want to be a stumbling block. That's what the counselor at school called it. Don't feel like a stumbling block. She said the same kind of things—the same questions you're asking. Wanted me to know it was their issue."

He shrugged.

I said, "You're not convinced."

"I kind of am, Doctor, but also . . . I mean they said it nearly every time they fought. So it's kind of obvious that it was a problem."

"That still doesn't make it your responsibility, Derek."

"I know that," he said. "I tell myself to keep knowing it, there's no point getting freaked out over it. I'll be at Hotchkins for three more years, anyway, and then hopefully I'll get into a good college and hopefully that will lead to other good stuff."

"What subjects are you interested in?"

"Everything, really," he said. "I guess if I had to pick favorites it would be math and science but basically I'm curious about everything."

"That's great."

He studied me.

I said, "Curiosity opens the world to you. It's a big factor in success."

"Really?"

"Really. So you're going to be set up financially and happy about going back to school."

"Exactly."

"We're not going to do this today, but next time I'll be administering some tests to you to measure your ability."

"Yes, Wendy said that. So they'd know how much schooling I'd need."

"Sounds like you're well informed."

"I hope so."

"But there's still the matter of who'll have legal custody—"

"Wendy," he said.

"Wendy Sugihara?"

"That's the plan, Doctor. If you—if you tell the judge and the judge says it's okay. She already has three adopted kids so she's used to the whole adopted thing. And Jack agrees. They told me it's what you call a consensus."

"Ah."

Broad smile. "That's why Wendy wanted to talk to you first. Why she said it would simplify everything. When you insisted, I didn't say anything because I figured you had a good reason."

"I did."

"But not anymore, huh?" he said. "Now that you know about Wendy."

"On the contrary, Derek. Especially now."

He squinted. "I don't get it."

"This is all about you," I said. "I wouldn't be doing my job if I didn't hear what you had to say first."

"Oh. Okay."

"Also, I need to make sure that you really are comfortable with the arrangement."

"Oh yeah, for sure. I am, promise. Her oldest is thirteen. Miles, very cool little kid. We like the same things. I won't be hanging with him that much because he'll be here and I'll be at school but we've been FaceTiming for a while and we'll keep doing it."

"How old are Wendy's other kids?"

"Elizabeth is eight and Sidney—that's a girl, too—is six."

"Is there a dad in the house?"

"William," he said. "He's a foot doctor. Has these giant shoes from Lakers and Rams in his waiting room. My feet used to point out, he made me these insoles."

He unlaced a sneaker, removed it, and drew out something black and foot-shaped. "My feet point the right way, now."

"Nice."

"Super-comfortable." He put the sneaker back on.

I said, "Sounds like a great situation all around."

"It is," said Derek Ruffalo. "It will be, I'll make sure of that."

"How?"

"By being a good person."

"Sounds like you take on a lot of responsibility."

"I do, Doctor. But that's good, right?"

"If it doesn't overburden you."

He laughed. "Why would it?"

We spent another half hour talking. Discussing math, science, videogames, BMX biking, his friends at school. Eventually, he veered back to what he liked about Wendy and William's house. Their three other kids. Them. Eventually he returned to the people who were relinquishing him.

"They have problems. I don't want to be one of them."

Uttered with conviction and just the slightest flicker of eyelash.

Time was nearly up and there's no point in opening up worm cans unless you're going to be sitting for a while and fishing.

I asked him if there was anything else he wanted to tell me.

"Just thanks for not seeing this as weird. So when do I come back for those tests?"

"How about tomorrow?"

"Sure. What will you be asking me?"

I smiled. "All kinds of things."

He smiled back. "You can't tell me."

"Nothing wrong with a bit of mystery."

He laughed. "Sure, why not. Wendy said you won't be taking my blood or giving me shots. Which I knew anyway, but she cares about me."

"That's for sure. If you have questions later today, here's my card."

He examined it. "Ph.D. You need top grades for that."

"You do."

"Maybe one day I'll get one. In chemistry or physics."

"Keep up the straight A's."

"Sure—how do you know?"

"Lucky guess."

He laughed. "But I still need those tests."

"People like numbers."

"I do, Dr. Delaware. I find them easy. The big number in my head is two."

"How so?" I said.

"I've been rescued twice."

We left the house together and walked down to the Escalade. Both lawyers must've seen us coming because they shot out of opposite doors. Edgy, like students waiting for test results.

I said, "Derek has educated me. Sounds like a great plan."

Jack Toth said, "There you go."

Wendy Sugihara looked ready to kiss me. Stepped forward and did, pressing her lips briefly to my cheek.

Toth said, "You won't get that from me, Doc."

Derek cracked up. Slapped his hand over his mouth.

She said, "Okay, fine, I'm a nerd," and hugged him. He leaned against her.

Jack Toth said, "Touching scene. We good to go now, Doc?"

I said, "Nice meeting all of you. Quite different from what I usually get from opposing counsel."

Quite different from the family situation I'd been dealing with since driving to a house in Bel Air.

"That," said Toth, "is because we're freakin' saints."

Wendy Sugihara said, "More like we've evolved

into human beings. Which is an accomplishment once you've been to law school."

She turned to Derek: "Hungry?"

"Kind of."

"Big shock there. Pizza okay?"

"Sure."

Toth said, "I'll pass, drop me back at my office. Got my girlish figure to maintain."

Wendy laughed. She said, "You first," and guided Derek toward the gleaming black vehicle.

About the Author

JONATHAN KELLERMAN has lived in two worlds: clinical psychologist and #1 **New York Times** best-selling author of more than fifty crime novels. His unique perspective on human behavior has led to the creation of the Alex Delaware series, **The Butcher's Theater, Billy Straight, The Conspiracy Club, Twisted, True Detectives,** and **The Murderer's Daughter.** With his wife, bestselling novelist Faye Kellerman, he co-authored **Double Homicide** and **Capital Crimes.** With his son, bestselling novel-ist Jesse Kellerman, he co-authored **The Burning, Half Moon Bay, A Measure of Darkness, Crime Scene, The Golem of Hollywood,** and **The Golem of Paris.** He is also the author of two children's books and numerous nonfiction works, including **Savage Spawn: Reflections on Violent Children** and **With Strings Attached: The Art and Beauty of Vintage Guitars.** He has won the Goldwyn, Edgar, and Anthony awards and the Lifetime Achievement Award from the American Psychological Association, and has been nominated for a Shamus Award. Jonathan and Faye Kellerman live in California.

jonathankellerman.com
Facebook.com/JonathanKellerman

LIKE WHAT YOU'VE READ?

Try these titles by Jonathan Kellerman,
also available in large print:

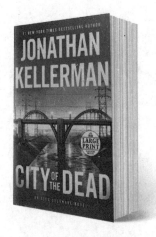

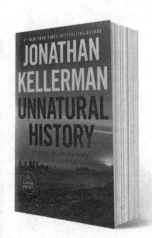

City of the Dead
ISBN 978-0-593-55876-8

Unnatural History
SBN 978-0-593-67838-1

The Burning
ISBN 978-0-593-50385-0

For more information on large print titles, visit
www.penguinrandomhouse.com/large-print-format-books